THE SAINT AND MR TEAL

FOREWORD BY
JOHN GOLDSMITH

THE ADVENTURES OF THE SAINT

Enter the Saint (1930), *The Saint Closes the Case* (1930),
The Avenging Saint (1930), *Featuring the Saint* (1931),
Alias the Saint (1931), *The Saint Meets His Match* (1931),
The Saint Versus Scotland Yard (1932), *The Saint's Getaway* (1932),
The Saint and Mr Teal (1933), *The Brighter Buccaneer* (1933),
The Saint in London (1934), *The Saint Intervenes* (1934),
The Saint Goes On (1934), *The Saint in New York* (1935),
Saint Overboard (1936), *The Saint in Action* (1937),
The Saint Bids Diamonds (1937), *The Saint Plays with Fire* (1938),
Follow the Saint (1938), *The Happy Highwayman* (1939),
The Saint in Miami (1940), *The Saint Goes West* (1942),
The Saint Steps In (1943), *The Saint on Guard* (1944),
The Saint Sees It Through (1946), *Call for the Saint* (1948),
Saint Errant (1948), *The Saint in Europe* (1953),
The Saint on the Spanish Main (1955), *The Saint Around the World* (1956),
Thanks to the Saint (1957), *Señor Saint* (1958), *Saint to the Rescue* (1959),
Trust the Saint (1962), *The Saint in the Sun* (1963),
Vendetta for the Saint (1964), *The Saint on TV* (1968),
The Saint Returns (1968), *The Saint and the Fiction Makers* (1968),
The Saint Abroad (1969), *The Saint in Pursuit* (1970),
The Saint and the People Importers (1971), *Catch the Saint* (1975),
The Saint and the Hapsburg Necklace (1976), *Send for the Saint* (1977),
The Saint in Trouble (1978), *The Saint and the Templar Treasure* (1978),
Count On the Saint (1980), *Salvage for the Saint* (1983)

THE SAINT
AND MR TEAL

LESLIE CHARTERIS

SERIES EDITOR: IAN DICKERSON

Text copyright © 2014 Interfund (London) Ltd.
Foreword © 2014 John Goldsmith
Introduction to "The Death Penalty" from *The First Saint Omnibus*, October 1939
Publication History and Author Biography © 2014 Ian Dickerson

Printed in the United States of America.

Published by Thomas & Mercer, Seattle

www.apub.com

ISBN-13: 9781477842690
ISBN-10: 1477842691

Cover design by David Drummond, www.salamanderhill.com

To Lawrence H. Wharton

My dear Lawrence,
A dedication to your noble self has long
been overdue, although you have been
on our highly exclusive Free List for some
time. Was it not you, in the beginning,
who officially pronounced the Immortal
Works worthy of introduction to the great
American Public . . . But that would be a
sordid commercial reason to give for such
an occasion as this. So let us say that it is
most especially because you have always
been one stalwart partner in the reviling of
all humbug and ballyhoo; because you were
not only with us in the Adventure of the
Unspeakable Landlubber, the Retreat from
Sarfend, and the Introduction to Total
Immersion, but also in many of the scenes
which you will find faithfully chronicled in
the last story in this volume; and because
you concoct such an excellent Salmon
Mayonnaise; that this book is offered for
your proper admiration.

Ever thine,
Leslie Charteris

PUBLISHER'S NOTE

The text of this book has been preserved from the original edition and includes vocabulary, grammar, style, and punctuation that might differ from modern publishing practices. Every care has been taken to preserve the author's tone and meaning, allowing only minimal changes to punctuation and wording to ensure a fluent experience for modern readers.

FOREWORD TO THE
NEW EDITION

In 1953, the journalist and author Richard Usborne published a seminal book called *Clubland Heroes*. It was an affectionate, nostalgia-tinged analysis and celebration of the fictional gentleman-adventurers whose exploits had thrilled him when he was a boy, the protagonists of three immensely popular novelists of the inter-war period: John Buchan's Richard Hannay, "Sapper's" Bulldog Drummond and Dornford Yates's Jonathan Mansel.

These characters had a great deal in common. They all enjoyed substantial private means and were rich enough not to let anything as vulgar as earning a living interfere with their adventuring. They were proudly upper-class and except in Hannay's case, Public School and Oxbridge. They had all had damned good wars. They drove Rolls-Royces. They were viscerally racist and anti-Semitic. They believed in rough justice, an eye for a tooth, in stepping in where plodding policemen feared to tread, or were unable to tread because of inferior birth and breeding. They regularly bumped off the villains on the grounds—if they thought about it at all—that they were simply saving the hangman the bother. Crucially, they were all members of London Clubs, those exclusive enclaves in the St. James's area, where the elite lunched and dined in splendour, wreathed in cigar smoke, waited on by silent, obsequious servants.

But there was another writer, competing in the same market, equally successful, equally adored by generations of school-boys. His name was Leslie Charteris and his hero was Simon Templar, the Saint.

Usborne does not ignore Charteris and the Saint entirely. He does something rather more disagreeable: he dismisses them both in a few disparaging lines. The Saint, he feels, is a lesser character than Hannay, Drummond, and Mansel; Charteris is a lesser writer than Buchan, Sapper, and Yates.

In the strict technical sense, Usborne is right not to include the Saint in his pantheon because Simon Templar would not have been seen dead in one of those stuffy St. James's clubs. Indeed, throughout the Charteris oeuvre the Saint is devastatingly satirical about the denizens of such places, with their snobbery, prejudices, prudery, and superannuated political opinions. (Hannay, Drummond, and Mansel were all firmly of the Conservative Right.) But in writing off the Saint as a character and Charteris as a prose stylist, Usborne was wrong.

I first encountered the Saint, as I did the other three, in the 1950s when I was banged up in a Prep School in Hertfordshire. Even for that dismal era, the school was a time warp, a little world of its own that would still have been comfortably familiar to Hannay, Drummond, and Mansel but which would have excited the Saint's mockery—and pity for its young inmates.

We were taught to worship Games and (a grimly Protestant) God. In the Cadet Corps we were trained to bayonet the "Hun"—as per the First World War—rather than the "Boche" of the Second World War. For competitive events—almost all sporting—the school was divided into sets named after military heroes: Roberts, Kitchener, Haig, and Beatty. Our physical horizons were bounded by the red brick turrets and walls of the school buildings, reminiscent of a Victorian prison, and fenced, gated playing fields and parkland. Beyond lay forbidden territory, strictly out of bounds, inhabited mainly by dangerous ruffians called oiks. Our intellectual horizons were limited to a curriculum designed for a sole purpose: to get one into a decent Public School. The food was abominable, the school rules numberless and enforced by the frequent swishing of cane and slipper.

Into this narrow, isolated realm stepped the Saint. He was dashing, debonair, didn't give a damn about rules and regulations, lived by his own code, went where he wanted to go, did what he wanted to do, leaving policeman and criminal alike gasping in his wake. He didn't drive a boring, boxy Rolls-Royce; he drove a sleek, superfast Hirondel. He was a citizen of the world, perfectly at home in any great city where, of course, he would know which was the best hotel, the finest restaurant, and where there was always an old friend to lend a hand in his latest endeavour. He was rich, yes, but the money didn't come from a country estate or a share portfolio: he earned it by creaming off his usual ten per cent of the booty or scooping a reward. He was a free spirit, open-minded, without a racist or anti-Semitic bone in his immaculately clothed body. His adventures sprang naturally out of his globe-trotting life, his insatiable curiosity about everything and everybody, his infallible nose for a mystery, his quixotic sense of justice. He was witty. He was clever. He had style, panache. He killed, certainly, but mostly in self-defence, and his preferred modus operandi was to step deftly aside and let dog eat dog. He never displayed the sadistic relish of Bulldog Drummond, the patriotic fervour of Richard Hannay, or the Old Testament righteousness of Jonathan Mansel. Most thrilling of all, perhaps, he lived openly with a woman, Patricia Holm, who was not his wife and whose charms could be only furtively and feverishly imagined.

Although I loved reading about Hannay, Drummond, and Mansel, they were, in a sense, only Senior Prefects writ large. They conformed to the rules—indeed, they strictly imposed them on others. They would triumph on the cricket field, the football pitch, and in the boxing ring and eventually rise to be Head Boy. The Saint, by contrast, might perhaps win the Poetry Prize but would undoubtedly be expelled.

He was completely different. He was a liberator. He pointed a finger, or rather two fingers, with a cigarette held nonchalantly between them, towards a wider, more sophisticated world. He showed that silly or irksome rules could and should be circumvented, pomposity laughed at, an individual path pursued.

So much for the character. What of the literary skills of his creator?

It was only years later, when I had the job of adapting some of the stories for the screen, that I came fully to appreciate what a superb writer Leslie Charteris was.

The first task of the adaptor is to analyze the plot. I quickly discovered that in terms of the overall impact of a given story, the plot plays a relatively minor role. Certainly, the plots are well, often brilliantly, constructed, with all the requisite twists and turns and surprises and—most important—a rigorous logic. But the real fascination lies elsewhere: in description, in the development of a particular situation or scene, above all, in dialogue. The prose is spare and sinewy where the pace of the narrative demands it, but where there is space for a pause, Charteris fills it with paragraph after paragraph, sometimes page after page, of highly entertaining, perfectly honed writing, with a lightness of touch and a refined humour worthy of P. G. Wodehouse. ("By the tum-tum of Tutankhamen!" the Saint exclaims to Mr Teal in the first story in the present collection. Bertie Wooster himself couldn't have put it better.)

The dyspeptic critic might dismiss all this as mere padding: Charteris either lacked the powers of invention or was simply too idle to construct an elaborate plot and made up for it by shoving in a lot of extraneous guff. This would be to miss the point completely. The minimisation of plot and maximisation of other elements is the warp and woof of the Charteris style. What other thriller writer would think of (or dare to proceed with) spicing up a murder mystery with satirical verse? And the verse itself is worthy of Ogden Nash:

> *Trained from an early age to rule*
> *(At that immortal Public School*
> *Whose playing fields have helped to lose*
> *Innumerable Waterloos),*
> *His brains, his wit, his chin, were all*
> *Infinitesimal . . .*

So how does Charteris, the prose stylist, measure up to the writers Usborne set above him? Take Sapper (the nom de plume of an officer-turned-prison governor called H. C. McNeile.) His literary skills can most charitably be described as workmanlike. There is none of the verve, vivacity, and pure relish for words that you find in Charteris. And the character of Drummond himself verges on the Fascistic. John Buchan is a much better writer, a fine writer in fact, but his plots rely unnervingly on coincidence and his attempts to reproduce the slang of the criminal classes, or even worse of Americans, are embarrassing. Dornford Yates is in a category of his own. He developed a unique style, full of archaisms and purple passages that some admire (I am one of them) and others find ludicrous. His plotting is superb, perhaps because his method was never to know himself, at the end of a day's writing, what was going to happen next. But he is most definitely an acquired taste.

By any standard, Leslie Charteris is worthy to stand beside Buchan and Yates—and well above "Sapper." And in *The Saint and Mr Teal* he is on top form. He was twenty-six when he wrote it, and it has all the freshness and vigour of an early work. The three stories are exciting, surprising, funny—and great, great fun. The character of the Saint is fully formed, with all the swashbuckling sparkle that kept him alive through the following decades and saw him emerge, in the form of the incomparable Roger Moore, as a globally recognized figure.

In the late 1970s I found myself one day in a remote fishing village on the coast of Brazil. When I told the locals that I was a writer they naturally asked me what I had written. I mentioned various novels and television shows, all of which were met with blank stares. But when I mentioned the Saint faces lit up, recognition was instant. It was smiles and ecstatic cries of *"El Santo! El Santo!"* all round. The Saint had travelled a long, long way. He is still travelling.

—John Goldsmith

THE SAINT AND MR TEAL

THE GOLD STANDARD

1

Simon Templar landed in England when the news of Brian Quell's murder was on the streets. He read the brief notice of the killing in an evening paper which he bought in Newhaven, but it added scarcely anything to what he already knew.

Brian Quell died in Paris, and died drunk; which would probably have been his own choice if he had been consulted, for the whole of his unprofitable existence had been wrapped up in the pleasures of the Gay City. He was a prophet who was without honour not only in his own country and among his own family, but even among the long-suffering circle of acquaintances who helped him to spend his money when he had any, and endeavoured to lend him as little as possible when he was broke—which was about three hundred days out of the year. He had arrived ten years ago as an art student, but he had long since given up any artistic pretensions that were not included in the scope of studio parties and long hair. Probably there was no real vice in him, but the life of the Left Bank is like an insidious drug, an irresistible spell to such a temperament as his, and it was very easy to slip into the stream in those days before the rapacity of Montmartre *patrons* drove the tourist pioneers across the river. They knew him, and charmingly declined to cash his cheques, at the Dôme, the Rotonde, the Select, and all the multitudinous *boîtes-de-nuit* which spring up around those unassailable institutions for a short season's dizzy popularity, and sink back just as suddenly into oblivion. Brian Quell had his fill of them all. And he died.

The evening paper did not say he was drunk, but Simon Templar knew, for he was the last man to see Brian Quell alive.

He heard the shot just as he had removed his shoes, as he prepared for what was left of a night's rest in the obscure little hotel near the Gare Montparnasse which he had chosen for his sanctuary in Paris. His room was on the first floor, with a window opening on to a well at the back, and it was through this window that the sharp crack of the report came to him. The instinct of his trade made him leap for the nearest swatch and snap out the lights without thinking what he was doing, and he padded back to the window in his stockinged feet. By that time he had realised that the shots could be no immediate concern of his, for the shots that kill you are the ones you don't hear. But if Simon Templar had been given to minding his own business there would never have been any stories to write about him.

He swung his legs over the low balustrade and strolled quietly round the flat square of concrete which surrounded the ground-floor skylight that angled up in to it like his own, but all of them except one were in the centre of the well. Other windows opened out on darkness. The lighted window attracted him as inevitably as it would have drawn a moth, and as he went towards it he observed that it was the only one in the courtyard besides his own which had not been firmly shuttered against any breath of the fresh air which, as all the world knows, is instantly fatal to the sleeping Frenchman. And then the light went out.

Simon reached the dark opening, and paused there. He heard a gasping curse, and then a hoarse voice gurgled the most amazing speech that he had ever heard from the lips of a dying man.

"A mos' unfrien'ly thing!"

Without hesitation, Simon Templar climbed into the room. He found his way to the door and turned on the lights, and it was only then that he learned that the drunken man was dying.

Brian Quell was sprawled in the middle of the floor, propping himself up unsteadily on one elbow. There was a pool of blood on the carpet beside him, and his grubby shirt was stained red across the chest. He stared at Simon hazily.

"A mos' *un*frien'ly thing!" he repeated.

Simon dropped on one knee at the man's side. The first glance told him that Brian Quell had only a few minutes to live, but the astonishing thing was that Quell did not know he was hurt. The shock had not sobered him at all. The liquor that reeked on his breath was playing the part of an anaesthetic, and the fumes in his brain had fuddled his senses beyond all power of comprehending such an issue.

"Do you know who it was?" Simon asked gently.

Quell shook his head.

"I dunno. Never saw him before in my life. Called himself Jones. Silly sora name, isnit? Jones . . . An' he tole me Binks can make gold!"

"Where did you meet him, old chap? Can you tell me what he looked like?"

"I dunno. Been all over place. Everywhere you could gerra drink. Man with a silly sora face. Never seen him before in my life. Silly ole Jones." The dying man wagged his head solemnly. "An' he did a mos' unfrien'ly thing. Tried to shoot me! A mos' unfrien'ly thing." Quell giggled feebly. "An' he saysh Binks can make gold. Thash funny, isnit?"

Simon looked round the room. There was no trace of the man who called himself Jones—nothing but an ash-tray that had been freshly emptied, Obviously the killer had stayed long enough to obliterate all evidence of his visit; obviously too, his victim had been temporarily paralysed, so that the murderer had believed that he was already dead.

There was a telephone by the door, and for a moment Simon Templar gazed at it and wondered if it was his duty to ring for assistance. The last thing on earth that he wanted was an interview even with the most unsuspecting police officer, but that consideration would not have weighed with him for an instant if he had not known that all the doctors in France could have done nothing for the man who was dying in his arms and did not know it.

"Why did Jones try to shoot you?" he asked, and Brian Quell grinned at him vacuously.

"Because he said Binksh could—"

The repetition choked off in the man's throat. His eyes wavered over Simon's face stupidly; then they dilated with the first and last stunned realisation of the truth, only for one horrible dumb second before the end . . .

Simon read the dead man's name from the tailor's tab inside the breast pocket of his coat, and went softly back to his room. The other windows on the courtyard remained shrouded in darkness. If anyone else had heard the shot it must have been attributed to a passing taxi, but there is a difference between the cough of an engine and the crack of an automatic about which the trained ear can never be mistaken. If it had not been for Simon Templar's familiarity with that subtle distinction, a coup might have been inscribed in the annals of crime which would have shaken Europe from end to end—but Simon could not see so far ahead that night.

He left Paris early the following morning. It was unlikely that the murder would be discovered before the afternoon; for it is an axiom of the Quarter that early rising is a purely bourgeois conceit, and one of the few failings of the French hotel-keepers is that they feel none of that divine impulse to dictate the manner of life of their *clientèle* which has from time immemorial made Great Britain the Mecca of holiday makers from every corner of the globe. Simon Templar had rarely witnessed a violent death about which he had so clear a conscience, and yet he knew that it would have been foolish to stay. It was one of the penalties of his fame that he had no more chance of convincing any well-informed policeman that he was a law-abiding citizen than he had of being elected President of the United States. So he went back to England, where he was more unpopular than anywhere else in Europe.

If it is true that there is some occult urge which draws a murderer back to the scene of his crime, it must have been an infinitely more potent force which brought Simon Templar back across the Channel to the scene of more light-hearted misdemeanours than Scotland Yard had ever before endured from the disproportionate sense of humour of any one outlaw. It was not so many years since he had first formulated the idea of making it his life work to register himself in the popular eye as something akin to a public institution, and yet in that short space of time his dossier in the Records Office had swollen to a saga of debonair lawlessness that made Chief Inspector Claud Eustace Teal speechless to contemplate. The absurd little sketch of a skeleton figure graced with a symbolic halo, that impudent signature with which Simon Templar endorsed all his crimes, had spread the terror of the Saint into every outpost of the underworld and crashed rudely into the placid meandering of all those illustrious members of the Criminal Investigation Department who had hitherto been content to justify their employment as guardians of the Law by perfecting themselves in the time-honoured sport of persuading deluded shop-assistants to sell them a bar of chocolate one minute later than the lawful hours for such transactions. The Robin Hood of Modern Crime they called him in the headlines, and extolled his virtues in the same paragraph as they reviled the CID for failing to lay him by the heels; which only shows you what newspapers can do for democracy. He had become an accepted incident in current affairs, like Wheat Quotas and the League of Nations, only much more interesting. He stood for a vengeance that struck swiftly and without mercy, for a gay defiance of all dreary and mechanical things.

"It's not my fault, sir," Chief Inspector Teal stated gloomily, in an interview which he had with the Assistant Commissioner. "We aren't in the Saint's class, and someday I suppose we shall have to admit it. If this was a republic we should make him dictator and get some sleep."

The Commissioner frowned. He was one of the last survivors of the old military school of police chiefs, a distinguished soldier of unimpeachable integrity, but he laboured under the disadvantage of expecting professional law-breakers to parade for judgment as meekly as the casual defaulters he had been accustomed to dealing with in Pondicherry.

"About two months ago," he said, "you told me that the Saint's arrest was only a matter of hours. It was something to do with illicit diamonds, wasn't it?"

"It was," Teal said grimly.

He was never likely to forget the incident. Neither, it seemed, were his superiors. Gunner Perrigo was the culprit in that case, and the police had certainly got their man. The only trouble was that Simon Templar had got him first. Perrigo had been duly hanged on the very morning of this conversation, but his illicit diamonds had never been heard of again.

"It should have been possible to form a charge," insisted the Commissioner, plucking his iron-grey moustache nervously. He disapproved of Teal's attitude altogether, but the plump detective was an important officer.

"It might be, if there were no lawyers," said Teal. "If I went into a witness-box and talked about illicit diamonds I should be bawled out of court. We know the diamonds existed, but who's going to prove it to a jury? Frankie Hormer could have talked about them, but Perrigo gave him the works. Perrigo could have talked, but he didn't—and now he's dead. And the Saint got away with them out of England, and that's the end of it. If I could lay my hands on him tomorrow I'd have no more hope of proving he'd ever possessed any illicit diamonds than I'd have of running the Pope for bigamy. We could charge him with obstructing and assaulting the police in the execution of their duty, but what in heaven's name's the use of running the Saint for a milk-and-water rap like that? It'd be the biggest joke that Fleet Street's had on us for years."

"Did you learn all the facts about his last stunt in Germany?"

"Yes. I did. And it just came through yesterday that the German police aren't in a hurry to prosecute. There's some big name involved, and they've got the wind up. If I was expecting anything else, I was betting the Saint would be hustling back here and getting ready to dare them to try and extradite him from his own country—he's pulled that one on me before."

The Commissioner sniffed.

"I suppose if he did come back you'd want me to head a deputation of welcome," he said scathingly.

"I've done everything that any officer could do in the circumstances, sir," said Teal. "If the Saint came back this afternoon, and I met him on the doorstep of this building, I'd have to pass the time of day with him—and like it. You know the law as well as I do. We couldn't ask him any more embarrassing questions than if he had a good time abroad, and how was his aunt's rheumatism when he last heard from her. They don't want detectives here any longer—what they need is a staff of hypnotists and faith healers."

The Commissioner fidgeted with a pencil.

"If the Saint came back, I should certainly expect to see some change in our methods," he remarked pointedly: and then the telephone on his desk buzzed.

He picked up the receiver, and then passed it across to Teal.

"For you, Inspector," he said curtly.

Teal took over the instrument.

"Saint returns to England," clicked the voice on the wire. "A report from Newhaven states that a man answering to Simon Templar's description landed from the Isle of Sheppey this afternoon. He was subsequently traced to an hotel in the town—"

"Don't talk to me like a fourth-rate newspaper," snarled Teal. "What have you done with him?"

"On the instructions of the Chief Constable, he is being detained pending advice from London."

Teal put the receiver carefully back on its bracket.

"Well, sir, the Saint *has* come back," he said glumly.

2

The Assistant Commissioner did not head a deputation of welcome to Newhaven. Teal went down alone, with mixed feelings. He remembered that the Saint's last action before leaving England had been to present him with a sheaf of information which had enabled him to clean up several cases that had been racking the brains of the CID for many months. He remembered also that the Saint's penultimate action had been to threaten him with the most vicious form of blackmail that can be applied to any police officer. But Chief Inspector Teal had long since despaired of reconciling the many contradictions of his endless feud with the man who in any other path of life might have been his closest friend.

He found Simon Templar dozing peacefully on the narrow bed of a cell in Newhaven police station. The Saint rolled up to a sitting position as the detective entered, and smiled at him cheerfully.

"Claud Eustace himself, by the tum-tum of Tutankhamen! I thought I'd be seeing you." Simon looked the detective over thoughtfully. "And I believe you've put on weight," he said.

Teal sank his teeth in a well-worn lump of chewing gum.

"What have you come back for?" he asked shortly.

On the way down he had mapped out the course of the interview minutely. He had decided that his attitude would be authoritative, restrained, distant, perfectly polite but definitely warning. He would tolerate no more nonsense. So long as the Saint was prepared to behave himself, no obstacles would be placed in his way, but if he was contemplating any further misdeeds . . . The official warning would be delivered thus and thus.

And now, within thirty seconds of his entering the cell, in the first sentence he had uttered, the smooth control of the situation which he had intended to usurp from the start was sliding out of his grasp. It had always been like that. Teal proposed and the Saint disposed. There was something about the insolent self-possession of that scapegrace buccaneer that goaded the detective into *faux pas* for which he was never afterwards able to account.

"As a matter of fact, old porpoise," said the Saint, "I came back for some cigarettes. You can't buy my favourite brand in France, and if you've ever endured a week of Marylands—"

Teal took a seat on the bunk.

"You left England in rather a hurry two months ago, didn't you?"

"I suppose I did," admitted the Saint reflectively. "You see, I felt like having a good bust, and you know what I am. Impetuous. I just upped and went."

"Pity you didn't stay."

The Saint's blue eyes gazed out banteringly from under dark level brows.

"Teal, is that kind? If you want to know, I was expecting a better reception than this. I was only thinking just now how upset my solicitor would be when he heard about it. Poor old chap—he's awfully sensitive about these things. When one of his respectable and valued clients comes home to his native land, and he isn't allowed to move two hundred yards into the interior before some flat-footed hick cop is lugging him off to the hoosegow for no earthly reason—"

"Now you listen to me for a minute," Teal cut in bluntly. "I didn't come here to swap any funny talk of that sort with you. I came down to tell you how the Yard thinks you'd better behave now you're home. You're going loose as soon as I've finished with you, but if you want to stay loose you'll take a word of advice."

"Shall I?"

"That's up to you." The detective was plunging into his big speech half an hour before it was due, but he was going to get it through intact if it was the last thing he ever did. It was an amazing thing that even after the two months of comparative calm which he had enjoyed since the Saint left England, the gall of many defeats was as bitter on his tongue as it had ever been before. Perhaps he had a clairvoyant glimpse of the future, born out of the deepest darkness of his subconscious mind, which told him that he might as well have lectured a sun-spot about its pernicious influence on the weather. The bland smiling composure of that lean figure opposite him was fraying the edges of his nerves with all the accumulated armoury of old associations. "I'm not suggesting," Teal said tersely. "I'm prophesying."

The Saint acknowledged his authority with the faintest possible flicker of one eyebrow—and yet the sardonic mockery of that minute gesture was indescribable.

"Yeah?"

"I'm telling you to watch your step. We've put up with a good deal from you in the past. You've been lucky. You even earned a free pardon, once. Anyone would have thought you'd have been content to retire gracefully after that. You had your own ideas. But a piece of luck like that doesn't come twice in any man's lifetime. You'd made things hot enough for yourself when you went away, and you needn't think they've cooled off just because you took a short holiday. I'm not saying they mightn't cool off a bit if you took a long one. We aren't out for any more trouble."

"Happy days," drawled the Saint, "are here again. Teal, in another minute you'll have me crying."

"You shouldn't have much to cry about," said the detective aggressively. "There's some excuse for the sneak-thief who goes on pulling five-pound jobs. He hasn't a chance to retire. You ought to have made a pretty good pile by this time—"

"About a quarter of a million," said the Saint modestly. "I admit it sounds a lot, but look at Rockefeller. He could spend that much every day."

"You've had a good run. I won't complain about it. You've done me some good turns on your way, and the Commissioner is willing to set that in your favour. Why not give the game a rest?"

The bantering blue eyes were surveying Teal steadily all the time he was speaking. Their expression was almost seraphic in its innocence— only the most captious critic, or the most overwrought inferiority complex could have found anything to complain about in their elaborate sobriety. The Saint's face wore the register of a rapt student of theology absorbing wisdom from an archbishop.

And yet Chief Inspector Claud Eustace Teal felt his mouth drying up in spite of the soothing stimulus of spearmint. He had the numbing sensation of fatuity of a man who has embarked on a funny story in the hope of salvaging an extempore after-dinner speech that has been falling progressively flatter with every sentence, and who realises in the middle of it that it is not going to get a laugh. His own ears began to wince painfully at the awful dampness of the platitudes that were drooling inexplicably out of his own mouth. His voice sounded like the bleat of a lost sheep crying in the wilderness. He wished he had sent someone else to Newhaven.

"Let me know the worst," said the Saint. "What are you leading up to? Is the Government proposing to offer me a pension and a seat in the House of Lords if I'll retire?"

"It isn't. It's offering you ten years' free board and lodging at Parkhurst if you don't. I shouldn't want you to make any mistake about it. If you think you're—"

Simon waved his hand.

"If you're not careful you'll be repeating yourself, Claud," he murmured. "Let me make the point for you. So long as I carry on like a little gentleman and go to Sunday School every week, your lordships will leave me alone. But if I should get back any of my naughty old ideas—if anyone sort of died suddenly while I was around, or some half-witted policeman lost sight of a packet of illicit diamonds and wanted to blame it on me—then it'll be the ambition of every dick in England to lead me straight to the Old Bailey. The long-suffering police of this great country are on their mettle. Britain has awoken. The Great Empire on which the sun never sets—"

"That's enough of that," yapped the detective.

He had not intended to yap. He should have spoken in a trenchant and paralysing baritone, a voice ringing with power and determination. Something went wrong with his larynx at the crucial moment.

He glared savagely at the Saint.

"I'd like to know your views," he said.

Simon Templar stood up. There were seventy-four steel inches of him, a long lazy uncoiling of easy strength and fighting vitality tapering down from wide square shoulders. The keen tanned face of a cavalier smiled down at Teal.

"Do you really want them, Claud?"

"That's what I'm here for."

"Then if you want the news straight from the stable, I think that speech of yours would be a knockout at the Mothers' Union." The

Saint spread out his arms. "I can just see those kindly, wrinkled faces lighting up with the radiant dawn of a new hope—the tired souls wakening again to beauty—"

"Is that all you've got to say?"

"Very nearly, Claud. You see, your proposition doesn't tempt me. Even if it had included the pension and the peerage, I don't think I should have succumbed. It would make life so dull. I can't expect you to see my point, but there it is."

Teal also got to his feet, under the raking twinkle of those very clear blue eyes. There was something in their mockery which he had never understood, which perhaps he would never understand. And against that something which he could not understand his jaw tightened up in grim belligerence.

"Very well," he said. "You'll be sorry."

"I doubt it," said the Saint.

On the way back to London Teal thought of many more brilliant speeches which he could have made but he had not made any of them. He returned to Scotland Yard in a mood of undiluted acid, which the sarcastic comments of the Assistant Commissioner did nothing to mellow.

"To tell you the truth, sir, I never expected anything else," Teal said seriously. "The Saint's outside our province, and he always has been. I never imagined anyone could make me believe in the sort of story-book Raffles who goes in for crime for the fun of the thing, but in this case it's true. I've had it out with Templar before—privately. The plain fact is that he's in the game with a few high-falutin' ideas about a justice above the Law, and a lot of superfluous energy that he's got to get rid of somehow. If we put a psychologist on to him," expounded the detective, who had been reading Freud, "we should be told he'd got an Oedipus Complex. He has to break the law just because it is the law. If we made it illegal to go to church, he'd be heading a revivalist movement inside the week."

The Commissioner accepted the exposition with his characteristic sniff.

"I don't anticipate that the Home Secretary will approve of that method of curtailing the Saint's activities," he said. "Failing the adoption of your interesting scheme, I shall hold you personally responsible for Templar's behaviour."

It was an unsatisfactory day for Mr Teal from every conceivable angle, for he was in the act of putting on his hat preparatory to leaving Scotland Yard that night when a report was brought to him which made his baby-blue eyes open wide with sheer incredulous disgust.

He read the typewritten sheet three times before he had fully absorbed all the implications of it, and then he grabbed the telephone and put through a sulphurous call to the department responsible.

"Why the devil didn't you send me this report before?" he demanded.

"We only received it half an hour ago, sir," explained the offending clerk. "You know what these country police are."

Chief Inspector Claud Eustace Teal slammed back the receiver, and kept his opinion of those country police to himself. He knew very well what they were. The jealousy that exists between the provincial CIDs and Scotland Yard is familiar to anyone even remotely connected with matters of criminal investigation; on the whole, Teal could have considered himself fortunate in that the provincial office concerned had condescended to communicate with him at all on its own initiative, instead of leaving him to learn the news from a late evening paper.

He sat on in his tiny office for another hour, staring at the message which had filtered the last ray of sunshine out of his day. It informed him that a certain Mr Wolseley Lormer had been held up in broad daylight in his office at Southend that afternoon and robbed of close on two thousand pounds by an intruder whom he never even saw. It would not have been a particularly remarkable crime by any standards if the caretaker who discovered the outrage had not also discovered a crude haloed figure chalked on the outer door of Mr Lormer's suite. And the one immutable fact which Chief Inspector Teal could add to the information given him was that at the very time when the robbery was committed the Saint was safely locked up in Newhaven police station—and Mr Teal was talking to him.

3

One of the charms of London, as against those of more up-to-date and scientific cities, is the multitude of queer little unscientific dwellings which may be found by the experienced explorer who wanders a mere hundred yards out of the broad regular thoroughfares and pries into the secrets of dilapidated alleys and unpromising courtyards. At some time in the more recent history of the city there must have been many adventurous souls who felt the urge to escape from the creeping development of modern steam-heated apartments planned with Euclidean exactitude and geometrically barren of all individuality. Wherever a few rooms with an eccentric entrance could be linked up and made comfortable, a home was established which in the days when there came a boom in such places was to repay a staggering percentage to the originality of its creators.

With his infallible instinct for these things, Simon Templar had unearthed this very type of ideal home within a matter of hours after he returned to London. His old stronghold in Upper Berkeley Mews, which he had fitted up years ago with all the expensive gadgets essential to a twentieth-century robber baron, had been the centre of an undue amount of official curiosity just before he embarked on his last hurried trip abroad. It no longer had any ingenious secrets to conceal from the inquisitive hostility of Scotland Yard, and the Saint felt in the mood for a change of scene. He found a suitable change in a quiet cul-de-sac, off the lower end of Queen's Gate, that broad tree-lined avenue which would be a perfect counterpart of the most Parisian boulevard if its taxis and inhabitants were less antique and moth-eaten. The home of his choice was actually situated in a mews which ran across the end of the cul-de-sac like the cross-bar of a T, but some earlier tenant had arranged to combine respectability with a garage on the premises, and had cut a street door and windows through the blank wall that closed the cul-de-sac, so that the Saint's new home was actually an attractive little two-storeyed cottage that faced squarely down between the houses, while the garage and mews aspect was discreetly hidden at the rear. It was almost perfectly adapted to the Saint's eccentric circumstances and strategic requirements, and it is a notable fact that he was able to shift so much lead out of the pants of the estate agents concerned that he was fully installed in his new premises within forty-eight hours of finding that they were to let, which anyone who has ever had anything to do with London estate agents will agree was no mean piece of lead-shifting.

Simon was personally supervising the unpacking of some complicated electrical apparatus when Mr Teal found him at home on the third day. He had not notified his change of address and it had taken Mr Teal some time to locate him, but the Saint's welcome was ingenuous cordiality itself.

"Make yourself at home, Claud," he murmured. "There's a new packet of gum in the sitting-room, and I'll be with you in two minutes."

He joined the detective punctually to a second, dusting some wood shavings from his trousers, and there was nothing whatever in his manner to indicate that he could anticipate any unpleasantness.

He found Teal clasping his bowler hat across his stomach and gazing morosely at an unopened package of Wrigley's Three Star which sat up sedately in the middle of the table.

"I just came in," said the detective, "to tell you I liked your alibi."

"That was friendly of you," said the Saint calmly.

"What do you know about Lormer?"

Simon lighted a cigarette.

"Nothing except that he's a receiver of stolen goods, an occasional blackmailer, and a generally septic specimen of humanity. He's quite a small fish, but he's very nasty. Why?"

Teal ignored the question. He shifted a wad of gum meditatively round his mouth, and then swept the Saint's face with unexpectedly searching eyes.

"Your alibi is good enough," he said, "but I'm still hoping to learn some more about your friends. You used to work with four of 'em, didn't you? I've often wondered how they all managed to reform so quickly."

The Saint smiled gently.

"Still the same old gang theory?" he drawled. "If I didn't know your playful ways so well, Claud, I'd be offended. It's not complimentary. You must find it hard to believe that so many remarkable qualities can be concentrated under one birth certificate, but as time goes on you may get used to the idea. I was quite a prodigy as a child. From the day when I stole the corsets off my old nannie—"

"If you're getting another gang together, or raking up the old lot," Teal said decisively, "we'll soon know all about it. What about that girl who used to be with you—Miss Holm, wasn't it? What's her alibi?"

"Does she want one? I expect it could be arranged."

"I expect it could. She landed at Croydon the day before we found you at Newhaven; I've only just learned that Lormer never saw the man who knocked him out and emptied his safe, so just in case it wasn't a man at all—"

"I think you're on the wrong Line," said the Saint genially. "After all, even a defective . . . detective—has got to consider probabilities. In the old days, before all this vulgar publicity, I could put my trade mark on every genuine article, but you must admit that times have changed. Now that every half-wit in the British Isles knows who I am, is it likely that if I contemplated any crimes I'd be such a fool as to draw Saints all over 'em? D'you think you could make any jury believe it? We got a reputation, Claud. I may be wicked, but I'm not waffy. It's obvious that some low crook is trying to push his stuff on to me."

Teal hitched himself ponderously out of his chair.

"I had thought of that argument," he said, and then, abruptly: "What's your next job going to be?"

"I haven't decided yet," said the Saint coolly. "Whatever it is, it'll be a corker. I feel that I could do with some good headlines."

"Do you think you're playing the game?"

Simon looked at the detective thoughtfully.

"I suppose my exploits don't improve your standing with the Commissioner. Isn't that it?"

The detective nodded.

"You make it very difficult for us," he said.

He could have said a lot more. Pride kept it back stubbornly behind his official detachment, but the sober glance which he gave the Saint was as near to a confession as he dared to go. It was not in his nature to ask favours of any man.

"I'll have to see what I can do," said the Saint.

He ushered Teal courteously to the door, and opened it to see a slim fair-haired vision of a girl walking up the road towards them. Teal watched her approach with narrowed and expressionless eyes.

The girl reached the door and smiled at him sweetly.

"Good-morning," she said.

"Good-morning," said Teal acridly.

He settled his hat and stepped brusquely past her, and Simon Templar closed the front door and caught the girl in his arms.

"Pat, old darling," he said, "I feel that life has begun all over again. With you around, and Claud Eustace dropping in every other day to have words . . . If we could only find someone to murder it'd just be perfect!"

Patricia Holm walked into the sitting-room and pulled off her hat. She helped herself to a cigarette from his case and surveyed him with a little smile.

"Don't you think there might be a close season for Teals? I'll never forget how it was when we left England. I hated you, boy—the way you baited him."

"It's a rough game," said the Saint quietly. "But I haven't baited him this time—not yet. The trouble is that the Ass. Com. holds poor old Claud personally responsible for our brilliance. It was a brain-wave of yours to raid Lormer directly you found I was in clink, but that alibi won't work twice. And Teal's just building up a real case. We'll have to be very careful. Anyway, we won't murder anyone in public . . ."

When the Saint went out that afternoon he carried a conspicuously large white envelope in his hand. At the corner of the cul-de-sac there was a big man patiently manicuring his nails with a pocket-knife. Simon posted his envelope in full view of the watcher, and afterwards suffered himself to be painstakingly shadowed through a harmless shopping expedition in the West End.

Late that night a certain Mr Ronald Nilder, whose agency for vaudeville artists was not above suspicion, received a brief letter in a large white envelope. It stated quite simply that unless he made a five-figure donation to the Actors' Orphanage within the week his relatives might easily suffer an irreparable bereavement, and it was signed with the Saint's trade-mark. Mr Nilder, a public-spirited citizen, immediately rang up the police. Chief Inspector Teal saw him and later had another interview with the Assistant Commissioner.

"Templar posted a large white envelope yesterday," he said, "but we can't prove it was the one Nilder received. If I know anything about the Saint, Nilder will get a follow-up message in a day or two, and we may be able to catch Templar red-handed."

His diagnosis of Saintly psychology proved to be even shrewder than he knew.

For the next couple of days Simon was busy with the work of adding to the comfortable furnishings of his house a selection of electrical devices of his own invention. They were of a type that he had never expected to find included in the fixtures and fittings of any ordinary domicile, but he considered them eminently necessary to his safety and peace of mind. He employed no workmen, for workmen are no less inclined to gossip than anyone else, and the kind of installations which were the Saint's speciality would have been a fruitful source of conversation to anyone. Wherefore the Saint worked energetically alone, and considered his job well done when at the end of it there were no signs of his activity to be found without a very close investigation. The watcher at the end of the cul-de-sac manicured his nails ceaselessly and had many enjoyable walks at the Saint's heels whenever Simon went out. Simon christened him Fido and became resigned to him as a permanent feature of the landscape.

It was near the end of the week when Simon emerged from his front door with another conspicuously large white envelope similar to the first tucked under his arm, and the plain-clothes man, who had definite instructions, closed his penknife with a snap and stepped forward as the Saint came abreast of him.

"Excuse me, sir," he said punctiliously. "May I have a look at your letter?"

The Saint stared at him.

"And who might you be?"

"I'm a police officer," said the man firmly.

"Then why are you wearing an Old Etonian tie?" asked the Saint.

He allowed the envelope to be taken out of his hand. It was addressed to Mr Ronald Nilder, and the detective ripped it open. Inside he found a flexible gramophone disc, and somewhat to his amazement the label in the centre bore the name of Chief Inspector Teal.

"You'd better come along with me," said the detective.

They went in a taxi to Walton Street police station, and there, after some delay, a gramophone was produced and the record solemnly mounted on the turntable.

The plain-clothes man, the Divisional Inspector, the sergeant on duty, and two constables gathered round to listen. Chief Inspector Teal had already been called on the telephone, and the transmitter was placed close to the gramophone for a limited broadcast. Someone set the needle in its groove and started it off.

"Hullo, everybody," said the disc, in a cracked voice. *"This is Chief Inspector Claud Eustace Teal speaking from Scotland Yard. The subject of my lecture today is 'How to Catch Criminals Red-Handed'—a subject on which my experience must be almost unique. From the day when I captured Jack the Ripper to the day when I arrested the Saint, my career has been nothing but a series of historic triumphs. Armed with a bottle of red ink, and my three faithful red herrings, Metro, Goldwyn, and Mayer, I have never failed to reduce my hands to the requisite colour. Although for many years I suffered from bad legs, eczema, boils, halitosis, superfluous hair, and bunions—"*

Simon gave Patricia a graphic account of the incident when he met her at lunch time.

"It was not Teal-baiting," he insisted. "It was a little deed of kindness—a little act of love. After all, is it right that Claud should be encouraged to prod his nose into my private correspondence? If we let him run amok like that, one day he might go too far. We have warned him off for his own good."

They celebrated suitably, and it was late that night when they returned home for a final plate of bacon and eggs before calling it a day. Simon paid off the taxi in Queen's Gate, and they walked up to the house together. The watcher at the corner of the road had gone—the Saint had not expected that Teal would urge him to stay on after that home-made gramophone record had been played.

It was so soon after he had finished installing his electric safety devices that Simon had not even started to anticipate results from them—they were provided for the more strenuous days which he hoped to enjoy before very long, when his return became more widely known and many more guilty consciences began to ask themselves whether their subterranean industries might prosper better if Simon Templar were removed from the catalogue of risks which no insurance company would cover. He had the front door key in his hand before he remembered that the latest product of his defensive genius was now in full working order. Quite casually he slid up a small metal panel under the knocker, and then his face went keen and hard. A tiny bulb set in the woodwork under the panel was glowing red.

Simon dropped the shutter over it again, and drew Patricia aside.

"We've had a visitor," he said. "I didn't think the fun would begin quite so soon."

There was nothing to show whether the visitor had taken his departure. Only one thing was certain—that someone or something had passed across the barrage of invisible alarms that Simon had arranged to cover every door and window in the place. The visitor might have left, but Simon was not disposed to bet on it.

He stood well to the side of the doorway, sheltered by the solid brickwork of the wall, while he reached round and slipped his key soundlessly into the lock at arm's length. Still keeping out of sight, he pushed the door softly back and felt under the jamb for the electric light switch. There was a flicker of fire and a deafening report, and then the light came on and Simon leapt through into the hall. He heard a patter of feet and the slam of a door, and raced through the kitchen to the back entrance on the mews. He got the door open in time to see a running figure fling itself into the back of an open car which was already speeding towards the street, and a second shot came from it before it turned out of the mews. The bullet flew wide and smacked into the wall, and Simon grinned gently and went back to Patricia Holm.

"There's one gunman in London who loses his nerve rather easily, which is just as well for us," he remarked. "But I wonder who it was?"

Curiously enough he had almost forgotten the man named Jones, who had done such an unfriendly thing to Brian Quell that night in Paris.

4

There were no further demonstrations of disapproval that night, although the Saint paid particular attention to the setting of his gadgets before he went to bed, and slept with one ear cocked. He came down to breakfast late the next morning, and was confronted by a shining little cylinder of brass in the middle of his plate. For a moment he stared at it puzzledly, and then he laughed.

"A souvenir?" he murmured, and Patricia nodded.

"I found it in the hall, and I thought you might like to put it in your museum."

Simon spread his napkin cheerfully.

"More 'Weapons I Have Not Been Killed With?'" he suggested "There must be quite a trunkful of them." He reached out a hand towards the cartridge case, and then drew it back. "Wait a minute— just how did you pick this thing up?"

"Why—I don't know. I—"

"Surely you can remember. Think for a minute. I want you to show me exactly how you took hold of it, how you handled it, everything that happened to it between the time when you saw it on the carpet and the time when it reached this plate . . . No—don't touch it again. Use a cigarette."

The girl took up the cigarette endways between her thumb and forefinger.

"That's all I did," she said. "I had the plate in my other hand, and I brought it straight in. Why do you want to know?"

"Because all clever criminals wear gloves when they open safes, but very few of them wear gloves when they're loading a gun." Simon picked up the shell delicately in his handkerchief, rubbed the base carefully where the girl's thumb had touched it, and dropped it into an empty match-box. "Thanks to your fastidious handling, we probably have here some excellent finger-prints of a rotten marksman—and one never knows when they might come in handy."

He returned to a plate of sizzling bacon and eggs with the profound gusto of a man who has slept like a child and woken up like a lion. Patricia allowed him to eat and skim through his morning paper in peace. Whatever schemes and theories were floating through his mercurial imagination, he would never have expounded them before his own chosen time, and she knew better than to try and drag them out of him before he had dealt satisfactorily with his fast.

He was stirring his second cup of coffee when the telephone bell roused him from a fascinating description of the latest woman Atlantic flier's underwear. He reached out a long arm, lifted the receiver, and admitted fearlessly that he was Mr Simon Templar.

"I trust you are well," said the telephone.

The Saint raised his eyebrows, and felt around for a cigarette.

"I'm very fit, thanks," he said. "How are you? And if it comes to that, who are you?"

A deep chuckle reached him from the other end of the line.

"So long as you don't interfere with me, that need not concern you. I'm sorry that you should have had such an unpleasant shock last night, but if my envoy had kept his head you would have felt nothing at all. On the other hand, his foolishness might still encourage you to accept a friendly warning."

"That's very kind of you," said the Saint thoughtfully. "But I've already got someone to see that my socks are aired, and I always take care not to get my feet wet—"

"I'm talking about more dangerous things than colds, Mr Templar."

Simon's gaze fell on the sheet of newspaper which he had been reading. Two columns away from the inventory of the lady aviator's wardrobe he saw a headline that he had not noticed before: and the germ of an inspiration suddenly flashed through his mind. "Another 'Saint' Threat," ran the heading of the column, in large black letters, and below it was an account of the letter that had been received by Mr Ronald Nilder . . . Patricia was watching him anxiously, but he waved her to silence.

"Dear me! Are you such a dangerous man—Mr Jones?" There was a long pause, and the Saint's lips twitched in a faint smile. It had been a shot clear into the dark, but his mind worked like that—flashing on beyond the ordinarily obvious to the fantastically far-fetched that was always so gloriously right.

"My congratulations." The voice on the line was scarcely strained. "How much did Quell tell you?"

"Plenty," said the Saint softly. "I'm sorry you should have had such an unpleasant shock, but if you had kept your head . . ."

He heard the receiver click down at the other end, and pushed the telephone away from him.

"Who was that?" asked Patricia.

"Someone who can think nearly as fast as I can," said the Saint, with a certain artistic admiration. "We know him only as Mr Jones— the man who shot Brian Quell. And it was one of his pals who disturbed the peace last night." The gay blue eyes levelled themselves on her with the sword-steel intentness that she knew of old. "Shall I tell you about him? He's a rather clever man. He discovered that I was staying in the hotel that night—on Quell's floor, with my window almost opposite his across the well. But he didn't know that before he did his stuff— otherwise he might have thought up something even cleverer. How he found out is more than we know. He may have accidentally seen my name in the register, or he may even have come back for something and listened outside Quell's door—then he'd made inquiries to find out who it could have been. But when he got back to England he heard more about me—"

"How?"

"From the story of your noble assault on Wolseley Lormer. Brother Jones decided to take no chances—hence last night. Also this morning there was another dose for him."

Simon pointed to the headlines that he had seen. It was while Patricia was glancing over them that a name in an adjoining paragraph caught his eye, and he half rose from his chair.

"And that!" His finger stabbed at the news item. "Pat—he can certainly think fast!"

He read the paragraph again.

UNIVERSITY PROFESSOR MISSING
SEQUEL TO PARIS SHOOTING TRAGEDY

Birmingham, Thursday.

Loss of memory is believed to be the cause of the mysterious disappearance of Dr Sylvester Quell, professor of electro-chemistry, who has been missing for twenty-four hours.

The professor's housekeeper, Mrs E. J. Lane, told a Daily

45

*Express representative that Dr Quell left his house as usual
at 10:30 a.m. on Wednesday to walk to his lecture-room. He
did not arrive there, and he has not been heard of since.*

*"The professor was very upset by his brother's sudden
death," said Mrs Lane. "He spoke very little about it, but I
know that it affected him deeply."*

*Dr Quell is acknowledged to be one of the foremost
authorities on metallurgy—*

Simon sprang out of his chair and began to pace up and down the room.

"Think it out from the angle of Comrade Jones. He knows I was in a position to know something—he knows my reputation—and he knows I'm just the man to pry into his business without saying a word to the police. Therefore he figures I'd be better out of the way. He's a wise guy, Pat—but just a little too wise. A real professional would have bumped me off and said nothing about it. If he failed the first time he'd've just tried again—and still said nothing. But instead of that he had to phone me and tell me about it. Believe it or not, Pat, the professional only does that sort of thing in story-books. Unless—"

"Unless what?" prompted the girl.

The Saint picked up his cigarette from the edge of the ash-tray, and fell into his chair again with a slow laugh.

"I wonder! If there's anything more dangerous than being just that little bit too clever, it's being in too much of a hurry to say that very thing of the other man. There's certainly some energetic vendetta going on against the Quell family, and since I've been warned to keep out I shall naturally have to be there."

"Not today, if you don't mind," said the girl calmly. "I met Marion Lestrange in Bond Street yesterday, and I promised to drop in for a cocktail this evening."

Simon looked at her.

"I think it might happen about then," he said. "Don't be surprised if you hear my melodious voice on the telephone."

"What are you going to do?" she asked, and the Saint smiled.

"Almost nothing," he said.

He kept her in suspense for the rest of the afternoon, while he smoked innumerable cigarettes and tried to build up a logical story out of the snatches of incoherent explanation that Brian Quell had babbled before he died. It was something about a man called Binks, who could make gold . . . But no consecutive sense seemed to emerge from it. Dr Sylvester Quell might have been interested—and he had disappeared. The Saint could get no further than his original idea.

He told Patricia Holm about it at tea-time. It will be remembered that in those days the British Government was still pompously deliberating whether it should take the reckless step of repealing an Act of 1677 which no one obeyed anyhow, and the Saint's feelings on the matter had been finding their outlet in verse when the train of his criminal inspiration faltered. He produced the more enduring fruits of his afternoon's cogitation with some pride.

> *"Wilberforce Egbert Levi Gupp*
> *Was very, very well brought up,*
> *Not even in his infant crib*
> *Did he make messes on his bib,*
> *Or ever, in his riper years*
> *Forget to wash behind his ears.*
> *Trained from his rawest youth to rule*
> *(At that immortal Public School*
> *Whose playing fields have helped to lose*
> *Innumerable Waterloos),*
> *His brains, his wit, his chin, were all*

Infinitesimal,
But (underline the vital fact)
He was the very soul of tact,
And never in his innocence
Gave anyone the least offence:
Can it be wondered at that he
Became, in course of time, M.P.?"

"Has that got anything to do with your Mr Jones?" asked Patricia patiently.

"Nothing at all," said the Saint. "It's probably far more important. Posterity will remember Wilberforce Gupp long after Comrade Jones is forgotten. Listen to some more:

"Robed in his faultless morning dress
They voted him a huge success;
The sober drabness of the garb
Fittingly framed the pukka sahib;
And though his many panaceas
Show no original ideas,
Gupp, who could not be lightly baulked,
Just talked, and talked, and talked, and talked,
Until the parliamentary clan
Prophesied him a coming man."

"I seem to have heard something in the same strain before," the girl remarked.

"You probably have," said the Saint. "And you'll probably hear it again. So long as there's ink in my pen, and I can make two words rhyme, and this country is governed by the largest collection of soft-bellied half-wits and doddering grandmothers on earth, I shall continue to castigate its imbecilities—whenever I have time to let go a tankard of old ale. I have not finished with Wilberforce."

"Shall I be seeing you after I leave Marion's?" she asked, and the Saint was persuaded to put away the sheet of paper on which he had been scribbling and tell her something which amazed her.

He expounded a theory which anyone else would have advanced hesitantly as a wild and delirious guess with such vivid conviction that her incredulity wavered and broke in the first five minutes. And after that she listened to him with her heart beating a little faster, helplessly caught up in the simple audacity of his idea. When he put it to her as a question she knew that there was only one answer.

"Wouldn't you say it was worth trying, old Pat? We can only be wrong—and if we are it doesn't cost a cent. If we're right—"

"I'll be there."

She went out at six o'clock with the knowledge that if his theory was right they were on the brink of an adventure that would have startled the menagerie of filleted young men and sophisticated young women whom she had promised to help to entertain. It might even have startled a much less precious audience, if she had felt disposed to talk about it, but Patricia Holm was oblivious of audiences—in which attitude she was the most drastic possible antithesis of Simon Templar. Certainly none of the celebrated or nearly celebrated prodigies with whom it pleased Marion Lestrange to crowd her drawing-room once a month would have believed that the girl who listened so sympathetically to their tedious autobiographies was the partner in crime of the most notorious buccaneer of modern times.

The cocktail party ploughed on through a syrupy flood of mixed alcohols, mechanical compliments, second-hand scandal, vapid criticism, lisps, beards, adolescent philosophy, and personal pronouns. Patricia attended with half her mind, while the other half wondered why the egotism which was so delightful and spellbinding in the Saint should be so nauseatingly flatulent in the assorted hominoids around her. She watched the hands of her wrist watch creep round to seven and seven-thirty, and wondered if the Saint could have been wrong.

It was ten minutes to eight when her hostess came and told her that she was wanted on the telephone.

"Is that you, Pat?" said the Saint's voice. "Listen—I've had the most amazing luck. I can't tell you about it now. Can you get away?"

The girl felt a cold tingle run up her spine.

"Yes—I can come now. Where are you?"

"I'm at the May Fair. Hop into a taxi and hurry along—I'll wait for you in the lounge."

She pulled on her hat and coat with a feeling somewhere between fear and elation. The interruption had come so exactly as the Saint had predicted it that it seemed almost uncanny. And the half-dozen bare and uninformative sentences that had come through the receiver proved beyond doubt that the mystery was boiling up for an explosion that only Simon Templar would have gone out of his way to interview at close quarters. As she ran down the stairs, the fingers of her right hand ran over the invisible outlines of a hard squat shape that was braced securely under her left arm, and the grim contact gave her back the old confidence of other dangerous days.

A taxi came crawling along the kerb as she stepped out into Cavendish Square, and she waved to it and climbed in. The cab pulled out again with a jerk, and it was then that she noticed that the glass in the windows was blackened, and was protected against damage from the inside by a closely-woven mesh of steel wire.

She leaned forward and felt around in the darkness for a door handle. Her fingers encountered only a smooth metal plate secured over the place where the handle should have been, and she knew that the man who called himself Jones was no less fast a thinker, and not one whit less efficient, than Simon Templar had diagnosed him to be.

5

Simon Templar refuelled his Duofold and continued with the biography of the coming politician.

> *And down the corridors of fame*
> *Wilberforce Egbert duly came.*
> *His human kindness knew no bounds:*
> *Even when hunting with the hounds*
> *He always had a thought to spare*
> *For the poor little hunted hare;*
> *But manfully he set his lips*
> *And did the bidding of the Whips.*
> *And though at times his motives would*
> *Be cruelly misunderstood,*
> *Wilberforce plodded loyally on*
> *Like a well-bred automaton*
> *Till 1940, when the vote*
> *Placed the Gupp party in the boat,*
> *And Wilberforce assumed the helm*

And laboured to defend the realm.

Simon glanced at his watch, meditated for a few moments, and continued:

> *And through those tense and tedious days*
> *Wilberforce gambolled (in his stays);*
> *The general public got to know*
> *That Gupp, who never answered "No,"*
> *Could be depended on to give*
> *Deft answers in the negative;*
> *And Royal Commissions by the score*
> *Added to Wisdom's bounteous store:*
> *The Simple Foods Commission found*
> *That turnips still grow underground;*
> *The Poultry Farms Commission heard*
> *That turkeys were a kind of bird;*
> *While in an office in the City*
> *The Famous Vicious Drugs Committee*
> *Sat through ten epic calendars*
> *To learn if women smoked cigars;*
> *And with the help Gupp's party gave*
> *Britannia proudly ruled the wave*
> *(Reported to be wet—but see*
> *Marine Commission, section D.)*

It was nearly seven o'clock when the Saint started his car and cruised leisurely eastwards through the Park. He had a sublime faith in his assessment of time limits, and his estimate of Mr Jones's schedule was almost uncannily exact. He pulled up in the south-west corner of

Cavendish Square, from which he could just see the doorway of the Lestranges' house, and prepared himself for a reasonable wait.

He was finishing his third cigarette when a brand-new taxi turned into the square and snailed past the doorway he was watching. It reached the north-east corner, accelerated down the east side and along the south, and resumed its dawdling pace as it turned north again. The Saint bent over a newspaper as it passed him, and when he looked up again the blue in his eyes had the hard glitter of sapphires. Patricia was standing in the doorway, and he knew that Mr Jones was beyond all doubt a fast mover.

Simon sat and watched the girl hail the taxi, and climb in. The cab picked up speed rapidly, and Simon touched his self-starter and hurled the great silver Hirondel smoothly after it.

The taxi swung away to the north and plunged into the streaming traffic of the Marylebone Road. It had a surprising turn of speed for a vehicle of its type, and the Saint was glad that he could claim to have the legs of almost anything on the road. More than once it was only the explosive acceleration of its silent hundred horse-power that saved him from being jammed in a tangle of slow-moving traffic which would have wrecked his scheme irretrievably. He clung to the taxi's rear number-plate like a hungry leech, snaking after it past buses, drays, lorries, private cars of every size and shape under the sun, westwards along the main road and then to the right around the Baker Street Crossing, following every twist of his unconscious quarry as faithfully as if he had been merely steering a trailer linked to it by an invisible steel coupling. It was the only possible method of making certain that no minor accident of the route could leave him sandwiched behind while the taxi slipped round a corner and vanished for ever, and the Saint concentrated on it with an ice-cold singleness of purpose that shut every other thought out of his head, driving with every trick of the road that he knew and an inexorable determination to keep his radiator nailed to a point in space precisely nine inches aft of the taxi's hind-quarters.

There was always the risk that his limpet-like attachment would attract the attention of the driver of the taxi, but it was a risk that had to be ignored. Fortunately it was growing dark rapidly after a dull and rainy afternoon; they raced up the Finchley Road in a swiftly deepening dusk, and as they passed Swiss Cottage Underground the Saint took the first chance of the chase—fell far behind the taxi, switched on his lights, tore after it again, and picked up the red glow-worm eye of its tail light after thirty breathless seconds. That device might have done something to allay any possible suspicions, and the lights of one car look very much like the lights of any other when the distinctive features of its coachwork are hidden behind the diffused rays of a few statutory candlepower.

So far the procession had led him through familiar highways, but a little while after switching on his lights he was practically lost. His bump of locality told him that they were somewhere to the east of the Finchley Road and heading roughly north, but the taxi in front of him whizzed round one corner after another until his bearings were boxed all round the compass, and the names of streets which occasionally flashed past the tail of his eye were unknown to him.

Presently they were running down a broad avenue of large houses set well back from the road, and the taxi ahead was slowing up. In a moment of intuitive understanding, the Saint held his own speed and shot past it; keeping the cab in his driving mirror, he saw it turning in through a pair of gates set in a high garden wall twenty yards behind him.

Simon locked his wheels round the next corner and pulled up dead. In a second he was out of the car and walking quickly back towards the driveway into which the taxi had disappeared.

He strolled quietly past the gates and took in as much of the lie of the land as he could in one searching survey under the slanted brim of his hat. The house was a massively gloomy three-storeyed edifice in the most pompous Georgian style, reminiscent of a fat archdeacon suffering an attack of liver with rhinoscerine fortitude, and the only light visible on that side of it was a pale pink bulb that hung in the drab portico like a forlorn plum in an orchard that the pickers have finished with. The neglected front garden was dappled with the shadows of a few laurel bushes and unkempt flower-beds. Of the taxi there was no sign, but a dim nimbus of light was discernible beyond the shrubbery on the right.

The Saint's leisured step eased up gradually and reached a standstill. After all, Mr Jones was the man he wanted to meet; this appeared to be Mr Jones's headquarters, and there were no counter-attractions in the way of night life to be seen in that part of Hampstead. The main idea suffered no competition, and a shrewd glance up and down the road revealed no other evening prowlers to notice what happened.

Simon dropped his hands into his pockets and grinned gently at the stars.

"Here goes," he murmured.

The dense shadows inside the garden swallowed him up like a ghost. A faint scraping of gears came to him as he skirted a clump of laurels and padded warily along the grass border of a part of the drive which circled round towards the regions where he had seen the light, and he rounded the corner of the house in time to see the taxi's stern gliding through the doors of a garage that was built on to the side of Mr Jones's manor. Simon halted again, and stood like a statue while he watched a vague figure scrunch out of the darkness and pull the doors shut behind the cab—from the inside. He surmised that there was a direct communication from the garage through into the house, but he heard a heavy bolt grating into its socket as he drew nearer to investigate.

The Saint sidled on past the garage to the back of the house and waited. After a time he saw two parallel slits of subdued radiance blink out around the edges of a drawn blind in a first-floor window; they were no more than hair-lines of almost imperceptible luminance etched in the blackness of the wall, but they were enough to give him the information he needed.

Down on the ground level, almost opposite where he stood, he made out another door—obviously a kitchen entrance for the convenience of servants, tradesmen, and policemen with ten minutes to spare and a sheik-like style with cooks. He moved forward and ran his fingers over it cautiously. A gentle pressure here and there told him that it was not bolted and he felt in his pocket for a slim pack of skeleton keys. At the third attempt the heavy wards turned solidly over and Simon replaced the keys in his pocket and pushed the door inwards by fractions of an inch, with the blade of his penknife pressing against the point where it would first be able to slip through. He checked the movement of the door at the instant when his knife slid into the gap, and ran the blade delicately up and down the minute opening. At the very base of the door it encountered an obstruction, and the Saint flicked the burglar alarm aside with a neat twist and an inaudible sigh of satisfaction, and stepped in.

Standing on the mat, with his back to the closed door, he put away the knife and snapped a tiny electric flashlight from its clip in his breast pocket. It was no longer than a fountain pen, and a scrap of tinfoil with a two-millimetre puncture in it was gummed over the bulb so that the beam it sent out was as fine as a needle. A three-inch ellipse of concentrated light whisked along the wall beside him, and rounded itself off into a perfect circle as it came to rest on another door facing the one by which he had entered.

Simon Templar's experience as a burglar was strictly limited. On the rare occasions when he had unlawfully introduced himself into the houses of his victims, it had nearly always been in quest of information rather than booty. And he set out to explore the abode of the man called Jones with the untainted zest of a man to whom the crime was still an adventure.

With one hand still resting lightly on the side pocket of his coat he opened the opposite door soundlessly and admitted himself to a large dimly illuminated central hall. A broad marble staircase wound up and around the sides of the hall, climbing from gallery to gallery up the three floors of the house until it was indistinguishable against the great shrouded emptiness of what was probably an ornate stained-glass skylight in the roof. Everything around was wrapped in the silence of death, and the atmosphere had the damply naked feel of air that has not been breathed for many months. A thin smear of dust came off on his fingers from everything he touched, and when he flashed his torch over the interior of one of the ground-floor rooms he found it bare and dilapidated, with the paint peeling off the walls and cobwebs festooning an enormous dingy gilt chandelier.

"Rented for the job," he diagnosed. "They wouldn't bother about the ground floor at all—not with kidnapped prisoners."

He flitted up the staircase without so much as a tap from his feather-weight crepe-soled shoes. A strip of cheap carpet had been roughly laid round the gallery which admitted to the first-floor rooms, and the Saint walked softly over it, listening at door after door.

Then he heard with startling clarity a voice that he recognised.

"You have nothing to be afraid of, Miss Holm, so long as you behave yourself. I'm sorry to have had to take the liberty of abducting you, but you doubtless know one or two reasons why I must discourage your friend's curiosity."

He heard the girl's calm reply:

"I think you could have invented a less roundabout way of committing suicide."

The man's bass chuckle answered her. Perhaps only the Saint's ears could have detected the iron core of ruthless menace that hardened the overtones of its full-throated heartiness.

"I'm glad you're not hysterical." A brief pause. "If there's anything within reason that you want, I hope you'll ask for it. Are you feeling hungry?"

"Thanks," said the girl coolly. "I should like a couple of sausages, some potatoes, and a cup of coffee."

Simon darted along the gallery and whipped open the nearest door. Through the gap which he left open he saw a heavily-built grey-haired man emerge from the next room, lock the door after him, and go down the stairs. As the man bent to the key, the Saint had a photographic impression of a dark, large-featured, smooth-shaven face; then he could only see the broad well-tailored back passing downwards out of view.

The man's footsteps died away, and Simon returned to the landing. He stood at the door of Patricia's room and tapped softly on the wood with his fingernails.

"Hullo, Pat!"

Her dress rustled inside the room.

"Quick work, boy. How did you do it?"

"Easy. Are you all right?"

"Sure."

"How's the window in there?"

"There's a sort of cage over it—I couldn't reach the glass. The taxi was the same. There's a divan bed and a couple of wicker arm-chairs. The table's very low—the legs wouldn't reach through the bars. He's thought of everything. Wash basin and jug of water on the floor—some towels—cigarettes—"

"What happened to the taxi-driver?"

"That was Mr Jones."

The Saint drew a thoughtful breath.

"Phew! And what a solo worker! . . . Can you hold on for a bit? I'd like to explore the rest of the establishment before I start any trouble."

"Go ahead, old chap, I'm fine."

"Still got your gun?"

"Sure."

"So long, lass."

The Saint tip-toed along the landing and prowled up the second flight of stairs.

6

There were no lights burning on the upper gallery, but a dull glimmer of twilight flittered up from the lamps below and relieved the darkness sufficiently for him to be able to move as quickly as he wanted to. With his slim electric flash in his hand he went around the storey from room to room, turning the door-handles with infinite care, and probing the apartments with the dancing beam of his torch. The first one he opened was plainly but comfortably furnished as a bedroom: it was evidently occupied, for the bed had not been made since it was last slept in, and a shaving brush crested with a mound of dried lather stood on the mantelpiece. The second room was another bedroom, tidier than the first, but showing the ends of a suit of silk pyjamas under the pillow as proof that it also was used. The door of the third room was locked, and Simon delved in his pocket again for a skeleton key. The lock was of the same type as that on the back door by which he had entered the house—one of those ponderously useless contraptions which any cracksman can open with a bent pin—and in a second or two it gave way.

Simon pushed the door ajar, and saw that the room was in darkness. He stepped boldly in, quartering the room with his weaving pencil of light. The flying disc of luminance danced along the walls and suddenly stopped, splashing itself in an irregular pool over the motionless form of a man who lay quietly on the floor as if asleep. But the Saint knew that he was dead.

He knelt down and made a rapid examination. The man had been dead about forty-eight hours—there was no trace of a wound but with his face close to the dead man's mouth he detected the unmistakable scent of prussic acid. It was as he was rising to go that he accidentally turned over the lapel of the dead man's coat, and saw the thin silver badge underneath—the silver greyhound of a King's Messenger.

The Saint came to his feet again rather slowly. The waters were running deeper than he had ever expected, and he felt an odd sense of shock. That slight silver badge had transformed the adventure at one glance from a more or less ordinary if still mysterious criminal problem to an intrigue that might lead anywhere.

As he left the room he heard the man called Jones coming up the stairs again. Peeping over the wooden balustrade, he saw that the man carried a tray—the catering arrangements in that house appeared to be highly commendable, even if nothing else was.

Simon slipped along the gallery without a sound. He opened two more rooms and found them both empty; then he paused outside another and saw a narrow line of light under the door.

He stood still for a few seconds, listening. He heard an occasional faint chink of glass or metal, and the shuffling of slippered feet over the carpet, but there were no voices. Almost mechanically he tried the door, and had one of the biggest surprises of his life when he felt it opening.

The Saint froze up motionless, with a dry electric tingle glissading over the surface of his skin. The way the door gave back under his light touch disintegrated the very ground from under his nebulous theory about the occupant of that room. In the space of four seconds his brain set up, surveyed, and bowled over a series of possible explanations that were chiefly notable for their complete uselessness. In the fifth second that ultimate fact impressed itself unanswerably on his consciousness, and he acknowledged it with a wry shrug and the decimal point of a smile. Theories were all very well in their place, but he had come to the house of Mr Jones on a quest for irrefutable knowledge, and an item of irrefutable knowledge was awaiting his attention inside that room. It remained for him to go in and get introduced—and that was what he had given up a peaceful evening in his own home to do.

He glanced downwards into the hall. There was no sound or movement from below. For a minute or two he might consider he had the field to himself—if he was quick and quiet about taking it over.

The door of the lighted room opened further, inch by inch, against the steady persuasion of his fingers, while his nerves were keyed up to check its swing at the first faint hint of a squeak out of the hinges. Gradually the strip of light at the edge widened until he could see part of the room. A grotesque confusion of metal and glass, tangled up with innumerable strands and coils of wire, was heaped over all the floor space that he could see like the scrap-heap of one of those nightmare laboratories of the future which appear in every magazine of pseudo-scientific fiction. The Saint's unscientific mind could grasp nothing but the bare visual impression of it—an apparently aimless conglomeration of burnished steel spheres and shining crystal tubes that climbed in and out of each other like a futurist sculptor's rendering of two all-in wrestlers getting acquainted. Back against the far wall ran a long work-bench of wood and porcelain surmounted by racks and shelves of glass vessels and bottles of multi-coloured mixtures. It was the most fantastic collection of incomprehensible apparatus that Simon Templar had ever seen, and yet in some ridiculously conventional way it seemed to have its perfect focus and presiding genius in the slender white-haired man in a stained and grimy white overall who stood at the bench with his back to the open door.

Simon Templar walked very quietly into the room and closed the door noiselessly behind him. He stood with his back leaning against it and his right hand circling comfortably round the butt of the automatic in his pocket, and cleared his throat apologetically.

"Hullo," he said.

The figure at the bench turned round sharply. He was a mild-faced man with a pair of thick gold-rimmed pince-nez perched slantwise on the end of a long fleshy nose, and his response was pitched in the last key on earth that the Saint had expected to hear.

"What the devil do you want?" he demanded.

To say that the Saint was taken aback means nothing. The effect on his emotional system was much the same as it would have been if the aged scientist had uttered a shrill war-whoop and begun to turn cartwheels over the test-tubes. Even in these days of free thought and speech the greeting seemed singularly unusual. When you have been at considerable pains, without appreciable hope of reward, to hunt along the trail of a kidnapped professor—when, in the process, you have been warned off the course with a couple of bullets, and have found it necessary to let yourself in for a charge of vulgar burglary in the good cause—you are definitely entitled to expect a fairly cordial welcome from the object of your rescue expedition.

Once before the Saint had been greeted something like that in rather similar circumstances, and the memory of that adventure was still fresh with him. It cut short the involuntary upward jerk of his eye-brows, and when he found an answer his voice was absolutely level and natural. Only an ear that was listening for it would have sensed the rapier points that stroked in and out of its casual syllables.

"I just came to see how you were getting on, Dr Quell."

"Well, why can't you leave me alone? How do you expect me to get any work done while I'm being pestered with your absurd questions every ten minutes?" The old man was gesticulating his disgust with everything from his feet to his forehead, till the glasses on his nose quivered with indignation. "What d'you think I am—a lazy schoolboy? Eh? Dammit, haven't you any work of your own?"

"You see, we don't want you to have a breakdown, professor," said the Saint, soothingly. "If you took a little rest now and then—"

"I had seven hours' rest last night. I'm not an invalid. And how would I get this done in time if I lay in bed all day? Think it would get done by itself? Eh?"

Simon took out a cigarette case and moved over to sit down on a conveniently shaped dome of metal.

"All the same, professor, if you wouldn't mind—"

The old man leapt towards him with a kind of yelp. Simon drew back hurriedly, and the professor glared at him, breathing heavily.

"Dammit, if you want to commit suicide, must you come and do it here?"

"Suicide?" repeated the Saint vaguely. "I hadn't—"

"Pish!" squawked the professor.

He snatched up a loose length of wire and tossed it on to the dome on which Simon had been preparing to rest himself. There was a momentary crackle of hot blue flame—and the wire ceased to resemble anything like wire. It simply trickled down the side of the dome in the shape of a few incandescent drops of molten metal, and Simon Templar mopped his brow.

He retreated towards the clear space around the door with some alacrity.

"Thanks very much, professor," he remarked. "Have you any more firework effects like that?"

"Bah!" croaked the professor huffily.

He went back to his bench and wiped his hands on a piece of rag, with every symptom of a society welfare worker removing the contamination of an afternoon with the deserving poor.

"Is there anything else you want to know?" he barked, and the Saint braced himself for the shot that had to be taken in the dark.

"When are we going to see some gold?"

The professor seemed on the verge of an outburst beside which his former demonstrations would pale into polite tea-table chatter. And then with a tremendous effort he controlled himself. He addressed the Saint with the dreadfully laboured restraint of a doting mother taking an interest in the precocities of a rival parent's prodigy and thinking what an abominable little beast he is.

"When you can use your eyes. When you can get some glasses powerful enough to show you something smaller than a haystack. Or else when you can improve on my methods and make gold run out of the bathroom tap. That's when." The old man stalked across to a cupboard and flung it open. "There. Look again. Try to see it. Borrow a microscope if you have to. But for heaven's sake, young man"—the quavering voice lost some of its self-control and rose two shrill notes—"for heaven's sake, don't utter any more blithering idiocies like that in my laboratory."

Simon stared into the cupboard.

He had never dreamed of seeing wealth like that concentrated in tangible form under his eyes. From floor to ceiling the cupboard was stacked high with it—great glittering yellow ingots the size of bricks reflecting the lamplight in one soaring block of tawny sleekness like the realisation of a miser's dream. The sight of it dazed him. There must have been over a million pounds' worth of the metal heaped carelessly into that tall rectangular cavity in the wall. And back and forth across his memory flashed the inane repetition of the dying young roué in Paris: "He says Binks can make gold . . ."

The professor's cracked voice broke in on him through a kind of fog.

"Well? Can you see it? Have you found your eyes at last? Eh? Does it begin to satisfy you?"

Simon had to fight for the smooth use of his tongue.

"Naturally, that's . . . er . . . very satisfactory, Dr Quell, but—"

"Very satisfactory. I should think so." The professor snorted. "Half a hundredweight every hour. Very satisfactory. Faugh! You're a fool—that's what you are. Dammit, if the rest of the Secret Service are as thick-headed as you, I don't know why the country should bother to have a Secret Service."

The Saint stood very still.

But he felt as if a light-bomb had exploded inside him. The mystery was opening out before his eyes with a suddenness that could only be compared with an explosion. The detached items of it whirled around like scattered aircraft in the beam of a searchlight, and fell luminously into formation with a precision that was uncanny. Everything fitted in its place: the murder of Brian Quell, the King's Messenger who lay dead in an adjoining room, the man who could make gold . . . the man called "Binks"—a queer nickname to be given to such a brilliant and irritable old magician by his dissolute young brother! And that last mordant reference to the Secret Service: an idea that was worthy of the genius of Mr Jones—so much simpler, so much more ingenious and effective than the obvious and hackneyed alternative of threats and torture . . . Most astounding of all, the proof that the essential pivot of the thing was true. Sylvester Quell—"Binks"—*could* make gold. He had made it—hundredweights of it. He was making more.

Simon heard him grousing on in the same cracked querulous voice.

"I don't know why I came here. I could have done better in my own laboratory. Look after me, eh? With the intelligence you've got, you couldn't look after yourself. What use d'you think you are? Why don't you go away and let me do my work? You're worse than that other man, with his stupid questions and his school-room tests. Does he think I don't know real gold when I make it?"

It was all quite clear to the Saint. The only question left was how he should act. He could give very little time now to arguments and discussions—escape from that house had become one of the paramount considerations of his life, a thing more vitally important than he had ever thought it could be.

His hand went back to his pocket, his thumb feeling around for the safety-catch of his automatic and pressing it gently out of engagement. Under straight dark brows the blue Saintly eyes centred on Quell like spear-points.

"Of course not, professor. But about the notes of your process—"

He was so intent on the scientist that the movement of the door behind him missed his ears. The crack of an automatic fired at close quarters battered and stung his ear-drums, and the bullet plucked at his coat. Somehow he was untouched—it is much easier to miss with an automatic than any inexperienced person would believe, and perhaps Mr Jones's haste made him snatch at the pull-off. The Saint spun round and fired from his pocket; his nerves were steadier, and he scored where he meant to score—on the gun in the big man's hand. The weapon dropped to the floor, and Simon stepped closer.

"Keep still."

The big man's face was twisted with fury. Behind him, Simon heard Quell's shrill whine.

"What does this mean, sir? Eh? Dammit—"

The Saint smiled.

"I'm afraid you've been taken in, professor. Our friend no more belongs to the Secret Service—"

"Than you do!" The big man's voice snarled in viciously. His fists were clenched and his eyes murderous—only the Saint's gun held him where he stood. "This is one of the men I warned you about, professor—he's trying to steal your secret, that's what it means! The damned traitor!—if I could only get my hands on him . . . For God's sake why don't you do something? He's probably one of the gang that killed your brother—"

"Stop that!"

The Saint's voice cracked through the room like a blade of lightning, but he saw where the big man's desperate clatter of words was leading to a fraction of a second too late. Quell leapt at him suddenly with a kind of sob, before Simon had time to turn. The professor's skinny hand wrestled with his gun wrist and hate-crazed talons clawed at his throat. Simon stumbled sideways under the berserk fury of the scientist's onslaught, and his aim on the man called Jones was hopelessly lost. They swayed together in the corner. Quell's hysterical breathing hissed and moaned horribly in the Saint's ears, and over the demented man's shoulder he saw Jones stooping with his left hand for the fallen gun.

The Saint saw certain and relentless death blazing across his path like an express train. With a savage gathering of all his muscles he shook the professor off and sent him reeling back like a rag doll. Quell's dreadful shriek rang in his ears as Simon leapt across the dividing space and kicked away the automatic that the big man's fingers were within an inch of touching.

The gun clanged heavily into a piece of metal on the far side of the room, and Simon caught the big man by one lapel of his coat and spun him round. The Saint's gun rammed into the big man's ribs with a brutal forcefulness that made the other wince.

"Don't try that again."

Simon's whisper floated into the other's ears with an arctic gentleness that could not have been driven deeper home by a hundred megaphones. It carried a rasping huskiness of meaning that only a fool could have mistaken. And Mr Jones was no fool. He stood frozen into stone, but the sweat stood out in glistening beads on his forehead.

The Saint flashed one glance sideways, and saw what Mr Jones had seen first.

Sylvester Quell was sitting on the floor with his back to the shining dome-like contrivance that Simon had seen in action. One hand still rested on the dome, as if by some kind of spastic attraction, exactly as it had involuntarily gone out to save himself when the Saint's frantic struggle sent him stumbling back against the machine, but the hand was stiff and curiously blackened. The professor's upturned face was twisted in a hideous grin . . . Whilst Simon looked, the head slipped sideways and lolled over on one shoulder . . .

7

A twitch of expression tensed over the face of the man who called himself Jones. His eyebrows were drawn down at the bridge of his nose, and strained upwards at the outside corners; the eyes under them were swollen and bloodshot.

"You killed him," he rasped.

"I'm afraid I did," said the Saint. "An unfortunate result of my efforts at self-defence—for which you were entirely responsible."

"You'll have a job to prove it."

The Saint's gentlest smile plucked for an instant at thin-drawn lips.

"I don't know whether I shall try."

He grasped the big man's shoulder suddenly and whirled him half round again, driving him back towards the door.

"Move on, comrade."

"Where are you going?"

"Downstairs, I've got a friend of mine waiting with claustrophobia, and I guess she's been locked up long enough for one day. And if she couldn't eat all those sausages I might find a home for one."

They went down the stairs step by step, in a kind of tango style that would have been humorous to anyone who was insensitive to the deadly tension of it. But Simon Templar was giving no more chances. His forefinger was curled tightly over the trigger for every foot of the way, and the big man kept pace with him in a silence that prickled with malignant vigilance. They came to the door of the room below, and the Saint stopped.

"Open it."

The big man obeyed, turning the lock with a key which he took from his trouser pocket. Simon kicked the door wider.

"This way, Pat."

He waited on the landing while the girl came out, never shifting his eyes from the big man's venomous stillness. Patricia touched his sleeve, and he smiled.

"Simon—then it wasn't you. I heard . . ."

"That scream?" Simon slipped an arm round her and held her for a moment. "Why— did you think my voice was as bad as that, old darling? . . . No, but it wasn't brother Jones either, which is a pity."

"Then who was it?"

"It was Dr Quell. Pat, we've struck something a little tougher than I expected, and it hasn't turned out too well. This is just once in our lives that Claud Eustace will be useful. Once upon a time we might have handled it alone, but I think I promised to be careful."

He looked at his prisoner.

"I want your telephone," he said.

The big man hesitated, and Simon's gun screwed in his ribs.

"C'mon. You can have indigestion afterwards." Simon released the girl. "And that reminds me—if you did leave one of those sausages . . ."

Again they descended step by step towards the hall, with the Saint using his free hand to feed himself in a manner that is rarely practised in the best circles. The telephone was in the hall, on a small table by the front door, and Simon turned his gun over to Patricia and walked across to it, chewing. He leaned a chair against the door and sat in it. The dial buzzed and clicked.

"Hullo . . . I want Chief Inspector Teal . . . Yeah—and nobody else. Simon Templar speaking. And make it snappy!"

The big man took a step towards him, his face yellow and his hands working. And immediately the girl's finger took up the slack of the trigger. It was an almost imperceptible movement, but Mr Jones saw it, and the steady deliberateness of it was more significant than anything that had entered his imagination since the gun changed hands. He halted abruptly, and the Saint grinned.

"Hullo. Is that you, Claud? . . . Well, I want you—Yeah—for the first time in my life I'll be glad to see you. Come right over, and bring as many friends as you like . . . I can't tell you on the phone, but I promise it'll be worth the trip. There's any amount of dead bodies in the house, and . . . Well, I suppose I can find out for you. Hold on."

He clamped a hand over the mouthpiece and looked across the table.

"What's the address, Jones?"

"You'd better go on finding out," retorted the big man sullenly.

"Sure." The Saint's smile was angelic. "I'll find out. I'll go to the street corner and see. And before I go I'll just kick you once round the hall—just to see my legs are functioning."

He lounged round the table, and their eyes met.

"This is two hundred and eight Meadowbrook Road," said the man grimly.

"Thanks a lot." Simon dropped into his chair again and picked up the telephone. "Two-o-eight, Meadowbrook Road, Hampstead—I'll be here when you come—O.K., Eustace."

He rose.

"Let's climb stairs again," he said brightly.

He took over the gun and shepherded the party aloft. The show had to be seen through, and his telephone call to Chief Inspector Teal had set a time limit on the action that could not be altered. It was a far cry from that deserted house to the hotel in Paris where Brian Quell had died, and yet Simon knew that he was watching the end of a coherent chain of circumstances that had moved with the inscrutable remorselessness of a Greek tragedy. Fate had thrust him into the story again and again, as if resolved that there should be no possibility of a failure in the link that bore his name, and it was ordained that he should write the end of the story in his own way.

The laboratory upstairs stood wide open. Simon pushed the big man in, and followed closely behind. Patricia Holm came last: she saw the professor huddled back against his machine with his face still distorted in the ghastly grimace that the death-agony of high-voltage electricity had stamped into his features, and bit her lip. But she said nothing. Her questioning eyes searched the Saint's countenance of carved brown granite, and Simon backed away a little from his captive and locked the door behind him.

"We haven't a lot of time, Jones," he remarked quietly, and the big man's lips snarled.

"That's your fault."

"Doubtless. But there it is. Chief Inspector Claud Eustace Teal is on his way, and we have one or two things to settle before he comes. Before we start, may I congratulate you?"

"I don't want any congratulations."

"Never mind, you deserve them." The Saint fished out his cigarette case with his left hand. Quite naturally he extracted and lighted a cigarette, and stole a glance at his wrist-watch while he did so. His brain worked like a taxi-meter, weighing out miles and minutes. "I think I've got everything taped but you can check me up if I go wrong anywhere. Somehow or other—we won't speculate how—you got to know that

Dr Quell had just perfected a perfectly sound commercial method of transmuting metals. It's been done already on a small scale, but the expense of the process ruled it right out as a get-rich-quick proposition. Quell had worked along a new line, and made it a financial cinch."

"You must have had a long talk with him," said the big man sardonically.

"I did . . . However—your next move, of course, was to get the process for yourself. You're really interesting, Jones—you work on such original lines. Where the ordinary crook would have tried to capture the professor and torture him, you thought of subtler methods. You heard of Quell's brother, a good-for-nothing idler who was always drunk and usually broke. You went over to Paris and tried to get him in with you, figuring that he could get Sylvester's confidence when no one else could. But Brian Quell had a streak of honesty in him that you hadn't reckoned with. He turned you down—and then he knew too much. You couldn't risk him remembering you when he sobered up. So you shot him. I was there. A rotten shot, Jones—just like the one you took at me this evening, or that other one last night. Gun work is a gift, brother, and you simply haven't got it."

The big man said nothing.

"You knew I knew something about Brian Quell's murder, so you tried to get me. That talk about an 'envoy' of yours was the bunk—you were playing the hand alone, because you knew there wasn't a crook on earth who could be trusted on a thing as big as this." The Saint never paused in his analysis, but his eyes were riveted to the prisoner's face, and he would have known at once if his shot in the dark went astray. Not the faintest change of expression answered him, and he knew he was right. Jones was alone. "By the way, I suppose you wouldn't like to tell me exactly how you knew something had gone wrong in Paris?"

"If you want to know, I thought I heard someone move in the corridor outside, and I went out to make sure. The door blew shut behind me, on an automatic lock. I had to stand outside and listen. Then someone really did come along the passage—"

"And you had to beat it." Simon nodded. "But I don't think you rang me up this morning just to make out how much I heard. What you wanted was to hear my voice, so that you could imitate it."

"He did it perfectly," said Patricia.

The Saint smiled genially.

"You see, Jones. If you couldn't have made your fortune as a gun artist, you might have had a swell career as a ventriloquist. But you wouldn't have it. You wanted to be a Master Mind, and that's where the sawdust came out. My dear old borzoi, did you think we'd never heard of that taxi joke before? Did you think poor little Patricia with all her experience of sin, was falling for a gag like that? Jones, that was very silly of you—quite irreparably silly. We've let you have your little joke just because it seemed the easiest way to get a close-up of your beautiful whiskers. If you'd left us your address before you rang off this morning we'd have been saved the trouble but as it was—"

"Well, what are you getting at?" grated the big man.

"Just checking up," said the Saint equably. "So you know how we got here. And I found that King's Messenger in the other room—that's what first confirmed what we were up against. Anyone making gold is one of the things the Secret Service sits and waits for all year round: one day the discovery is going to be genuine, and the first news of it would send the international exchanges crazy. There'd be the most frightful panic in history, and any Government has got to be watching for it. That King's Messenger had the news—you were lucky to get him."

The big man was silent again, but his face was pale and pasty.

"Two murders, Jones, that were your very own handiwork," said the Saint, "And then—the professor. Accidental, of course. But very unfortunate. Because it means that you're the only man left alive who knows this tremendous secret."

Simon actually looked away. But he had no idea what he looked at. The whole of his faculties were concentrated on the features which were still pinned in the borders of his field of vision, watching with every sense in his body for the answer to the question that he could not possibly ask. That one thing had to be known before anything else could be done, and there was only one way to know it. He bluffed, as he had bluffed once before, without a tremor of his voice or a flicker of his eyes . . .

And the most impressive thing about the big man's expression was that it did not change. The big man took the Saint's casual assertion into his store of knowledge without the slightest symptom of surprise. It signified nothing more to him than one more superfluous blow on the head of a nail that was already driven deep enough. He glared at the Saint, and the gun in the Saint's hand, without any movement beyond a mechanical moistening of his lips, intent only on watching for the chance to fight that seemed infinitely improbable . . . And the Saint tapped the ash from his cigarette and looked at the big man again.

"I got nearly everything out of Dr Quell before you interrupted us," he said, clinching the assertion of utter certainty. "It was clever of you to wheedle Quell's process out of him bit by bit—and very useful that you had enough scientific knowledge to understand it. I suppose Quell's sphere of service was running out about this time, anyway— you'd have got rid of him yourself even if there'd been no accident. A very sound and prudent policy for a Master Mind, Jones, but just a shade too dangerous when the scheme springs a leak like me."

"Cut it short," snarled the big man. "What more d'you want? The gold's there—"

"Yes, the gold's certainly there," said the Saint dispassionately. "And in about ten minutes the police will be here to gape at it. I'm afraid that can't be helped. I'd like to get rich quick myself, but I've realised tonight that there's one way of doing it which is too dangerous for any man to tackle. And you don't realise it, Jones—that's the trouble. So we can't take any risks."

"No?"

"No." Simon gazed at the big man with eyes that were very clear, and hard as polished flints. "You see, that secret's too big a thing to be left with you. There's too much dynamite tied up in it. And yet the police couldn't do anything worth a damn. They're bound by the law, and it's just possible you might beat a murder rap. I don't know how the evidence might look in front of a jury, and of course my reputation's rather shop-soiled, and you may be a member of parliament for all I know . . . Are you following me, Jones? The police couldn't make you part with your secret—"

"Neither could you."

"Have your own way. As it happens, I'm not trying. But with a reputation like mine it'd be a bad business for me to shoot you. On the other hand, there could always be another accident—before the police arrived."

The man called Jones stood with his arms hanging loosely at his sides, staring at the Saint unblinkingly. In those last few minutes he had gone suddenly quiet: the snarl had faded out of his voice and left a more restrained level of grim interrogation. His chin was sunken tensely on his powerful chest, and under the thick black eyebrows his eyes were focusing on the Saint with the stony brightness of brown marble.

He hunched his muscular shoulders abruptly—it was the only movement he made.

"Is that a threat?" he asked.

"No." Simon was just as quiet. "It's a promise. When the police arrive they're going to find that there's been another accident. And the fact will be that you, Jones, also fell against that machine."

8

The big man leapt forward as he finished speaking. Simon knew that that was coming—he was ready and waiting for it. There was no other way about it, and he had been prepared for it ever since one question had been answered. He had never intended to shoot after they returned to the laboratory, whatever happened, but he snatched his gun away out of range of the wild grab that Jones made for it, and tossed it neatly across to Patricia. She caught it at her knees, and the Saint slipped under the big man's arms and jammed him against the door. For an instant they strained against each other face to face, and the Saint drew a deep breath and spoke over his shoulder.

"Don't shoot, Pat," he said. "Get over in the corner and stay out of the way. The gun's for you to get out with if anything goes wrong."

The big man heaved up off the door in a mighty jerk, and hurled the Saint back with all the impetus of his superior weight. He shook off the Saint's grip with a writhing effort of his arms—Simon felt the man's biceps cording under his hands before the grip was broken, and knew that he was taking on nothing easy. The force of his opponent's rush drove him to within a yard of the deadly steel dome; then he recovered his balance, and stopped the man with a couple of half-arm jolts to the stomach that thudded into their mark like pistons hitting a sandbag. Jones grunted, and went back on his heels, dropping his hands to guard, and the Saint shot out a snake-like left for the exposed chin. The big man took it on the side of his jaw, deliberately, and snatched at the flying wrist as the blow landed.

His fingers closed on it like iron clamps, twisting spitefully. He had every ounce of the strength that his build indicated, and he was as hard as teak all over—the Saint had felt that when he landed with those two staggering blows that would have broken most men in the middle. What was more, he had been trained in a school of fighting that knew its stuff: he never gave the Saint a chance to make a boxing match of it. Simon swerved away from the dome and kicked up his knee, but the big man edged back. The Saint's left arm was clamped in an agonising arm-lock, and he was wrenched ruthlessly round again towards the dome. The leverage of the hold was bearing him down to his knees; then with a swift, terrific kick he straightened his legs under him and swung his right fist over in a smashing blow at the back of the man's neck. The man coughed, and crumpled to his hands and knees, and Simon tore his wrist out of the grip and fell on top of him.

They rolled over together, with the Saint groping for a toe-hold. One of the big man's insteps came under the palm of his hand, and he hauled it up and bent it over with a brutal efficiency that made his victim gasp. But the big man was wise to that one—the hold only hurt him for a couple of seconds, before he flung it off with a mighty squirm of his body that pitched the Saint over on his face. In an instant the big man's legs were scissoring for a clasp round the Saint's neck and shoulders, and his hands were clamping again on the Saint's wrist. Simon heard his muscles creaking as he strained against the backward pressure that was slowly straightening his arm. Once that arm was locked out straight from the shoulder, with the elbow over the big man's knee-joint, he would have to move like a supercharged eel to get away before a bone was snapped like dry wood. He fought it desperately, but it was his one arm against the big man's two, and he knew he was losing inch by inch. His free hand clawed for a nerve centre under one of the thighs that were crushing his chest: he found it, and saw the big man wince, but the remorseless straightening of his arm went on. In the last desperate moment that he had, he struggled to break the nutcracker grip around his upper body. One of the big man's shoes came off in his hand, and with a triumphant laugh he piled all his strength into another toe-twist. The man squeaked and kicked, and Simon broke away. As he came up on all fours, the other rolled away. They leapt up simultaneously and circled round each other, breathing heavily.

"Thanks for the fight," said the Saint shortly. "I never cared for cold-blooded killings."

For answer the big man came forward off his toes like a charging bull, but he had not moved six inches before the Saint's swift dash reached him. Again those pile-driving fists jarred on the weak spot just below the other's breast-bone. Jones grabbed for a strangle-hold, but the drumming of iron knuckles on his solar plexus made him stagger backwards and cover up with his elbows. His mouth opened against the protest of his paralysed lungs, and his face went white and puffy. Simon drove him to the door, and held off warily. He knew that the big man was badly hurt, but perhaps his helplessness looked a little too realistic . . . The Saint feinted with a left to the head, and in a second the big man was bear-hugging him in a wild rush that almost carried him off his feet.

They went back towards the gleaming dome in a fighting tangle. Simon looked over his shoulder and saw it a yard away, with its brilliant surface shining like silver around the charred blackness of the professor's hand. The strip of wire that he had seen melted on it had left streaky trails of smeared metal down the curved sides, like the slime of a fantastic snail. The Saint saw them in an instant of photographically vivid vision in which the minutest details of that diabolical apparatus were printed for ever on his memory. There must have been tens of thousands of volts pulsing invisibly through that section of the secret process, hundreds of amperes of burning annihilation waiting to scorch through the first thing that tapped them with that crackle of blue flame and hiss of intolerable heat which he had seen once and heard again. His shoes slipped over the floor as he wrestled superhumanly against the momentum that was pressing him back towards certain death: the big man's face was cracked in a fiendish grin, and he heard Patricia cry out . . . Then one of his heels tripped over the professor's outstretched legs, and he was thrown off his balance. He put all his strength into a frantic twist of his body as he fell, and saw the dome leap up beside him, a foot away. The fall knocked half the wind out of his body, and he fought blindly away to one side. Suddenly his hands grasped empty air, and he heard Patricia cry out again.

The splitting detonation of a shot racketed in his ears as he rolled up on one elbow. Patricia had missed, somehow, and the big man was grappling for the gun.

Simon crawled up and flung himself forward. As he did so, the big man saw his own gun lying in the corner where the Saint had kicked it, and dived for it. Simon caught him from behind in a circling sweep, locking the big man's arms to his sides at the elbows: but the big man had the gun. The Saint saw it curling round for a backward shot that could not help scoring somewhere; he made a wild grab at the curving wrist and caught it, jerking it up as the trigger tightened, and the shot smashed through the floor. Simon flung his left leg forward, across the big man's stance. The steel dome was a yard away on his left He heaved sideways, across the leverage of his thigh, and sprang back . . .

The man's scream rang in his ear as he staggered away. Once again that spurt of eye-aching blue flame seared across his eyes, and turned suddenly orange. The big man had hit the dome with his shoulder, and his coat was burning: the smell of singeing cloth stung the Saint's nostrils, and the crack of cordite sang through his head as the galvanic current clamped a dead finger convulsively on the trigger and held it there rigidly in one last aimless shot . . .

"And we still don't know his real name," murmured the Saint.

He pushed a handkerchief across his brow, and looked at Patricia with a crooked grin. Patricia was fingering her wrist tenderly, where the big man's crushing grip had fastened on it. She looked back at the Saint with a pale face that was still hopelessly puzzled.

"That's your fault," she said.

"I know." The Saint's eyes had a mocking twist in their inscrutable blue that she couldn't understand. "You see, when you've made up your mind about a thing like brother Jones's demise, the only way is to get it over quickly. And Claud Eustace will be along soon. But I promise you, Pat, I've never hated killing anyone so much—and there was never anyone who'd've been so dangerous to my peace of mind if he'd stayed alive. If you want any excuses for it, he'd got two deliberate murders on his own hands and one more for which he was deliberately responsible, so he only got what was coming to him."

She waited alone in the room of death while the Saint vanished along the landing towards one of the bedrooms. It took the Saint a few minutes to repair the damage which the fight had done to his immaculate elegance, but when he had finished there was hardly a trace of it—nothing but a slight disorder that could have been caused by a brief scuffle. He used the dead man's hairbrushes and clothes brush and wrapped a handkerchief round his hand before he touched anything. Everything went back on the dressing-table exactly as he had found it, and he returned to the girl with a ready smile.

"Let's finish the clean-up, Pat—I don't know that we've a lot of time."

He went over the floor with keen restless eyes. Two cartridge-cases he picked up from odd corners where they had rolled away after the snap action of the recoil had spewed them out of a pistol breech. He identified them as the products of his own gun, for he had marked each of them with a nick in the base. They went into his pocket; the others, which testified to the shots which Jones had fired, he left where they lay, and added to them the souvenir which he had preserved in a match-box from his breakfast-table that morning. He searched the room once more for any other clues which he might have overlooked, and was satisfied.

His hand fell on Patricia's shoulder.

"Let's go," he said.

They went down to the hall. Simon left her again while he went out into the garden. His automatic, and the shells he had picked up, went deep under the earth of a neglected flower-bed, and he uprooted a clump of weeds and pressed them into a new berth where they would hide the marks of freshly-turned earth.

"Don't you ever want me to know what you're up to?" asked Patricia when he came back, and the Saint took her by the arm and led her to a chair.

"Lass, don't you realise I've just committed murder? And times is not what they was. I've known much bigger things than this which were easy enough to get away with before Claud Eustace had quite such a life-and-death ambition to hang my scalp on his belt, but this is not once upon a time. We might have run away and left the mystery to uncover itself, but I didn't think that was such a hot idea. I'd rather know how we stand from the start. Now sit down and let me write some more about Wilberforce Gupp—this is a great evening for brain work."

He propelled her gently into the chair, and sat himself down in another. An envelope and a pencil came out of his pocket, and with perfect calm and detachment, as if he were sitting in his own room at home with a few minutes to spare, the amazing Saint proceeded to scribble down and read aloud to her the epilogue of his epic.

> *"Thus, on good terms with everyone,*
> *Nothing accomplished, nothing done,*
> *Sir Wilberforce, as history knows,*
> *Earned in due course a k-night's repose,*
> *And with his fellow pioneers,*
> *Rose shortly to the House of Peers,*
> *Which nearly (but not quite) woke up*
> *To greet the noble Baron Gupp.*
> *Citizens, praise careers like his,*
> *Which have made England what she is,*
> *And prove that only Lesser Breeds*
> *Follow where a stuffed walrus leads."*

He had just finished when they both heard a car swing into the drive. Feet crunched over the gravel, and heavy boots grounded on the stone outside the front door. The resonant clatter of a brass knocker curtly applied echoed through the house.

Simon opened the door.

"Claud Eustace himself!" he murmured genially. "It seems years since I last saw you, Claud. And how's the ingrowing toe-nail?" He glanced past the detective's bulky presence at the four other men who were unloading themselves and their apparatus from the police car and lining up for the entrance. "I rather thought you'd be bringing a party with you, old dear, but I don't know that the caviar will go all the way round."

The detective stepped past him into the hall, and the other men followed. They were of various shapes and sizes, deficient in sex appeal but unconversationally efficient. They clumped themselves together on the mat and waited patiently for orders.

Mr Teal faced the Saint with a certain grimness. His round pink face was rather more flushed than usual, and his baby-blue eyes were creased up into the merest slits, through which pinpoints of red danger-lights glinted like scattering embers. He knew that he had taken a chance in coming to that house at all, and the squad he had brought with him multiplied his potential regrets by more factors than he cared to think about. If this was one of the Saint's practical jokes, Chief Inspector Teal would never hear the last of it. The whole CID would laugh itself sick—there were still giggles circulating over the gramophone-record incident—and the Assistant Commissioner's sniff would flay him till he wanted to find a quiet place to die. And yet he had had no choice. If he was told about a murder he had to go out and investigate it, and his private doubts did not count.

"Well?" he barked.

"Fairly," said the Saint. "I see you brought the homicide squad."

Teal nodded briefly.

"I gathered from what you told me that a murder had been committed. Is that the case?"

"There are certainly some dead bodies packed about the house," admitted the Saint candidly. "In fact, the place is making a great start as a morgue. If you're interested—"

"Where are these bodies?"

Simon gestured impressively heavenwards.

"Upstairs—at least, so far as the mortal clay is concerned, Eustace."

"We'll go up and see them."

Curtly Teal gave his orders to the silent squad. One man was left in the hall, and Patricia stayed with him. The others, who included a finger-print expert with a little black bag, and a photographer burdened with camera and folding tripod, followed behind. They went on a tour that made every member of it stare more incredulously from stage to stage, until the culminating revelation left their eyeballs bulging as if they were watching the finale of a Grand Guignol drama coming true under their noses.

9

Chief Inspector Teal twiddled his pudgy fingers on his knees, and studied the Saint's face soberly, digesting what he had heard.

"So after that you allowed this man Jones to kidnap Miss Holm so that you could follow him and find out his address?" he murmured, and the Saint nodded.

"That's about it. Can you blame me? The guy Jones was obviously a menace to the community that we ought to know more about, and it was the only way. I hadn't the faintest idea at that time what his graft was, but I figured that anything which included wilful murder in its programme must be worth looking into. I was all bubbling over with beans after that bust I told you about—talking of busts, Claud, if you ever go to the Folies Bergère—"

"Yes, yes," interrupted the detective brusquely. "I want you to tell me exactly what happened when you got here."

"Well, naturally I had to break into the house. I went up to the first floor and heard Jones talking to Miss Holm in the room where he'd taken her. I hid in another room when he came out to get her some food; then I went and spoke to Miss Holm through the door—which

Brother J. had remembered to lock. We exchanged some bright remarks about the weather and the Test Match prospects, and then I carried on with the exploration. On the way I found that King's Messenger. Then Jones came upstairs again and I lay low for quite a while, cautious like. After a time I got tired standing about, and I went in search of him. I came up outside this laboratory door and listened. That's when I heard what it was all about. Jones was just wheedling what sounded like the last details of the process out of Quell—the science I know wouldn't cover a pinhead, but Jones seemed quite happy about it."

"Can you remember any part of what you heard?"

"Not a thing that'd make sense—except the outstanding bit about the gold. Quell was making gold, there's not a doubt about it. You can see it for yourself. I gathered that Jones had told the old man some yarn about saving England from going off the gold standard—manufacturing an enormous quantity of the stuff under the auspices of the Secret Service, and unloading it quietly in a way that'd put new life into the Bank of England—and Quell, who probably wasn't so wise to the ways of crime as he was to the habits of electrons and atoms, had fallen for it like a dove. Anyway, Jones was happy."

"And then?"

"There was a frightful yell. I've never heard anything like it. I burst in—the door wasn't locked—and saw the professor doing a last kick beside that machine. Jones must have pushed him on to it in cold blood. The old man had told him everything he wanted to know, and made him a lot of specimen gold as well, and Jones hadn't any further use for him. Jones heard me come in, and spun round, pulling a gun. He tripped over the professor's legs and put out a hand to save himself—then he saw his hand was going on the machine, and he pulled it away. He fell on his shoulder, and it burned him just the same. I suppose the current jiggered his muscles like it does on those electric machines, and he went on shooting all round the place for a second or two."

Teal looked round at the finger-print expert, who was busy at the bench.

"Have you done those shells?" he asked.

"Just finished, sir."

Simon raised his eyebrows.

"What's the idea?" he inquired.

"I don't know whether you've thought of wearing gloves when you're loading a gun," said the detective blandly, and the Saint did not smile.

He allowed the expert to take impressions of his finger-tips on a special block, and waited while the man squinted at them through a magnifying-glass and checked them against the marks which he had developed on the spent cartridge cases which had been picked up. Teal went over to his side and stood there with a kind of mountainous placidity which was not the most convincing thing Simon Templar had ever seen.

"There's no similarity, sir," pronounced the expert at length, and a glimmer of blank disbelief crossed the detective's round face.

"Are you sure?"

"It's quite obvious, sir. The prints are of totally different types. You can see for yourself. The prints on the shells are spirals, and this gentleman's prints—"

"Don't call him 'this gentleman,'" snapped the detective. "This is Simon Templar, known as the Saint—and you know it too."

"Why not try Jones's finger-prints?" suggested the Saint mildly. "It seems simpler than suspecting me automatically. I've told you—I'm not in this party. That's why I sent for you."

Teal regarded the two contorted bodies thoughtfully. The photographer had finished his work and he was packing his exposed plates away in a satchel. The detective took a step forward.

"I should take a lot of care, if I were you," murmured the Saint. "I'd hate you to have an accident, and I suppose the juice is still functioning."

They went round the room circumspectly. Someone discovered a collection of switches, and reversed them. A likely looking terminal was disconnected by a man who donned rubber gloves for the purpose. Finally they approached the dome again, and one of the men tossed bits of wire on to it from various angles. Nothing happened, and eventually Teal knelt down and tried to detach the gun from the dead man's hand. He remained alive, but it took the efforts of two other men to unlock the terrific clutch of the dead man's fingers.

Teal straightened up and clicked out the magazine.

"Two shots here." He jerked the sliding jacket. "One in the breech . . . We picked up four shells, and four shots have been fired in this room." Teal turned the figures over in his head as if he loathed them. The chagrin showed on his face, and Simon Templar relaxed gently. It was the one risk that he had to take—if Jones's gun had contained more shells it would have been a tougher proposition, but seven was a possible load. "You're lucky," Teal said venomously.

He turned the gun over in his hand, and suddenly he stiffened.

"What's that?"

He displayed a thin silvery scratch on the blue-black steel, and Simon gazed at the mark along with the other detectives.

"It looks as if it had hit something," said one of them.

"I'll say it does," grunted Mr Teal.

He crawled round the room on his hands and knees, studying the bullet scars that had already been discovered. One of them occupied him for some time, and he called over one of the other men to join him. There was a low-voiced colloquy, and then Teal rose again and dusted the knees of his trousers. He faced the Saint again.

"That shot there was a ricochet," he said, "and it could have come off Jones's gun."

"Shooting round corners and hitting itself?" drawled the Saint mildly. "You know, you're a genius—or rather Jones must have been. That's an invention that's been wanted for years. Damned useful thing in a tight corner, Claud—you aim one way, and the bullet comes back and hits the man standing behind you—"

"I don't think that was it," said the detective short-windedly. "What kind of gun are you carrying these days?"

Simon spread out his hands.

"You know I haven't got a licence."

"Never mind. We'll just look you over."

The Saint shrugged resignedly, and held out his arms. Teal frisked him twice, efficiently, and found nothing. He turned to the odd man.

"You'd better get busy and dig out all the bullets. We'll be able to tell from the marks of the rifling whether they were all fired from the same gun."

A trickle of something like ice-cold water fluttered down Simon Templar's spine. That was the one possibility that he had overlooked— the one inspiration he had not expected the plump detective to produce. He hadn't even thought that Teal's suspicions would have worked so hard. That gramophone record must have scored a deeper hit than he anticipated—deeper perhaps than he had ever wanted it to be. It must have taken something that had rubbed salt viciously into an old and stubbornly unhealed wound to kindle an animosity that would drive itself so far in the attempt to pin guilt on a quarter where there was so much prima-facie innocence.

But the Saint schooled himself to a careless shrug. The least trace of expression would have been fatal. He had never acted with such intensity in his life as he did at that moment, keeping unruffled his air of rather bored protest. He knew that Teal was watching him with the eyes of a lynx, with his rather soft mouth compressed into a narrow line which symbolised that unlooked-for streak of malice. "I can't help it if you want to waste time making a damned fool of yourself," he said wearily. "If there's a scratch on that gun it's probably there because Jones *did* happen to bang it on something. If there's a ricco anywhere, it's probably one that bounced off some of the apparatus—there's any amount of solid metal about, and I told you how Jones was thrashing around when the current got him. Why go trying to fix something on me?"

"Only because I'm curious," said the detective inflexibly. "You've had quite a lot of jokes at our expense, so I'm sure you won't mind us having a harmless little fun at yours."

Simon took out his cigarette case.

"Am I to consider myself under arrest—is that the idea?"

"Not yet," said Teal, with a vague note of menace sticking out of the way he said it.

"No? Well, I'm just interested. This is the first time in my life I ever behaved like a respectable citizen and gave you your break according to the rules, and I'm glad to know how you take it. It'll save me doing anything so damned daft again."

Teal stripped the wrapping from a wafer of spearmint with a sort of hard-strung gusto.

"I hope you'll have the opportunity of doing it again," he said. "But this looks like the kind of case that would have interested you in other ways, and I shouldn't be doing my duty if I took everything for granted."

Simon looked at him.

"You're wrong," he said soberly. "I tell you, Teal, when I saw that guy Jones dying all that went through my mind in a flash. Before he killed Quell—before I came through the door—I'd heard enough to know what it meant. I knew I could have taken him prisoner, made him work the process for me—had all the wealth I wanted. You know what one can do with a bit of persuasion. I could have taken him away from this house and left everything as it was—Quell and the King's Messenger mightn't have been found for weeks, and there'd have been nothing in the world to show that I'd ever been near the place. I could have done in real earnest what Jones was trying to kid Quell he was doing. I could have manufactured gold until I'd built up a balance in the Bank of England that would have been the sensation of the century. I could have played fairy godmother in a way that would have made me safe for ever from your well-meant persecutions, Claud. I could have paid off the National Debt with one cheque—my own free gift to Great Britain. With love and kisses from the Saint. Think of it! I could have named my own price, I might have been dictator— and then there might have been some more sense in the laws of this nit-witted community than there is now, Certainly you'd never have dared to touch me so long as I lived—there'd have been a revolution if you'd tried it. Simon Templar—the man who abolished income-tax. My God, Teal, I don't think anyone's ever been able to dream a miracle like that and see it within his reach!"

"Well?"

Teal was chewing steadily, but his eyes were fixed on the Saint's face with a solid attentiveness that had not been there before. Something in the Saint's speech commanded the respect that he was unwilling to give—it was drawn from him in spite of himself. Simon's sincerity was starkly irresistible.

"You know what happened. I passed up the idea. And I don't mind telling you, Claud, quite honestly, that if Jones hadn't died as he did, I should have killed him. There you are. You can use that as evidence against me if you like, because this time I haven't a thing on my conscience—just for once."

"What made you pass up the idea?" asked Teal.

Simon took the cigarette from his mouth, and answered with an utter frankness that could have been nothing but the truth.

"It would have made life too damned dull!"

Teal scratched his chin and stared at the toe-cap of one shoe. The odd man had finished digging out bullets; he dropped them into a match-box and stood by, listening like the others.

"You know me, Claud," said the Saint. "I was just tempted—just in imagination—for that second or two while I watched Jones die and his bullets were crashing round me. And I saw what a deadly frost it would have been. No more danger—no more risk—no more duels with Scotland Yard—no more of your very jolly backchat and bloody officiousness as per this evening.

"Claud, I'd have died of boredom. So I gave you your break. I left everything as it was, and phoned you straight away. There was no need to, but that's what I did. Jones was dead of his own accord, and I'd nothing to be afraid of. I haven't even touched an ounce of the gold—it's there for you to take away, and I suppose if the Quell family's extinct the Government will get it and I won't even be offered a rebate on my income tax. But naturally, like the poor dumb boobs you are, you have to sweat blood trying to make me a murderer the one time in my life I'm innocent. Why, you sap, if I'd wanted to get away with anything—"

"It's a pity you couldn't have saved Jones and done what you thought of all the same," said Teal, and the change in his manner was so marked that the Saint smiled. "It might have done the country some good."

Simon drew at his cigarette and hunched his shoulders.

"Why the hell should I bother? The country's got its salvation in its own hands. While a nation that's always boasting about its outstanding brilliance can put up with a collection of licensing laws, defence-of-the-realm Acts, seaside councillors, Lambeth conventions, sweepstake laws,

Sunday-observance Acts, and one fatuity after another that's nailed on it by a bunch of blathering maiden aunts and pimply hypocrites, and can't make up its knock-kneed mind to get rid of 'em and let some fresh air and common sense into its life—when they can't do anything but dither over things that an infant in arms would know its own mind about—how the devil can they expect to solve bigger problems? And why the blazes should I take any trouble to save them from the necessity of thinking for themselves . . . ? Now, for heaven's sake make up your mind whether you want to arrest me or not, because if you don't I'd like to go home to bed."

"All right," said Teal. "You can go."

The Saint held out his hand.

"Thanks," he said. "I'm sorry about that gramophone record. Maybe we can get on better in the future—if we're both very good."

"I'll believe that of you when I see it," said Teal, but he smiled.

Simon pushed his way through the knot of waiting men to the door.

At the foot of the stairs the detective who had been left with Patricia barred his way. Teal looked over the gallery rail and spoke down.

"It's all right, Peters," he said. "Mr Templar and Miss Holm can go."

Simon opened the front door and turned to wave the detective a debonair good-bye. They went out to where the Saint had left his car, and Simon lighted another cigarette and waited in silence for the engine to warm. Presently he let in the clutch and they slid away southwards for home.

"Was it all right?" asked Patricia.

"Just," said the Saint. "But I don't want such a narrow squeak again for many years. There was one vital piece of evidence I'd overlooked, and Teal thought of it. I had to think fast—and play for my life. But I collared the evidence as I went out, and they'll never be able to make a case without it. And do you know, Pat?—Claud Eustace ended up by really believing me."

"What did you tell him?"

"Very, very nearly the whole truth," said the Saint, and hummed softly to himself for a long while.

He drove home by a roundabout route that took them over Westminster Bridge. In the middle of the bridge he dipped into his pocket and flung something sideways, far out over the parapet.

It was a small box that weighed heavily and rattled.

Back at Scotland Yard, a puzzled detective-sergeant turned his coat inside out for the second time.

"I could have sworn I put the match-box with those bullets in my pocket, sir," he said. "I must have left it on the bench or something. Shall I go back and fetch it?"

"Never mind," said Mr Teal. "We shan't be needing it."

THE MAN FROM ST LOUIS

1

A certain Mr Peabody, known to his wife as Oojy-Woojy, was no fool. He used to say so himself, on every possible occasion, and he should have known. He was a small and rather scraggy man with watery eyes, a melancholy walrus moustache, and an unshakable faith in the efficiency of the police and the soundness of his insurance company—which latter qualities may provide a generous explanation of an idiosyncrasy of his which in anyone else would have been described as sheer and unadulterated foolishness.

Mr Peabody, in fact, is herewith immortalized in print for the sole and sufficient reason that he was the proprietor of a jewellery shop in Regent Street which the Green Cross gang busted one night in August. Apart from this, the temperamentalities, destiny, and general Oojy-Woojiness of Mr Peabody do not concern us at all, but that busting of his shop was the beginning of no small excitement.

Mr Peabody's idiosyncrasy was that of displaying his choicest wares in his window—and leaving them there for the passing crowd to feast their eyes upon. Not for him the obscurity of safes and strong-rooms: that was only the fate of the undistinguished bulk of his stock, the more commonplace articles of vertu. His prize pieces were invariably set out behind the glass on velvet-lined shelves lighted by chastely shielded bulbs. An act of deliberate criminal foolishness, from the point of view of almost anyone except Mr Peabody. From the point of view of the Green Cross boys, an act of sublime charity.

It was a very good bust, from the point of view of a detached connoisseur—carried out with all the slick perfection of technique of which the Green Cross boys were justly proud. The coup was no haphazard smash-and-grab affair, but a small-scale masterpiece of which every detail had been planned and rehearsed until the first and only public presentation could be guaranteed to flutter through its allotted segment of history with the smooth precision of a ballet. Mr Peabody's emporium had been selected for the setting out of a list of dozens of other candidates simply on account of that aforesaid idiosyncrasy of his, and every item to be taken had been priced and contracted for in advance.

Joe Corrigan was booked to drive the car; Clem Enright heaved the brick, and Ted Orping, a specialist in his own line, was ready with the bag. In the space of four seconds, as previously timed by Ted Orping's stop-watch, a collection of assorted bijouterie for which any receiver would cheerfully have given two thousand pounds in hard cash vanished from Mr Peabody's shattered window with the celerity of rabbits fading away from a field at the approach of a conjuror with an empty top-hat, A gross remuneration, per head of the parties concerned, of five hundred pounds for the job—if you care to look at it that way. Fast money, for on the big night the performance went through well within scheduled limits.

It was precisely two o'clock in the morning when Clem Enright's brick went through Mr Peabody's plate-glass, and the smash of it startled a constable who was patrolling leisurely down his beat a matter of twenty yards away. Ted Orping's hands flew in and out of the window with lightning accuracy while the policeman was fumbling with his whistle and lumbering the first few yards towards them. Before the Law had covered half the distance the job was finished, and the two Green Cross experts were piling into the back of the car as it jolted away and gathered speed towards Oxford Circus. The stolen wagon whizzed over the deserted cross-roads as the first shrill blast of alarm wailed into the night far behind.

"Good work," said Ted Orping, speaking as much for his own share in the triumph as anybody else's.

He settled back in his corner and pulled the brim of his hat—a broad-shouldered, prematurely old young man of about twenty-eight, with a square jaw and two deep creases running down from his nose and past the corners of his thin mouth. He was one of the first examples of a type of crook that was still new and strange to England, a type that founded itself on the American hoodlum, educated in movie theatres and polished on the raw underworld fiction imported by F. W. Woolworth—a type that was breaking into the placid and gentlemanly paths of old-world crime as surely and ruthlessly as Fate. In a few years more his type was no longer to seem strange and foreign, but in those days he was an innovation, respected and feared by his satellites. He had learned to imitate Transatlantic callousness and pugnacity so well that he was no longer conscious of playing a part. He had the bullying swagger, the taste for ostentatious clothes, the desire for power, and he said "Oh, yeah?" with exactly the right shade of contempt and belligerence.

"Easy pickings," said Clem Enright.

He tried to ape Ted Orping's manner, but he lacked the physical personality. He was a Cockney sneak-thief born and bred, with the pale peaked face and shifty eyes of his inheritance. Alone and sober, his one idea was to avoid attracting attention, but in the shelter of Ted Orping's massive bravado he found his courage expanding.

He also lolled back in the seat, and produced a battered yellow packet of cigarettes.

"Fag?"

Ted Orping looked down his nose.

"Y'ain't still smokin' those things?"

He twitched the packet out of the Cockney's fingers and flipped it over the side. A rolled-gold cigarette case came out of his pocket and pushed into Clem Enright's ribs under a black-rimmed thumbnail.

"Take 'alf a dozen."

Clem helped himself, and struck a match. They lounged back again, exhaling the fumes of cheap Turkish tobacco with elaborate relish. Either of them would secretly have preferred the yellow gaspers to which they were accustomed, but Ted Orping insisted on their improved status.

Suddenly he leaned forward and punched the driver on the shoulder.

"Hey, Joe! Time you were turning east The Flying Squad ain't after us tonight."

The driver nodded. They were speeding up the west side of Regent's Park, and the driving mirror showed no lights behind.

"And easy on the gas," Ted snapped. "You don't want to be copped for dangerous driving."

The car spun round a bend with a sharpness that sent Ted Orping lurching back into his corner, and held its speed. They drove east, and turned south again.

Ted Orping scowled. He wanted all his colleagues to acknowledge him as the boss, the Big Fellow, whose word was law—to be obeyed promptly and implicitly. Joe Corrigan didn't seem to cotton to the idea. And he had broad shoulders too—and grey Irish eyes that didn't flinch readily. Independent. Maybe too independent, Ted Orping thought. It was Joe Corrigan who had insisted that they should go into a pub and have a bracer before they did the job, and who had got his way against Ted Orping's opposition. Maybe Joe was getting too big for his boots . . . Ted ran a hand over the hard bulge at his hip, thoughtfully. Four or five years ago the independence of Joe Corrigan would never have stimulated Ted to thoughts of murder, but he had been taught that when a guy got too big for his boots he was just taken for ride.

The car swung left, violently, and then to the right again. They were droning down a street of sombre houses on the east side of the park. One or two upper windows were lighted, but there were no pedestrians about—only another long-nosed silvery-grey speed wagon drawn up by the kerb with its side lights dimmed, facing towards them.

All at once their brakes went on with a screaming force that jerked the two men behind forward in their seats. They skidded to a stop by the pavement, with their bonnet a dozen feet away from the nose of the silver car.

Ted Orping cursed and hitched himself farther forward. His broad hand crimped on the driver's shoulder.

"What the hell—?"

He fell back as the driver turned . . . with his jaw dropping.

The two Green Cross boys sat side by side, staring at the face of the man in the heavy leather coat that had been worn by Joe Corrigan when they set out. It was a lean sunburnt face, recklessly clean-cut and swashbuckling in its rakish keenness of line, in which the amazingly clear and mocking blue eyes gleamed like chips of crystal. There was a coolness, an effrontery, a fighting ruthlessness about it that left them momentarily speechless. It was the most dangerously challenging face that either of them had ever seen. But it was not the face of Joe Corrigan.

"The jaunt is over, boys," said the face amiably. "I hope you've had a good time and caught no colds. And thanks for the job—it was about the best I've been able to watch. You two ought to take it up professionally—you'd do well."

Ted Orping wetted his lips.

"Who are you?" he asked.

The driver smiled. It was a benevolent, almost seraphic smile, that bared a glint of ivory-white teeth, and yet there was nothing reassuring about it. It was as full of the hair-trigger threat of sudden death as the round hollow snout of the gun that slid up over the back of the seat in the driver's hand. Ted Orping had seen smiles like that in the movies, and he knew.

"I am the Saint," said the driver gently. "I see you've heard of me. Perhaps you thought I'd gone out of business. Well, you can work it out. I'm sorry about Joe, but he kind of had an accident coming out of that pub. It seemed as if you were left without a driver, but I hated to disappoint you—so I took his place . . . You might keep your hands on your lap, Ted—it makes me nervous when they're out of sight."

The muzzle of the gun shifted slightly, so that Ted Orping looked down the barrel. His hands ceased to stray behind him, and lay still.

The Saint reached a long arm over to the floor at Ted Orping's feet, and picked up the bag. He weighed it, speculatively and judiciously under the two Green Cross boys' noses.

"A nice haul—as you were both saying," he murmured. "I couldn't have done better myself. But I think it's worth too much money for you lads to have all to yourselves. You might want to move up another stage in life and take to cigars—and cigars, Ted, need a strong tum-tum when you aren't used to them. So I'll just take care of it for you. Give my love to Joe and the rest of the gang, and if you hear any more of those rumours about my having retired you'll know what to say. And I hope you'll say it. It cannot be too widely known—"

Ted Orping came to life, grimly and desperately. It may have been that the actual sight of so much hard won wealth vanishing into the hands of the mocking hijacker in front spurred him to the gamble; it may have been that he had to prove to himself that he wasn't afraid of any other man who carried a gun; or it may only have been the necessity of retaining Clem Enright's respect. Whatever his motive was, he took his chance, with a blaze of sheer animal courage.

He hurled himself forward out of his seat and grabbed at the gun in the Saint's hand. And the Saint pressed the trigger.

There was no report—only a sharp liquid hiss. A shining jet of ammonia leapt from the muzzle of the gun like a pencil of polished glass, and struck Ted Orping accurately on the bridge of his nose. It sprayed out over his face from the point of impact, burning his eyeballs with its agonising sting and filling his lungs with pungent choking vapours. Orping fell back with a gasp, and Simon Templar opened the door.

He stepped out on the pavement, and his gun still covered the two men. Clem Enright cringed away.

"So long, Clem," said the Saint genially.

He ran down to the other car. The engine was ticking smoothly over as he reached it, and he swung himself nimbly in beside the girl who sat waiting at the wheel. The car swung out and skimmed neatly past the front wheels of the motionless bandit wagon ahead, and the Saint turned to wave a farewell to the two helpless men as they went by.

Then he sank back with a laugh and lighted a cigarette.

"Haven't you ever noticed that the simplest ideas are usually the best?" he remarked. "That old water-pistol gag, for instance: could anything be more elementary, and yet more bright and beautiful? I see that our technique is not yet perfect, Pat—all we need is to discover some trick with the smell of the Ark still wafting fruitily about it, and we could clean up the world."

Patricia Holm steered the huge Hirondel round another corner and the wind caught her fair hair as she turned to smile at him.

"Simon," she said dispassionately, "you have no conscience."

"None," said Simon Templar.

He was wearing a dinner jacket under his leather coat, and Joe Corrigan's cap went into a pocket in the car. Half an hour later they were strolling into the Breakfast Club for a celebratory plate of bacon and eggs and a final turn round the minute dance floor. And to any casual observer who saw the Saint drifting debonairly through the throng of elegant idlers, exchanging words with an acquaintance here and there, straightening the head waiter's tie, and at last demolishing a large dish of the Club's world-famous speciality, it would have been difficult to believe that the police and the underworld alike reckoned him the most dangerous man in England—or that a matter of mere minutes earlier he had been giving a convincing demonstration that his hand had lost none of its cunning.

It amused Simon Templar to be taken for one of those elegant idlers, just as it amused him to be known for something totally different in other and no less exclusive circles. He was due to derive a great deal of amusement from the fact that a certain gentleman from St. Louis counted him the most serious obstacle to a well-planned campaign that was just coming to maturity.

2

The city of St. Louis was not particularly proud of Tex Goldman. It knew him as a man who had successfully "beaten the rap" on five notorious occasions, who was no less at home with typewriters and pineapples than he was with the common heater, who had a choice selection of judges and police captains eating out of his hand, and who secured whatever subscriptions to the funds of "protection" that he set out to collect. He ranked third on the city's roll of public enemies, and he made no secret of his aspirations to an even higher position, but nearly nine months ago an unfortunate incident had dictated a lengthy holiday. Tex Goldman had taken on the task of reducing a recalcitrant section of the Chinese laundry proprietors to a proper sense of their responsibilities, and in the process one of his bullets had found its mark in the heart of the leader of a powerful Tong. Before nightfall the war gongs were beating for him, and Tex Goldman, who was no coward, took the advice of his friends and left St. Louis for his health.

He headed for New York, and felt homesick. He was used to being recognised as a big shot, but he found that Manhattan Island scored him as a small town hoodlum. When it formed any other estimate of him, the result was a warning to watch his step and pipe down. The Great White Way had its own emperors, who were not disposed to encourage competition. If he had been a smaller man he could probably have found a billet for his heater in one of the Broadway Czars' bodyguards; if he had been bigger he might have negotiated for a little kingdom of his own; but Tex Goldman in those days came just between the useful extremes, and he wasn't wanted. Also he had a tip that the Tong's hatchet men were close behind him. There was plenty of jack in his pocket, and for reasons known only to himself his thoughts wandered to a holiday in the Old World.

He came to England, looked around, and thought of business.

He was a big man running to fat, a little thin on top, with a round blue jowl and cold black eyes. A killer by nature and experience, of the authentic type that Ted Orping tried to emulate. He wore a yellow belted overcoat and a solitaire diamond in his tie, and the one thing he knew all about was how to pay for such adornments without wearing himself out in honest labour. He studied London, and called it soft.

"There's a fortune to be picked up here by any man who ain't too particular," he said, "But you got to get organised. What's the use of a few bum stickup men who've scarcely learnt to tell one end of a rod from the other? They're just nibbling at it—and they got the police scared already. All they want is pulling together by a man who knows the racket, and that guy's name is Tex Goldman."

He said that to Mr Ronald Nilder, who was not a willing audience.

"You won't get away with it over here," said Mr Nilder. "They're hot on murder in this country, and you can't bribe the police over anything big."

"You gotta show me," said Tex Goldman.

He extinguished a half-smoked cigar, and lighted a fresh one. Tex Goldman never smoked more than half a cigar, and he paid two bucks for each of them.

"Can't bribe the dicks, huh? Are you telling me that no policeman ever took graft? Sure, the London police are wonderful—they ain't even human . . . Forget it, Nilder. You can bribe anyone if you make it big enough. Cuts in police pay mean men who want more money, and they get a sense of grievance that eases their consciences."

Mr Nilder sat on the edge of a chair and twirled the handle of his umbrella. He was a well-fed and nattily-dressed little man with close-set eyes and a loose lower lip. Tex Goldman knew what he was, despised him heartily, and intended to make use of him.

"I don't like it, Mr Goldman."

"You ain't asked to like it or not like it," said the man from St. Louis bluntly. "All you got to do is take your orders from me and cash your shakedown, and you can put your feelings where they belong. You got a dandy little motor launch, and you got connections on the other side of the ditch. You just be a good boy and run the guns over for me as I order 'em, or do anything else I tell you with that boat of yours, and you and me will mix in fine. Otherwise Scotland Yard might hear some more about your vice racket."

Mr Nilder winced slightly. He disliked hearing his business described so candidly. The Cosmolite Vaudeville Agency, which he controlled, was a prosperous organisation that supplied cabaret artists to every part of Europe and South America. Frequently the cabarets concerned were not so purely artistic as they might have been, but since the girls who went there had no relatives there were no embarrassing inquiries. Mr Nilder was not troubled with moral scruples. He was a simple tradesman, like a green-grocer or a butcher, supplying a continuous demand, and his sole object was to avoid the attention of the police. The "cabaret" game was already almost played out, but there were other and less widely advertised channels which Mr Ronald Nilder knew.

"It means prison if we're caught, Mr Goldman," he said.

"It means prison if you're caught doing other things," said Goldman, significantly. "But don't worry—I shouldn't ask you to do any shooting. All you gotta do is run those heaters, and you start Monday."

He peeled a dozen ten-pound notes off a thick pack, and slipped them contemptuously across the table. Nilder picked them up, fingered them nervously, and pushed them into his pocket. He knew that Goldman could order him about as he willed—he was afraid of the big man from St. Louis, afraid of his cold black eyes and deep masterful voice, even more afraid of what the man from St. Louis could have told the police. But he was not happy. Violence was not in his line—not even when he had to take no active part in it, and was still paid generously.

He rose, and picked up his hat.

"All right, Mr Goldman. I'll be going."

"Just a minute."

Tex Goldman came out of his chair, stepped across to the smaller man. He caught Nilder by the lapel of his coat, quite gently, but his cold black eyes drilled into the other's brain like jagged iron.

"Talking of telling things to the dicks don't sound so good between friends, Nilder. Let's say I just mentioned it in case you didn't feel like listening to reason. You don't want to go thinking up any ideas like that by yourself. You play ball with me, and I'll play ball with you. But any time you think it might pay you to squeal . . ."

He never sounded like finishing the sentence. And Ronald Nilder went away with that deliberate half-threat ringing in his head, and the memory of Tex Goldman's grim stare before his eyes.

The interview took place at Tex Goldman's apartment. Tex had started his sojourn in London at a West End hotel, but with the prospect of a longer stay in front of him he had moved out to an apartment of his own in an expensive modern block near Baker Street. It was the nearest approach he could find to the American model to which he was accustomed, and on the whole it suited him very well. The rent was exorbitant, but it had the advantage of being on the first floor with an emergency fire-escape exit down to an alley-way which communicated with a dirty lane in the rear.

It was eight o'clock when Nilder left. Goldman dressed himself leisurely in a new suit of evening clothes, put on a white panama hat, and went down to W1. He dined at the Berkeley, without haste, and went on later to a night club that was still waiting to be invaded by the after-theatre patrons. There was a girl there who came to his table—he had met her there regularly before. Tex Goldman ordered champagne.

"Guess you're too good for this, baby," he said. "Why don't you take a rest?"

He had asked that before, and she made the equivalent of every other answer she had given him.

"Would I get a lot of rest in your flat?"

Tex Goldman grinned, and discarded another half-smoked cigar. He knew what he wanted, knew how to get it, and had an infinite capacity for patience in certain directions.

It was after two o'clock when he left the club—and the girl—and took a taxi back to Baker Street. In his apartment, he exchanged his tail coat for a silk dressing-gown, removed his collar and tie, and settled himself in an arm-chair over an evening paper.

Half an hour later his bell rang, and he went to open the door. A red-eyed Ted Orping stood outside, looking rather dishevelled in spite of his flashy clothes, with Clem Enright a little behind him.

"Well?"

There was trouble plainly marked on every feature of Ted Orping's face, ratified in the peaked countenance of Clem Enright, but Tex Goldman showed no emotion. He let the Green Cross boys past, closed the door after them, and followed them through to the sitting-room.

Clem Enright sat awkwardly on the edge of an upright chair, while Ted Orping flung himself asprawl in an arm-chair and kept his hat on. Naturally it was Ted Orping who was the spokesman.

"Boss—we were hijacked."

Goldman gauged the length of his cigar-butt calmly.

"How?"

"It was Corrigan's fault. Joe said he must have a drink before we did the job, an' drove us round to Sam Harp's. Sam don't care what time it is if he's awake. We had a couple, an' come out—Clem an' me first, an' Joe last. Least we thought it was Joe. We got in the car an' drove off. We could only see what we thought was Joe's back, driving, an' we went up Regent Street to Pea-body's. Did the job properly, just as it'd been fixed, an' hopped back in the wagon. There was a copper—a bull—on the beat, but he never got near us. We went around Regent's Park, an' then this guy cut out of it an' stopped. I still thought it was Joe. I asked him what he was playin' at, then he turned round. It wasn't Joe."

"Who was it?"

"The Saint." Ted looked at Goldman grimly, and wiped his mouth on the back of his hand. "He stuck us up with a gun, an' took the bag. I went for him, an' his gun squirted ammonia in my face. He had another wagon fixed for his getaway. I was blind for a quarter of an hour. Clem had to drive me here."

Tex Goldman's cigar had gone out. He shredded it into the wastepaper basket.

"Where's Corrigan?"

"I dunno. We come straight here. There wasn't nothing we could do."

Goldman sat down. His square stubby fingers drummed on the arm of his chair, while his narrowed black eyes remained fixed on Ted Orping's face.

"We ain't here to be hijacked," he said. "We're here for all we can get. Get it quick—no mistakes—and scram. No one's gonna give us the runaround. Not dicks, Saints, nor anyone else. Anyone that gets in the way—well, it'll be just too bad about him. You got a gun. It's meant to be used. Back where I come from, we shoot fast and often. It saves trouble."

"Sure."

The black eyes swivelled round to Clem.

"You got a gun, Enright?"

"N-no, sir."

Goldman hitched open a drawer and dragged out a heavy blue-black automatic and a box of cartridges. He tossed the items, one after another, across the room to the little Cockney.

"You got one now—and I didn't give it you for ornament. There's no room for pikers or double-crossers in this racket. Anyone that don't toe the line is only safe in one place. Anyone—understand?"

"Y-yes, sir."

Clem Enright turned the gun over in his hand, felt the weight of it, tested his fingers round the grip. He put it away in his pocket reluctantly, with the box of cartridges, his eyes gleaming. He drew a deep breath and held some of it back, making his chest appear larger, and conscious all the time of Ted Orping's critical scrutiny.

"I'll use it, Mr Goldman," he said.

The whirr of the front door buzzer broke in on them sharply, sounding again and again insistently.

Tex Goldman raised the lid of a cigar-box.

"See who it is, Ted."

Orping slouched up and went out. The front door opened, and Joe Corrigan came bursting through into the sitting-room. Ted Orping followed him in. Corrigan's hair was awry, his tie loose and askew, and his clothes looked as if he had been pulled backwards through a hedge.

He stood just inside the room, breathing heavily, glancing from one face to another.

Goldman surveyed him with distaste.

"What d'you mean by coming here like that?" he demanded harshly. "Are you aiming to tell the world I'm in the habit of entertaining a pack of hoboes in my apartment at three o'clock in the morning?"

"I'm sorry," Corrigan said stolidly. "I thought I'd better come here at once and tell you what happened."

"I've heard most of it. What happened to you?"

Corrigan rubbed the palms of his hands down his trousers.

"We went to Sam Harp's and I was coming out last. Ted was in a hurry to go, and I stayed to pay for the last round. There's a dark corridor between Sam's private room and the side door, and as I came down there I was caught from behind. There was two of 'em—whoever they were—and they had a handkerchief with chloroform on it. I sort of passed out. When I woke up I was lying on a heap of bricks in a building lot just next to Sam's."

"What did Harp say about it?"

"He didn't know anything. Said he locked the door after he let us in, and couldn't see that anyone had forced it."

"Have you any idea who the other guy was—besides the Saint?"

"I don't know, Mr Goldman. I didn't hear neither of them speak—"

Corrigan's voice died away. The cold black eyes of Tex Goldman screwed down to vicious pin-points, and were boring into his face with an inclement ferocity that appalled him. Ted Orping started up—one abrupt menacing movement. Clem Enright moved his feet restlessly, his mouth opening in stupid perplexity.

Tex Goldman's cigar waved a slight gesture of restraint.

"You didn't seem surprised when I mentioned the Saint, Corrigan," said the gunman silkily. "Who told you that was who it was?"

"I don't . . . Nobody told me, Mr Goldman. I . . . I s'pose—"

THE SAINT AND MR TEAL

"You skunk!"

Goldman moved with startling suddenness, swiftly and savagely. He pulled himself out of his chair and stepped up to within a foot of the Irishman. His eyes never left the other's face. One of his hands grasped the man's coat collar; the other dived into Corrigan's pockets, one after another, like a striking snake. It came out of one trouser pocket with a roll of new one-pound notes.

He flung Corrigan back. Ted Orping seized Corrigan from behind as the Irishman's fists clenched.

"You dirty double-crossing rat! So you sold us to the Saint!"

Goldman tore the notes across and across, and scattered them over the floor.

"Get out of here!"

"Listen, Goldman—I didn't—"

"*Get out!*"

Ted Orping twisted the man round and pushed him towards the door. Corrigan's eyes flamed, and he took a pace back into the room. Orping's hand touched his hip.

Then Joe Corrigan turned on his heel and left the apartment.

Tex Goldman looked at Orping steadily. There was a question in Ted Orping's gaze, another question in Tex Goldman's. Temporarily forgotten in his corner, Clem Enright shuffled his feet again, open-mouthed.

"There's only one way to deal with traitors," Goldman said.

Ted Orping nodded. He shrugged with the callous understanding that he had been taught, and pulled down the brim of his hat. He went out without a word.

He caught Joe Corrigan in the street.

"Walk a little way with me, Joe?"

"You get away from me," grated Corrigan surlily. "I don't want your company."

Ted Orping took his arm.

"Aw, come on, Joe. You don't understand the boss. He's a great guy, but naturally he has to be suspicious. You must admit what you said didn't sound right. I just took his part so's I could try an' make things right for you when he cools off."

"I never double-crossed anyone," said Corrigan. "I dipped a toff's wallet on a bus this morning, and got those notes."

"O' course, Joe. That's what he ought to have thought of, I understand."

They walked up Baker Street from the Marylebone Road crossing. Near the top, a few yards from Regent's Park, Orping steered the other off to the right into a dimly-lighted mews. They went a little way down it, and Corrigan stopped.

"What's the idea?" he demanded sullenly. "We don't want to go this way."

Ted Orping looked left and right.

"This'll do," he said.

"What for?"

"Just to give you what's coming to you, rat."

He fired three times before Joe Corrigan could speak.

3

Simon Templar came back from Amsterdam a few days later. The items of jewellery which sometimes came his way were never fenced in England—the Saint was far too notorious for that, and caution in the right place was still his longest suit. He travelled by roundabout routes, for his movements were always a subject of absorbing interest to the watchful powers of Scotland Yard. That particular trip took him the best part of a week, but it was worth three thousand pounds to him.

He felt no remorse on account of Mr Peabody. The insurance companies would cover most if not all of the loss, and Mr Peabody had definitely asked for it. As for those insurance companies, Simon felt that the blow would not be likely to shake their stock to its foundations. In a misguided moment of altruistic zeal he had once attempted to insure his own life, and had discovered that so long as he undertook not to fly aeroplanes, travel in tropical parts, enter into naval or military service, become a lion-tamer or a steeple-jack, or in fact do anything whatsoever that might by any conceivable chance endanger the life of a reasonably healthy and intelligent man, the insurance company would be charmed to accept his premiums. His opinion of insurance companies was that they were bloated organisations which were delighted to take anybody's money over risks that had been eliminated from every angle that human ingenuity could foresee. They were fair game so far as he was concerned, and his conscience was even more pachydermatous than usual over their rare misfortunes.

But he came back to a London in which the insurance companies were more worried than they had been for many years.

Patricia Holm met him in the Haymarket, where the Air Union bus decanted him after an uneventful journey from Ostend. One of the first things he saw was a crimson evening newspaper poster proclaiming "Another Bank Hold-up," but he was not immediately impressed. They strolled up to Oddenino's for a cocktail and she sprang the news on him rather suddenly.

"They got Joe Corrigan," she said.

Simon raised his eyebrows. He read the newspaper cutting which she handed him, and smoked a cigarette.

"Poor devil! . . . But what a fool! He shouldn't have gone back—at least, I thought he'd have the sense to put up a good story. Goldman must have caught him out somehow . . . Tex is clever!"

The cutting simply described the finding of the body and its identification. Corrigan was a man of doubtful associations with three convictions to his name, and the police were hopeful of making an early arrest.

"I saw Claud Eustace in Piccadilly the day before yesterday," said Patricia. "He as good as told me they hadn't a hope of getting the man who did it."

"I suppose it'd be a long shot if the night porter in Tex's block recognised the photograph," said the Saint thoughtfully. "It isn't particularly flattering to Joe. And the whole Green Cross bunch would have their alibis." He speared a cherry and frowned at it. "Tex might have done it himself—or else it was Ted Orping. I don't see Brother Clem as a cold-blooded killer."

"There've been some odd-looking men hanging about Manson Place," she told him, and the Saint's eyebrows slanted again—dangerously.

"Any trouble?"

"No. But I've been taking care not to come home late at night."

Simon sipped his Bronx and gazed at the Bacchanalian array of shakers and glasses stencilled on the coloured glass behind the bar.

"I expect things would be quiet. Tex isn't the lad to waste his energies on side issues when there's big stuff in the offing. Now that I'm home, South Kensington may get unhealthy. Glory be, Pat—wouldn't you love to see the faces of the local trouts if Tex started spraying SW7 with Tommy guns for my benefit?"

It was characteristic of him to turn off the menace with a flippant remark, and yet he knew better than anyone what a threat hung over others in London beside himself—others who had a far sounder claim than he to object to a lavish expenditure of ammunition. The Saint had never cared to live safely, but there were others who held their lives less lightly.

Before dinner was over he had learned more. Things had been happening quickly in London while he had been away, and behind them all he could see the guiding hand of the man from St. Louis. After the fiasco of the Peabody raid it seemed as if Goldman had gone all out for a restoration of confidence in his followers. The work was rapid, ruthlessly thorough, a desperate bid for power under the standards of sudden death. The day after the Peabody raid another jeweller's shop had been successfully smashed in Bond Street, and on the same night a small safe deposit off the Tottenham Court Road had been blasted open and half emptied while masked men with revolvers held a small crowd at bay and covered the escape of the inside party before the police reached the scene. In those cases the victims were discreet rather than valorous.

It was different at the Battersea branch of the Metropolitan Bank, which the same men held up the following midday. A cashier attempted to reach for a gun under the counter, and was shot dead where he stood. The gang escaped with over two thousand pounds in cash.

While officialdom was still humming with that outrage, another bank in Edmonton was similarly held up, but with the warning of the Metropolitan Bank murder fresh in their memories, the staff showed no resistance.

Conferences were held, and special reserves of armed men in plain clothes were called out to cover as many likely spots as possible. But the police were again out-guessed. The next day, an excess of confidence on the part of the management concerned allowed a private car bearing the week's pay envelopes for half a dozen branches of a popular library to leave a bank in the city. It was intercepted at its first stop, the messenger sandbagged, and fifteen hundred pounds in cash stolen. A constable on point duty saw the incident and tried to pursue the bandits' car on the running board of a commandeered taxi. He was shot off it by the fugitives and seriously injured, but it was expected that he would live.

The tale went through a sequence of bare-faced brigandage that was staggering.

"We're getting 'em scared," Tex Goldman said. "That's the only way to do it. Hit 'em, and keep on hitting. Don't give 'em time to think. In a month or two they'll be begging for mercy."

"You bet," said Orping.

He had automatically become Goldman's aide-de-camp, and held his position by his own audacity. It was he who had shot the Metropolitan Bank cashier—in a week he had become a confirmed killer, with two notches on his gun and the bravado of experience. "Basher" Tope, who had shot the policeman, ran him a fair second.

Ted Orping poured out a dose of brandy from a silver hip-flask. He had learned that trick too, and he used it often. Alcohol braced his recklessness up to a point at which murder meant nothing.

"The guy I'm wantin' to see again is the Saint," he said.

"You'll get your chance," said Goldman. "We'll know about it the minute he comes home. I'd like to see him myself."

He might or might not have been pleased to know that Simon Templar shared that wish with him in no uncertain manner.

As far as the Saint was concerned, the desired opportunity came his way with a promptness for which he had only a stretch of coincidence to thank. On the night when some of the events already mentioned were told to Simon they had dined at a favourite restaurant of theirs in Beak Street, a quiet little Spanish eating-house where the food was good and cheap and the crowd neither fashionable nor pseudo-Bohemian. It was some time after eleven o'clock when they left, and wandered through side streets towards Shaftesbury Avenue with the vague idea of having another cup of coffee somewhere before going home. They were just turning a corner when Simon saw the man from St. Louis emerging from a doorway. In a flash Simon had caught Patricia's arm and jerked her back into the narrow lane from which they had just been turning. He leaned against the wall, covering her with his body, with his broad back turned to the Yankee gunman.

"Tex himself!" he said. "Pretend to be powdering your nose—get out a mirror."

His ambition to see Tex Goldman again included a time and place of his own choosing, with the circumstances carefully reviewed and his plan of campaign completely polished—not a chance encounter in a back street that would do little more than advertise his return.

In the girl's mirror he saw Goldman step into a taxi and drive off. Patricia saw the gunman for the first time.

"That's the boy who's causing all the trouble. And I wonder what he's doing around here tonight?"

They walked on, and Simon studied the doorway that had exhaled the new menace to the peace of London. A small illuminated sign over the lintel announced it as the Baytree Club. The door was open, but all that could be seen was a short passage leading to a flight of stairs, from beyond which came subdued sounds of music. It appeared to be one of those centres of furtive gaiety which one passes almost without noticing in daylight, and which suddenly become attractive when the neon signs wake up and the unprepossessing street outside is hidden in a kindly gloom.

The Saint stood on the opposite pavement with a cigarette drooping from the corner of his mouth, and surveyed the premises in a contemplative silence. A private car turned into the street and drew up outside the doorway to exude two men who went down the passage and up the stairs.

"Feel like a spot of night life, Pat?" queried the Saint.

There was a promise of mischief in his gaze. It might have come to anything or nothing, as the Fates decreed, but he felt that he would like to know more about the place where Tex Goldman descended to common or garden frivolity.

She nodded.

"O.K., boy."

They were crossing the road when the Saint's keen ears became aware that the music inside the club had stopped. There was nothing very remarkable in that, for even the most energetic orchestras must rest for a few moments now and then to expand their lungs and gargle. And yet it made the Saint hesitate. Somehow he associated that stoppage with the arrival of the two men who had just gone in—and the peculiar fact that their car was still standing outside, where parking was not allowed. Perhaps the glimpse he had had of Tex Goldman leaving the same premises a few minutes before had made him unduly suspicious. He turned off diagonally along the road, drawing Patricia with him. He seemed to hear the muffled sounds of some commotion inside the club—a commotion that was rather more than the usual babble of conversation that springs up between dances.

And then he heard the sound of feet pelting down the stairs.

He guided Patricia into the nearest porch as if he were merely an innocent young citizen taking his girlfriend home from a movie, and again used her mirror inconspicuously. He saw the two men dash out of the doorway and plunge into their car, and before they disappeared he had seen that the lower halves of their faces were covered by their white evening scarves.

The car pulled out and whirled up the street, passing them where they stood. Other feet were pounding down the steps of the club, and Simon looked round and saw the owner of the first pair reach the pavement. He was a frantic-looking young man with his bow tie draggling loose down his shirt-front, and he yelled "Police!" in a voice that echoed down the street. In a few seconds he was joined by others with the same cry. One or two pale-faced girls crowded out behind the leading men.

Simon glanced after the departing car. He could still see its tail light as it was swinging round the next corner, and his hand flew to his hip . . .

It stayed there. His other hand followed suit, on the other hip. With his coat swept back behind his forearms, he lounged over towards the panic-stricken mob on the pavement. A police whistle was shrilling somewhere nearby. He might have been able to do some damage to the bandits' car, but the official attention to his tactics might have been more embarrassing than the damage would have been worth. He was not yet ready to take the law into his own hands.

The frantic-looking young man confirmed his guess of what had happened.

"They held us up—it must have been the gang that's been holding up all the banks. Took all our money and the girls' jewellery. We couldn't do anything, or some of the girls might have got hurt . . . I say! Officer—"

A running policeman had appeared and the young man joined the general surge towards him. Simon faded away from the group and rejoined Patricia.

"Let's stick around," he said. "If I know anything, Claud Eustace will be along."

He was right in his diagnosis. The chattering crowd gradually filtered back into the club to make its several statements, under the constable's pressure, and a couple of plain-clothes men arrived from Marlborough Street. After a while another taxi entered the street and released a plump familiar figure. Simon buttonholed him.

"What ho, Claud!" he murmured breezily. "This is a bit late in life for you to take up dancing. Or has someone been trying to buy a box of chocolates after nine o'clock?"

The detective looked at him with a rather strained weariness.

"What are you doing here, Saint?"

"Taking an after-dinner breather. Giving the gastric juices their ozone. I just happened to be around when the fun started."

"Did you see the men?"

Simon nodded.

"Yes. But they were half-masked, of course. I got the number of the car, but it looked new, so I suppose it was stolen."

Teal rubbed his chin.

"If you can wait till I've finished here I'd like to have a talk with you."

"OK. We'll toddle along to Sandy's and sniff some coffee. See you there."

The Saint took Patricia's arm, and they strolled through to Oxenden Street. Three-quarters of an hour later Chief Inspector Teal came in and took his place at the counter.

"Did you get anything useful?" asked the Saint.

"Nothing," said Teal shortly. "The men had scarves over their faces, as you said. They were both in evening dress, which lets you out."

Simon sighed.

"That bee in your bonnet buzzes an awful lot," he protested. "Can't you think up anything better than that?"

"You've been abroad for a week, haven't you?"

"I have. Drinking good beer and associating with some stout Huns. The Secret Service must have been working overtime."

"I didn't suspect you seriously." Teal stirred three lumps of sugar into his cup. "This wholesale murder isn't in your line, is it? A wretched clerk and one of our own uniformed men shot down in a week—and nothing to show for it. It fairly makes your blood boil."

The detective's round face was unwontedly hollow in the cheeks. The failures of the last few hectic days were making their mark on his ponderous self-assurance.

"We've tried all the regulars," he said. "The Green Cross boys are the nucleus of it, we know, but so far they've been able to work a system of alibis that have left us flat. Most of them have come into a lot of money that they can't account for since this trouble started, but that isn't a crime. We had one of their best men in the other day—a fellow named Orping. He was playing the American gangster to the life. Between ourselves, we knocked him about a bit—you know what can be done—but we couldn't shake a thing out of him. I don't like that American line that Orping's got hold of. It looks ugly."

"Any idea where the stuff's being fenced?"

"I'm afraid not. I don't think it's being fenced in this country at all."

Simon Templar smiled inwardly, but he forebore to point a moral.

"Who's the Big Noise?" he asked, and the detective shrugged grimly.

"If we knew that, the trouble would be practically over. There are rumours that it's some sort of Yank, and all the registered aliens have come under observation, but we haven't learned much. Whoever he is, he's got his men right under his thumb, I've never met so many oysters before. The story is that Corrigan was one of the bunch who threatened to squeal, and what happened to him has put the fear of God into everyone else who might have talked."

The Saint pushed his hands into his pockets and gazed at the detective with a faint suggestion of mockery.

"It must have made you wish I was on the road again, Claud. It's something to think that you may have admitted that my reign of terror wasn't so bad after all."

Mr Teal finished his coffee and unwrapped a wafer of chewing gum. His baby-blue eyes looked the Saint over with a certain seriousness.

"If you only had the sense to keep out of the newspapers, and save the Assistant Commissioner from practising sarcastic remarks on me," he said, "I shouldn't be sorry if you were on the road for a while. You can do things that we can't do officially. We're trying to get special powers, but you know what that's likely to mean. It may take us months—and men will be killed every day while we're helpless. There's only one way to deal with this sort of thing. You've got to fight guns with guns, killing with killing, fear with fear."

They separated on an arrangement to lunch together in three days' time, which was the friendliest parting they had had for many months. It rather tickled Simon to think how the advent of a common enemy might make a branded outlaw almost persona grata with the Law, merely because his killings were more discriminate.

Patricia and the Saint drove boldly back to Manson Place in a taxi. There was a man tinkering with a motorcycle at the open end of the cul-de-sac: Simon saw him look up as the taxi passed, and reckoned that Tex Goldman would shortly be receiving some interesting news.

Curiously enough, it did not occur to him that a sharp pair of eyes in the car that had carried the holdup men away from the Baytree Club might have noticed him where he stood in the street a few doors from the scene of the crime.

He paid off the taxi, and mounted the short flight of steps to the front door of his temporary home circumspectly. The man at the corner still tinkered with his motorcycle. Simon slid aside the pivoted metal plate under the knocker, and studied the indicator bulb which it concealed to make sure that no one had entered the house in his absence before he called Patricia to join him. He kept his right hand in his pocket while he unlocked the door and let her through, and his eyes never ceased their watchful survey of the street, but his precautions were a matter of routine. He was not expecting trouble immediately.

"It's rather a pity I let those Green Cross boys know who I was," he said.

There were several letters waiting for him, and he sat on the table in the sitting-room and read them while Patricia Holm went to the kitchen to find him a bottle of beer.

She came back with a tray. He heard her put it down, and then he heard a crash.

"Never mind the glass," he said, without looking round. "We can always burgle Woolworth's for some more. Break the lot if you feel like it."

"Simon . . . I didn't—"

The Saint took his eyes off the letter he was reading. A motorcycle was roaring away with an open exhaust. He saw the broken window, and the shining metal cylinder that lay on the floor, and he moved like a streak of lightning.

The force of his rush hurled the girl bruised and shaken on to the settee, and the next instant the Saint's weight was flung on the back of it. The heavy piece of leather-upholstered furniture was toppled over by the impact, so that they lay sheltered behind it. In another split second the thunder of the explosion deafened them and the air was full of the whine of flying metal.

4

Patricia Holm looked up from her crossword puzzle.

"Give me a word for 'sack' in three letters, boy. 'M,' 'A,' something."

"Bag," suggested the Saint.

The girl eyed him sinisterly.

"What d'you mean—'bag'? I said—"

"Eb, A. G.," insisted the Saint adenoidally. "Bag. With a code id the doze."

They were having breakfast in the kitchen, for the sitting-room was uninhabitable. A representative from a firm of decorators whom the Saint had telephoned came round at eleven and inspected the mess wisely.

"It looks as if there'd been an explosion, sir," he said.

"You're wrong," said the Saint. "A man came in here and sat on a pin after putting baking powder on his gooseberries in mistake for sugar. We're still looking for him."

An assurance was given that the firm would set to work to make good the damage as quickly as possible, and Simon bathed and dressed himself with unaltered cheerfulness. Any philosophically-minded man in his position could have found something to be cheerful about that morning, for it was a miracle that the Saint was alive. If the pineapple expert had not misjudged the length of his fuse the end of all Saint Stories would have been written in a sticky splash.

Chief Inspector Teal himself called in later. He had the report of the explosives man who had been sent down from the Yard to view the damage. The bomb was a home-made affair of the jam-tin type, but it might have been none the less effective for that. The assortment of broken nails and scrap-iron with which it had been lined had pocked the walls and ceiling like a burst of shrapnel, and slit to ribbons the upholstery that had saved the Saint's and Patricia's lives.

"I'm wondering why they should have bothered about you," said Teal.

"Passing over the insult to my fame," drawled the Saint, "maybe someone overheard your suggestion to me last night. Or else there's someone in the gang with a grudge against me—Basher Tope is a Green Cross boy, and you may remember that I once had words with him. But don't take it to heart, Claud—I expect your turn will come."

Teal turned his chewing gum over somnolently.

"You haven't been interfering already, have you?" he inquired, and the Saint smiled.

"I never interfere, Claud. You know that."

"All the same, I think I'd change my address if I were you," said the detective.

Simon stood at the broken window after he had gone and gazed down the road. The motorcycle man was no longer in sight, and it was unlikely that he would return. The crowd which had filled the road after the explosion the night before had had its eyeful and dispersed, and there were no curious sightseers to replace it that morning. London had taken the attempt on the Saint's life with considerable sang-froid.

There were no suspicious loiterers on the vista on which the Saint looked out, but Simon Templar was not deceived.

"There might be something in Claud's idea as far as you're concerned, Pat," he said. "Ted Orping will be trying again, if none of the others do."

"How long is this going on for?" she asked.

"Until Tex Goldman is the Big Shot of London, or material for a front-page inquest," said the Saint. "Tex thinks the first and I think the second."

She slipped a hand through his arm. He was not utterly surprised at her gaiety.

"Gee, boy, it's thrilling!"

"You're a wicked little girl," said the Saint solemnly, "and if anybody hears you talk like that you'll find yourself thrown out of the YWCA on your ear . . . But don't get the idea that London is going to be like Chicago. There are no gangs coming over here. It's just a wildcat scheme out of Tex Goldman's head, but there may be lots of skylarking and song before the swelling goes down."

The general public's interest in Simon Templar's fate was demonstrated more enthusiastically in newsprint than in person. Harassed editors in search of new headlines connected with the gang menace to London seized on the bombing incident joyfully with an unspoken prayer of thanksgiving for the fact that it happened in time for them to find a position of suitable prominence for it before the country editions went to bed. Morning newspapers work under the tragic disadvantage compared with their brethren of the evening, for they are unable to rush out special editions at any hour of the day in order to scoop an exclusive story. This was the kind of event that they lived for.

The pashas of Fleet Street shared the Saint's knowledge that no seriously Chicago-esque wave of lawlessness was on its way, but it takes more than that to stop an experienced news editor. Fleet Street grabbed at the temporary orgy of violent crime, as it appeared to the public at the moment, with both hands. The Saint's escape was featured on the front page of every national daily, and in it, naturally, was mentioned the essential point that Simon Templar had survived the attack.

This fact was the subject of a short-tempered conference in the neighbourhood of Baker Street.

"Let me go after him with a gun, boss," said Ted Orping. "I'll get him for you."

"Yeah—you'd get him like you got him last time," replied Tex Goldman sourly. "You're just a beginner, and from what I hear that guy was toting a gun before you were weaned. You ain't much to look at, but you're more use alive than dead."

Orping scowled. He had almost thought out a fittingly belligerent retort when Goldman put away his cigar and waved him to silence.

"Back in St. Louis, when a guy had to be bumped off, we had a way of doing it. I'll tell you what it was. We found an empty apartment, or a room, or sump'n, that had a window fixed so's you could see his door. Then a coupla choppers, or maybe sometimes just one, would sit up in that window and watch till he came out. They had a machine-gun, and they didn't care how long they waited. Some time he had to come out, and then he got his."

"How could we get a machine-gun?" asked Orping sceptically.

"We couldn't—not yet," said Goldman. "But we can get a rifle, can't we? And half the houses in that street are boarding-houses or apartments, ain't they? We'll get him—maybe tomorrow."

The simple feasibility of the idea impressed itself gradually on Ted Orping. He nodded.

"I'll do it," he said.

"You won't," said Tex Goldman, without emotion. "With a rifle, it wants a guy who can shoot. Tope can shoot, and I'll be wanting you for another job."

Extraordinarily enough, this was no less than the truth. During the Great War, Basher Tope had found himself pressed into the army with the coming of conscription, and had actually contrived to spend nearly six months of his service outside the military prisons which opened their doors to him as automatically as had the civil prisons with which he was so familiar. The only good mark on his military record was that he had passed his musketry courses with flying colours. It was a rather unexpected accomplishment to find a man like that, but good shots are born a thousand times more often than they are made. Basher Tope had the gift, and Tex Goldman selected him uncompromisingly for the second assault.

He appeared in Manson Place that afternoon, wearing a stained black suit and hat and an impressive beard. In the fourth house which he tried he secured a front bed-sitting room on the ground floor from which he had a perfect view of Simon Templar's front door. He called himself Schwartz, a traveller for a Leipzig firm of publishers, and spoke English so badly that his Hoxton accent was undetectable among the dense clutter of other accents with which his guttural speech was interspersed. He said he required a room only for two days and could not stand hotels.

Unfortunately for him, he discarded his beard in the privacy of his room before he went to bed that night. Simon Templar, scanning the street from behind drawn curtains through a pair of field-glasses, saw him through the window and knew what to expect.

"Tex isn't wasting any time," he said.

His reply to the threat called for two curious articles of which at least one is not an ordinary purchasable commodity, but a closed car had been standing near his back door in the mews all day, and he knew it would not be easy to go out and do his shopping.

He telephoned to an hotel, and to a firm of removers, and at half-past four a motor van drew up outside his front door and two men in green baize aprons disembarked and rang the bell. They were admitted, and a few minutes later they came out again with a large wardrobe trunk. It was loaded into the van, and delivered half an hour later to the hotel. Simon stepped out of it in his room, went unnoticed down the stairs, and in due course was shown up to his room again.

It stands to the credit of his remarkable knowledge of queer markets that he was able to make his purchases in a very short time.

At half-past ten the following morning another van drew up outside the Saint's house. This time the men unloaded a large packing-case, and carried it inside. Half an hour later they brought it out again, and Basher Tope, at his window, did not notice that it appeared to be just as heavy when it came out as when it went in.

He stole a few minutes from his post to telephone Tex Goldman.

"Templar seems to be moving out," he said. "'E sent orf some luggage and a packin'-case."

"I thought he would," said Goldman, with satisfaction. "Get back to your window and see you don't miss him."

There was a fast car outside the door of the house where Basher Tope had found his lodgings, waiting to take its part in his escape as soon as his job was done. The landlady came up to his room after lunch, and he paid her bill and muttered something about leaving that night. That left him free to depart at any time he pleased without exciting attention, and his task seemed easy. The fast car was only provided in case of unforeseen accidents.

There was certainly an accident, and it was certainly unforeseen.

Shortly afterwards Clem Enright, in a new brown-check suit and a bowler hat, called round with a message.

"The boss says you're to get 'im before eight o'clock, an' 'e don't care 'ow yer do it."

"I'll get 'im if it's possible," growled Tope.

Clem Enright found him unresponsive to a line of conversation about "real men like you an' me wot means to get wot we goes after," and departed huffily in a few minutes. There was a shabby loafer knocking his pipe out on the bumpers of the car as Enright came out, but Clem paid him no attention. Basher Tope had not noticed him, though he had been hanging around there for half an hour.

Simon Templar only required the street to himself for a couple of minutes to do what he had to do, but it took him all that time to get it.

He had left the house in the packing-case in which he had returned to it, but one of his purchases had gone in with him and had not come out again. Patricia Holm stayed there to attend to it.

The shabby loafer shuffled out of Manson Place a quarter of an hour after Enright had gone, and in three-quarters of an hour more, by devious routes, he became Simon Templar again. It was as Simon Templar that he rang up Chief Inspector Teal.

"If you've any time to spare, Claud, you might like to get the man who shot your policeman. He's staying in Manson Place, and his present job is to murder me."

"Whereabouts is he?" asked the detective eagerly, and Simon grinned into the mouthpiece.

"What's lighting-up time these days? About seven-thirty, isn't it? . . . Well, why don't you blow down to Queen's Gate about then? Hang around the corner of Manson Place and watch for the excitement."

Basher Tope had a boring afternoon, sitting in his window with a loaded rifle on his knee and his eyes glued to the green-painted door out of which he expected his target to emerge. The twilight came down while he watched, and a lamplighter went round the cul-de-sac to confirm the fact that it was getting near the time limit that Tex Goldman had given him.

And then, at seven-thirty exactly, a ground floor window in the Saint's house suddenly sprang into a square of light.

Basher Tope leaned forward. He could see clearly into the room, which looked like a dining-room. At one end of the table with his back to the window, he could see the head and shoulders of a man in a grey suit who seemed to be absorbed in a book.

Basher Tope turned sideways, and cuddled the stock of the gun slowly into his right shoulder.

A knock came on the door of his room. It made him jump, although he knew the door was locked.

"'Oo's that?" he grunted.

"A gentleman called Smith rang up, Mr Schwarz," said his landlady's voice. "He told me to ask you when's Mr Brown going out."

It was a prearranged message, and it showed that Tex Goldman was getting impatient. Basher Tope showed his teeth.

"Tell 'im 'e go out now."

He listened to the woman's footsteps receding along the hall, and nestled his cheek once more against the stock of his rifle. Carefully he aligned the sights, the foresight exactly splitting the V of the back-sight, and the tip of it resting steadily at six o'clock on a point just below where the Saint's left shoulder-blade should have been. His forefinger tightened on the trigger . . .

Plop!

He could see the dark hole made by the bullet, and his target flopped forward. Even so he fired two more shots to make certain— one more to the heart, one to the back of the head. Then he unscrewed the silencer rapidly, folded the gun over its central hinge, and packed it away in a plain black hand-bag. He unlocked the door and went out to the waiting car. The engine answered the self-starter instantly.

Chief Inspector Teal idly watched the car turn into Queen's Gate, and then he found Simon Templar beside him.

"Well?" prompted the detective.

"That was Basher Tope," said the Saint casually, jerking a thumb after the retreating car. "He's just killed me."

"What d'you mean—he's just killed you?" snapped the detective. "Why didn't you—"

"I mean, he thinks he has. As a matter of fact, he's pumped three bullets into a tailor's dummy with an old coat of mine on, and it fell over when Pat pulled a string. It's too bad about Basher."

Teal looked down towards the Saint's house and saw three splintery stars in the glass of the lighted window. It seemed as if he was about to say something, but he never said it. The crash of an explosion hit the left side of his face like a blow, and he turned quickly. Less than a hundred yards up Queen's Gate he saw the car that had carried the bearded man away swerving wildly across the road, and the whole of one shattered side of it seemed to be hanging loose.

The car jumped the kerb, ran across the pavement, and piled itself up with a second crash against a strip of area railings that bent over like reeds under the impact. Passers-by began running towards it, but Teal stood where he was. His baby-blue eyes returned to the Saint's face.

"What does that mean?" he asked.

Simon slid out a cigarette case. His own eyes were just as steady as Teal's—perhaps even steadier—and he shook his head with a slow motion of great sorrow.

"The way I figure it out, Claud," he said, "I think you'll find he must have had some sort of bomb on board, in case the rifle didn't work. It must have short-circuited, or something, and gone off. It's just too bad about him."

5

Simon took Patricia back to the hotel where he had booked a suite. They went there with the comforting feeling that they were not being followed, since at that moment there was no one available to follow them, and had a cocktail in the lounge with the knowledge that it would be sheer bad luck if any of the ungodly happened to come upon them there. Temporarily they had disappeared into the wide world, so far as Tex Goldman's information was concerned.

This hotel was the Dorchester, where the Saint had taken two small but luxurious rooms, with bath, overlooking Hyde Park. They were commended by the fact that they were faced by no other buildings from which shots might be fired, and although they cost twelve pounds a day Simon was untroubled by the thought of what the Sunday night orators a short distance away at Marble Arch might say about his extravagance if they knew. The accommodation satisfied that instinct in him which demanded the best of everything at any price, and he was not proposing to pay for it himself.

"It is a fascinating thought," said the Saint, nibbling a chip potato, "that there are well over forty million living souls in this great England.

If every one of them gave me sixpence, none of them would really miss it, and I should be a millionaire."

"You'd better start collecting," said Patricia.

"I'm afraid it would take too long," said the Saint regretfully.

"Especially when we got north of the Tweed. No—we shall have to muck along with what we can collect in lumps from just a few people. Which reminds me that it must be nearly three months since we last thought of Mr Nilder."

It was quite true that Simon Templar's memory had almost lost hold of that natty and unsavoury little gentleman. Three months ago he had sent him through the post a polite intimation that a gift of about ten thousand pounds to the Actors' Orphanage would be in order, but that had been rather more of a derisive gesture to Mr Teal than a proposal of serious dimensions. The other exciting things that had happened about that time had driven the idea out of his head, but now it came back to him out of the blue.

He felt that a brief Interlude of change from the somewhat strenuous circumstances of his war with Tex Goldman would do him good. Ordinary gang wars, after all, were not strictly in his line. They provided a definite interest in life, and a plentiful supply of skylarking and song, but taken continuously they were a heavy diet. Simon Templar required his share of the lighter things as well.

No one knew better than the Saint that Scotland Yard was perfectly capable of taking care of the ordinary and open forms of law-breaking. In the Saint's various arguments with the Tex Goldman mob, he had done very little more than could have been done by any detective with an original turn of mind and an equal freedom from responsibility to the stolidly unimaginative Powers who draw princely salaries for encumbering with red tape and ballyhoo the perfectly simple process of locating ungodliness and smacking it on the nose. His self-appointed mission was far more concerned with the ugly twists of ungodliness which rarely come within the ken of Scotland Yard at all—and which, if they do come within that myopic ken, are usually found to be so studiously legal that Officialdom can find nothing to do about them.

The profession of Mr Nilder came very fairly into that category.

At that moment Simon Templar knew little about him. A word of information had come his way through one of the mysterious channels by which such words reached his ears. It was a word that would have meant nothing to Scotland Yard, but to the Saint it opened up an avenue of fascinating speculations which he knew he would have to explore someday. Three months ago he had seized on it blindly for a passing need, and now it seemed to him that the time was ripe for investigating it further.

"We ought to know more about Ronald," said the Saint.

It was quite natural for him to turn aside like that to such a comparatively trivial affair, though his life had been called for twice in the last two days and the Green Cross boys were still combing London for him with their message of death. Numbers of beefy men were drawing their weekly pay envelopes for looking after the Green Cross boys, but he was not included in the distribution.

Mr Ronald Nilder left London the next morning, as a matter of history—alone, and driving the modest two-year-old Buick which was the limit of his ostentation on the road, Simon Templar, also as a matter of history, went with him—though Mr Nilder did not know this.

The preparation of successful buccaneering raids on the aforesaid members of the ungodly requires an extensive knowledge of the victims' habits. The actual smacking of them on the nose is very spectacular and entertaining to behold, but although it is those high spots of privateering that the chronicler is happiest to record, it is still tediously true that if there were no dull periods of preparation there would be no high spots. You have to get to the top of the Eiffel Tower before you can dive off, and the elevator is often out of order.

Simon figured it was a nice day for a drive. London was in the grip of its brief summer. From Aldgate to the Brompton Road, locked lines of grumbling traffic edged along their routes in rackety crawls of a few feet at a time, and subsided again into jammed immobility with a ceaseless belching of blue smoke and mephitic fumes—an unforgettable procession of tribute to the singular genius of the Authorities who had organised enormous gangs of workmen to dig up roads and excavate new and superfluous Underground stations at every point where their activities could set a capstone on the paralytic confusion. The slobbering sultans of Whitehall thought about the colossal tax on petrol, and rubbed their greasy hands gleefully at the idea of the tens of thousands of gallons that were being spewed out into space for the pleasure of keeping engines running between two-yards snail's-rushes; while the perspiring public stifled in the fetid atmosphere, and wondered dumbly what it was all about—being constitutionally incapable of asking why their money should be paid into the bank balances of Traffic Commissioners nominally employed to see that such conditions should not exist. London, in short, was just the same as it always was, except for the temperature, and the Saint felt almost kindly disposed towards Mr Nilder as the dusty Buick picked up speed as they left Kingston, and he was led rapidly out into the cleaner air of Surrey.

With these bolshevistic reflections to divert him, the Saint had an easy part to play as the hind quarters of a loose tandem that headed by the most direct road to Bursledon. Mr Nilder did not know the Saint's car, and he did not know the Saint, and Simon made no particular effort to hide himself. After all, there is nothing very startling about two motorists trailing to the same destination at approximately the same average speed, and the Saint did not feel furtive that morning.

They ran into Bursledon with fifty yards between them, and there Mr Nilder's car swung off sharply to the right down a lane that led along the backs of the many dockyards that line the river. Simon drove on across the bridge, parked at the side of the road, and returned on foot.

He stood in the middle of the bridge and leaned his elbows on the parapet, gazing down along the lines of houseboats and miscellaneous other craft that were moored in the stream. The mingled smells of paint and tar and sea-water drifted to his nostrils down the slight sultry breeze, and he could hear the clunk of spasmodic hammering from one of the yards on his right. Somehow it brought back to him a nostalgia of other and perhaps better days when he had been free to go down to limpid tropical seas under the swelling white sails of a schooner, and his forays against the ungodly had been fought under the changing skies of forbidden pearling grounds. All at once that twist of retrospect made him envy the men he had left behind—bad men and all. And for one moment of memory he felt tired of the grubby ratting through smirched city streets which had claimed him for so long . . .

And then he saw a dinghy putting out from the shore, and Mr Ronald Nilder in the stern.

His cigarette canted up alertly, and the blue far-seeing eyes ranged out over the water. In a few moments he was able to pick out the dinghy's objective—a trim white fifty-foot motor cruiser that rode lazily at its moorings in mid-stream. It looked fast—faster than anything else in the perspective—and at the same time it had a sweetly proportioned breadth of beam that guaranteed it seaworthy as well.

The Saint launched himself off the parapet and strolled along to the lane down which Nilder's car had disappeared. Wandering through the yards, he had glimpses of the cruiser which showed him Ronald Nilder's progress in a series of illuminating snapshots. He saw the dinghy come alongside, and the oarsman holding it steady while Nilder climbed aboard. Then he saw Nilder disappearing into the cabin, and the oarsman making the dinghy fast to a cleat on the stern. Then the oarsman going forward over the cabin roof and lowering himself into the cockpit. Then Nilder appearing again beside him, having exchanged his grey homburg for a white-topped yachting cap, and not looking very nautical even then . . .

By which time the Saint was leaning on the bows of an old ML hull directly opposite the *Seabird*—he was close enough to read the name painted on a shining white lifebuoy.

A whiskered old salt a couple of yards away was parcelling the ends of a frayed length of rope; Simon caught his eye, and waved vaguely towards the *Seabird*.

"That's a nice boat," he said.

The old salt looked out over the water and spat.

"Not bad, sir, if you like that sorter thing, I wouldn't be seen dead in it, sir, if you ask me."

"Nothing like sail, eh?" murmured the Saint sympathetically.

"Ar," said the old salt, spitting emotionally. "Now yer talkin'. Them jiggery things is all right fer ladies an' fancy toffs, but wot I says is, give me a man's boat every time."

Simon screwed up his eyes. The *Seabird* had cast off, and was sliding smoothly down towards the Channel. The man who had rowed the dinghy held the wheel, and Ronald Nilder stood with his hands in his pockets and gazed backwards towards the bridge benevolently.

"All the same," Simon remarked, "she looks as if she could stand some weather."

"She goes to France all right," conceded the salt reluctantly. "The gentleman wot owns 'er often does it. Says 'e likes to look inside a casino now an' then."

The saint proffered a packet of cigarettes and switched a casual glance round the yard. Parked up beside the wall of a boat-house he saw the shape of a car under a waterproof dust-cover, and identified the number on the exposed plate.

"Looks as if she might have gone there today," he said, indicating the Buick.

"Shouldn't be surprised if she 'ad," said his informant, accepting the smoke. "Can't be going for long, though, because the gentleman said 'e'd be back tomorrow."

Simon nodded thoughtfully, and lounged back on the ML.

"I suppose you haven't got a little motor-boat for hire, have you?" he asked.

The old salt's scornful attitude towards power underwent a rapid change when he found that the Saint professed his complete personal indifference to the merits of canvas. Yes, he had an excellent motor-boat. It was, he implied, such an exceptional motor-boat that it could not be included in any general denunciation of mechanical craft. It could be chartered by the day, the week, the month, the year, or, presumably by the century, and it was the property of a gentleman wot owned racehorses wot always seemed to win when 'e said they would, which naturally raised its virtues to a pitch that surpassed perfection.

Simon looked it over, decided that it would suit him, and arranged to take it out the next morning.

"I just feel like floating around and doing a spot of fishing," he said.

He drove down to the inn at Warsash, and put a call through to Patricia.

"Ronald has gone to hit up the casinos, and I'm going to buy some string and bend a pin," he said. "We may say 'Ship ahoy!' to each other at seven bells."

With a tremendous effort, which could only have been inspired by an unfaltering loyalty to his sense of duty, he managed to breakfast at six o'clock the next morning, and to parade at the boat yard at seven with a reasonably professional-looking array of gear. He chugged down to the Solent, and cruised up and down opposite the mouth of the

Hamble with a cigarette in his mouth and a baited line over the side. Moreover, he caught a fish which greatly lowered his estimation of piscine intelligence.

And whilst he was doing that he produced a Thought.

There are boats tooling in and out of here every day during the season, and nobody gives a damn. It isn't the shortest crossing to the French coast, but for anyone running cargo it must have its advantages.

It was nine o'clock when he sighted the *Seabird*'s bow wave making up the Solent towards him, and it told him that Ronald Nilder's boat could certainly move fast. It was making over twenty knots, and he had very little time to prepare for the scene which he intended to stage.

He let his line go to the bottom, and shut off the idling motor. He was directly in the *Seabird*'s course as she headed for the entrance of the river, and as she came within hailing distance he stood up and flagged her vigorously, yelling some despairing sentence about a breakdown. It was an even chance that Nilder would ignore his signals and cut round him, but the Saint's luck was working that day. He saw the cruiser's white bow wave sink down, and the water foaming astern as her engines went into reverse. She manoeuvred deftly alongside him, and they rolled together in the slight swell.

"I'm awfully sorry to trouble you," said the Saint, "but my motor's conked out, and I haven't any oars or anything."

"Where do you want to get to?" asked Nilder.

He stood in the cockpit, with his cap tilted to what he obviously thought was a rakish angle.

"Bursledon," said the Saint. "But I expect someone could come out to me from wherever you're going to—"

"We're going there ourselves. We'll take you in tow."

At a nod from Nilder the helmsman went aft and flung out a rope. He seemed to comprise the entire crew of the *Seabird*, and seen at close quarters he appeared noticeably lacking in that winsome benignity of countenance which is found on the dials of governors of infant orphanages.

Simon made the rope fast, and Nilder leaned over the side.

"Why don't you come up here?" he suggested amiably. "I'm afraid you'll get rather wet if you stay where you are."

Simon had proposed to get aboard somehow from the beginning but he had not expected such a prompt invitation. He climbed into the cockpit rather watchfully, with a tiny question mark roving through his mind. It was a perfectly normal invitation in itself, but if Nilder was revealing a little more astuteness than the Saint had credited him with . . . And then the morning breeze wafted over to him the fragrance of Ronald Nilder's breath, and Simon realised that the man was more than a little drunk.

"It's quite a coincidence that we should meet again so soon, isn't it?" Nilder remarked suddenly, as the engines picked up again and the one-man crew took the wheel. "I had an excellent view of you in my driving mirror yesterday."

His close-set eyes were fixed on the Saint with the peculiarly rigid stare of mild intoxication, and Simon understood in a flash that Ronald Nilder had oiled himself up to the exact stage of tiddliness at which a man becomes conscious of a verve and brilliance which no one else can perceive and which he himself never knew he possessed.

Simon returned the man's stare coolly. He had set out that morning with no intention of doing anything desperate, but he was always ready to adapt his style to circumstances. And Ronald Nilder was being so frantically and unnecessarily clever that he was asking for a suitable retort with both hands.

"Why, yes—it does seem odd, doesn't it?" murmured the Saint.

He tapped the helmsman gently on the shoulder, and the man half turned. In that position, the point of his jaw offered itself to the Saint's fist as a target that could not in common politeness be ignored. Simon duly obliged—gracefully, accurately, and with a detonating release of energy that lifted the helmsman clear on to the balls of his feet before he dropped.

"Perfectly priceless weather isn't it?" murmured the Saint conversationally.

He spun the wheel hard over, so that the *Seabird* heeled to starboard and came about in a flat skid. Simon straightened her up smoothly and let her run south, away from the river mouth.

His eyes returned to Nilder's face with a blue challenge of devilment to match his smile. It was on such moments of inspired unexpectedness that the Saint's greatness was founded. Looking at Ronald Nilder, he saw that the tipsy courage which had induced the man to take such a recklessly incalculable bull by the horns had wheezed down like a punctured tyre. There was a kind of panic in Ronald Nilder's face, and he was trying clumsily to draw a gun.

Simon took it away from him quite good-humouredly, and dropped it over the side.

"You know, that's another mistake, Ronald," said the Saint calmly. "Respectable yachtsmen never pull guns when their crew are assaulted. They just go mauve in the frontispiece and say, 'What the devil, sir, is the meaning of this outrage?'"

Nilder stared at him whitely, and the Saint declutched the engine and allowed the *Seabird* to lose way.

"And now that the audience has gone to sleep, Ronald," he remarked, "I'll tell you a secret. While I was sitting out here hoping that some young fish who'd never heard of my reputation would accept one of my worms, I thought to myself what a useful base this would be for anyone who didn't want to advertise his cargo." He saw Nilder crouch a little and did not smile. "I'm afraid several girls must have been sorry they accepted an invitation to go yachting with you. But

what do you bring back with you on the return journey, Ronald?—
that's what worries me."

Nilder licked his lips and did not answer.

Then a hand like steel gripped his arm, and a brown face that had
lost all its geniality looked down into his.

"Shall we go and look?" said the Saint.

He thrust Nilder through the door that led into the saloon aft.
There were a couple of wicker hampers on the table, and Simon
surveyed them thoughtfully. That of course was the simplest way of
bringing any reasonably sized cargo ashore.

"Champagne and caviar sandwiches?" drawled the Saint. "That's
just what the doctor ordered for me."

He pushed Nilder on to one of the sofa berths, and snapped up the
lid of one of the baskets.

He was not quite sure what he expected to find but it was certainly
not what he saw. He looked at it in silence for several seconds, and then
he raised the lid of the other hamper. The contents of that one were
the same.

"So it's Tommy guns, is it?" he said quietly. "I wondered when that
was coming. And how long have you known Tex Goldman?"

Still Nilder did not answer.

Without losing sight of him for an instant, Simon carried out the
hampers one by one and dumped them overboard into the deepest part
of the Solent. He came back and lifted Nilder off the sofa by his collar.

"I asked you a question, you horrible little scab," said the Saint.
"How long have you known Tex Goldman?"

Nilder shook his head in a dumb travesty of stubbornness. And
the Saint's fist crashed into his mouth and knocked him back against
the bulkhead.

"If you don't talk now you won't smile for months," said the Saint equably. "It'll be too painful. I don't like you, and I loathe your trade. How long have you known Tex Goldman?"

Nilder wiped his bleeding lips.

"I don't know him, I tell you. What right have you—"

But in three more minutes he was glad to talk.

"I knew him six years ago, before he went to America. He was flying kites—passing bad cheques. He got to know something about a girl I . . . I found a job for. She was only fifteen but how was I to know? It wasn't my fault . . . He was deported. Then when he came back he made me help him. It was blackmail. I didn't want to do it—"

"That's nearly all I want to know," said the Saint "How many trips have you made so far?"

"This is the first—I swear it is—"

Simon flung him back into a corner.

"That's as much of your voice as I can stand, Ronald—really."

He went and found the small cramped engine-room, and drained every drop of oil out of the sumps into an empty two-gallon can which he found. In instalments, he poured it away over the side, without letting Nilder see what he was doing, and then he returned to the saloon.

"I expect you'll be leaving the country as soon as you can," he said. "If it will help you to see the indications for a spot of travel, I may tell you that if I ever see you again the rest of your travelling will be done behind two black horses with flowers round you. And you won't make any complaints about this little voyage before you go, because if I were arrested I should feel fearfully talkative."

"You'll pay for this, you dirty bully!" snarled Nilder furiously. "Goldman will have something to say to you—"

"I shouldn't be surprised," said the Saint contemptuously. "Tex has the guts to say it, which you haven't."

He climbed out of the saloon by the after door, and hauled up his own motor-boat.

Thirty seconds later he was creaming up the river towards Bursledon, while the *Seabird* drifted on down the Solent on the falling tide.

6

He was back at Warsash in another twenty minutes, and as he stepped out of his car beside the inn he was just able to catch a sight of the *Seabird* turning to race up towards the Hamble. Even while he paused to watch it for a moment, the bow wave sank down and the ship's bows began to yaw round as she lost way. Simon grinned happily to himself, and went through to the dining-room.

He twitched his nostrils appreciatively at the aroma of crisping bacon which greeted him. Three hours in the fresh sea air after the sketchy meal he had swallowed at six a.m., plus a certain amount of useful exercise, had done their full share towards setting up his appetite to its ordinary matutinal proportions.

"I'll have two fried eggs, lots of bacon, and about a quart of coffee," he said to the waitress who had already served him with one breakfast that day. "After that, I might be able to toy with three more eggs, a pound of mushrooms, and a lot more bacon. Go out and tell them to kill the pig, Gladys."

While at least part of his order was being executed he went to the telephone and put another call through to Patricia.

"Hullo, darling," he said. "This is very late for you to be up."

"I have been to bed," said the girl.

"So have I," murmured the Saint breezily. "But not for long. I don't think this early rising is healthy—the prospect of it takes such a lot of kick out of the night before, and I hate having my morning tea by moonlight."

"How did the fishing go?"

"Pretty well." Simon glanced round him cautiously but there was no one within earshot. "When last observed, Brother Ronald was running into a lot of trouble. I ran all the oil out of his engines, and unless he thought of greasing them with his own perspiration they've seized up in a way that'll take days to unstick. The *Seabird* won't be making any more voyages for a while."

Patricia laughed softly.

"When are you coming home, boy?"

"Well—this is Friday, isn't it? I seem to remember that we have a date for lunch with Claud Eustace Teal. I'll meet you at the Bruton at twelve-thirty."

He went back to his second breakfast with the contented knowledge that another and very different conversation must have been seething over the London wire at about that time, and he was right.

Ronald Nilder did not think it expedient to go into details.

"The Saint caught me in the Solent, Goldman. He didn't say it was him, but it couldn't have been anyone else. He threw the guns overboard and beat me up."

Tex Goldman had the gift of not wasting time on useless bad language.

"Get back here as quick as you can," he said grimly. "I'll have something waiting for the Saint."

Simon Templar, however, had an equally valuable gift which had stood him in good stead before. On that Friday morning it worked at full pressure. He had a very clear conception of Tex Goldman's psychology. Wherefore he drove back to London by way of Leatherhead and Epsom, and Ted Orping waited for him at the end of the Portsmouth Road in vain.

It was a minute or two before twelve-thirty when he entered the doors of Lansdowne House, but Patricia was waiting for him. The Saint ordered cocktails, and told her the detailed history of his early morning escapade.

"If you came back by a roundabout way, I expect Nilder's got home about the same time," she said, and Simon smiled.

"I doubt it, old darling," he said calmly. "I stuck my penknife through both his back tyres and the spare for luck, so he could either wait for someone to repair the damage or catch a train that won't get him in for another quarter of an hour. That'll make it a bit too much of a rush for him to catch the two o'clock via Boulogne, so he can either make a dash for the four o'clock Dover-Calais or wait for the eight-twenty via Dieppe or the nine o'clock via Havre—my familiarity with these timetables is remarkable," said the Saint modestly. "In any case, he'll have to go to his bank first, that's all I'm interested in."

The girl looked at him curiously.

"There was a time when he wouldn't have got off so lightly," she said.

Simon leaned back with his long legs stretched out in front of him, and watched the smoke from his cigarette curling towards the ceiling.

"I know. But we weren't so businesslike in those days, and the income-tax wasn't five bob in the pound. Besides which, the activities of the great Claud Eustace weren't quite so near the mark. No, Pat—in the autumn of his life this young man's fancy lightly turns to thoughts of subtler things, which includes ingenious methods of getting his dirty work done for him. And I think I know a far, far neater way."

And then he looked round and saw the oval figure of Chief Inspector Teal crossing the lounge towards them. He hitched himself up and called for more Martinis.

"Tell us about things," he murmured.

"There's nothing much to tell," said the detective sleepily, sinking into a chair. "We're still working, and we'll get our men before long. I suppose you read about the Underground hold-up last night?"

Simon shook his head.

"I haven't seen a morning paper."

"They wounded two men and got away with over three thousand pounds in cash—the booking-office takings from several stations. That's where it's so difficult. They've got us guessing all the time. First it's jeweller's shops; then we guard those, and it's banks. Then we watch the banks, and it's a night club. Now it's the Underground. We can't possibly protect every place in London where you can find large sums of money, and they know it."

"No more clues?"

"We're working on several lines," said the detective, with professional vagueness, but Simon Templar was not impressed.

"As I see it," he said, "your trouble is to get hold of the man up top who's producing all these smart ideas. It's no good knocking off Green Cross boys here and there—you can always keep tabs on them in the ordinary way, and it's just this unknown bloke who's got control of 'em who's making 'em dangerous for the time being."

Teal nodded.

"That's about it."

"And if you did find this unknown bloke, he'd probably turn out to be so unknown that all the evidence you could get against him wouldn't hang a mosquito."

"That's often the trouble," said Teal gloomily. "But we can't work any other way."

THE SAINT AND MR TEAL

"Let's have some lunch," said the Saint brightly.

Throughout the meal he played the perfect host with a stern devotion to the book of etiquette that Patricia could not understand. He talked about racing, beer, aeroplanes, theatres, politics, sparking-plugs, dress reform, and cancer—everything that could not be steered to any subject that the detective might find tender. Most particularly he avoided saying anything more about the Green Cross boys or their unknown leader, and more than once Teal looked sideways at him with a kind of irritated puzzlement.

It was not like the Saint to show such an elaborate desire to keep possibly painful matters out of discussion, and the symptom made Mr Teal feel a dim uneasiness.

At two o'clock he excused himself with a muttered hint of official business, and Simon accompanied him to the door. Teal twiddled his bowler hat and stared at him somnolently.

"You're keeping something back," he said bluntly. "I can't make you tell me if you don't want to, but I suppose you realise that these shootings will go on until we get the man who's at the back of it."

"That reminds me," said the Saint. "Can you give me the names of all the people who've been shot up since the fashion started—including the policeman?"

He wrote down the names Teal gave him on the back of an envelope, and waved the detective a cheery farewell without saying anything in answer to his implied question—a fact which did not dawn clearly upon Mr Teal until he was half-way down Berkeley Street.

Simon went back to Patricia, and his eyes were gay and dangerous.

"This is where we work very fast," he said. "London stinks in my throat, and we need a holiday. Wouldn't you like to get hold of a ship and sail out into the great open seas?"

"But what do we do now?" she asked, and the Saint tilted his eyebrows in teasing mysteriousness.

"One item of the agenda is to have words with Clem Enright. Thank God, Corrigan told me where he hangs around when he's not doing anything—otherwise it might have been difficult."

He was lucky enough to find Clem Enright at his third attempt, in a public-house near Charing Cross station, but he made no fuss about his discovery. Clem Enright, in fact, did not know that it had been made.

Clem in his earlier days had haunted the public bars of the taverns where he drank, but recently, under the patronising tuition of Ted Orping, he had learned to walk quite unselfconsciously through the saloon entrance. Clem was handling more money than he had ever had in his life before, and in the daze of his new-found affluence he was an apt pupil.

He sat behind a whisky and soda—"Only bums drink beer," insisted Ted—with his derby hat tipped cockily over one ear in what was meant to be an imitation of Ted Orping's swagger, listening to a lecture from his hero.

"Protection," said Ted Orping impressively. "That's what we're goin' for. Protection."

"I thought that was somethink to do wiv politics," said Clem hazily.

"Not that sort of protection, you chump," snarled the scornful Ted, "Who cares about that? I mean protection—like they do it in America. Ain't you never heard of it? What I mean is, you say to a guy: 'Here you are with a big business, an' you never know when some gang may hold you up or chuck a bomb at you. You pay us for protection, an' we'll see nothing happens to you.'"

"But I thought we was doing the 'old-ups," said Clem.

Ted Orping sighed, and spat a loose strand of tobacco through his teeth.

"Course we are, fathead. That's just to show 'em what may happen if they don't pay. Then when they're all frightened, we come an' talk about protection. We get just as much money, an' we don't have to work so hard."

"Sounds all right," said Clem.

He took a drink from his glass, and tried to conceal his grimace. He'd never cared for whisky and never would, but it cost twice as much as beer, and a toff always had the best. They were toffs now—Ted Orping said so. They owned cigarette cases, had their nails manicured, and changed their shirts twice a week.

"This is a big thing," said Ted, leaning sideways confidentially. "It's goin' to grow an' grow—there ain't no limits to it. An' we're in at the beginnin', like the guys who started motor cars an' wireless. An' what are they now? Look at 'em!"

"Marconi," hazarded Clem helpfully, "Austin, Morris, 'Enry Ford—"

"Millionaires," said Ted. "That's what. And why? Because they were in first. Just like we are. An' we can be millionaires too. Ain't Tex told you what them guys in Chicago live like? Sleepin' in silk sheets, tickin' off judges, an' havin' the mayor to dinner off gold plates. That's what we'll be like one day. Have another drink."

He went to the bar to have the glasses replenished and came back to the corner where they were sitting. A barmaid began to cry "Time, please!" and Ted put his tongue out at her impudently.

"We won't have none of this, either," he said. "We'll have it in our own homes, an' nobody can say 'Time' there. Why, we're better off in England, because there ain't no Third Degree here."

"Wot's that mean?" asked Clem.

"Well, when you get pinched they don't treat you friendly like they do here. They don't just ask you a few questions which you needn't answer, an' then lock you up till you see the beak in the mornin'. What they do is, they take you into a room, about half a dozen bloody great coppers, an' they make you talk—whether you know anything or not."

Enright regarded him owlishly.

"'Ow do they do that?"

"They know how," said Ted Orping. "There's nothing they won't do to make you confess. Keep you without water, bash you about, beat you with a rubber hose, grind your teeth down with a dentist's drill— just any torture they can think of. You got to be tough to keep your trap shut when they do things like that."

Clem Enright shuddered as Orping proceeded to explain other methods of persuasion that he had read of. Clem didn't feel tough— not in that way. He had had his arms twisted often enough by bigger boys in his ragamuffin youth to know what acute physical pain was like, and he didn't fancy any of its more agonising refinements.

"Time please," said the barmaid again, and a shirt-sleeved potman began to take up the refrain as he collected glasses off the tables with every circumstance of the spiteful satisfaction which public-house employees seem to feel when they enforce that fatuous law.

"Come on," said Ted finally. "Let's get out of here."

He turned his glass defiantly upside down and swaggered out of the bar, with Clem following him. On the pavement they paused.

"Where are you goin'?" asked Ted. "I got a date with a dame."

He had spent three hours in a cinema the day before and learnt several new words.

"I'll go down to the revolver range and practise a bit of shooting," said Enright.

"Right-ho," said Ted heartily. "You can't get too much practice, but don't let 'em know you got a gun of your own. See you tonight."

They separated there, and Clem Enright walked slowly and a little unsteadily down Villiers Street. He was always conscious of his inferior toughness in the presence of Ted Orping, who had killed two men and wounded others. The weight of the automatic in his hip pocket gave him the feeling of being a genuine desperado only occasionally—at other times it seemed to bulk out under his clothes like a poached pheasant, and he went into a cold sweat at the momentary expectation of feeling a heavy hand on his shoulder and hearing familiar words of invitation murmured genially in his ear. Of late he had spent a lot of his money on ammunition at the range, and had once scored a target of twenty-four at twelve paces.

They didn't believe he had it in him to be tough—that was the trouble. He was a good man with the brick in a smash-and-grab, and he could drive a car pretty well in an emergency, but they didn't class him as a man to take the initiative in any violence. And it rankled. He was as good as they were, but they had never let him play a prominent part in a hold-up. He had a sense of injustice about it, and in his daydreams he lived for the glory of the day when he could demand the right to equality with them by virtue of the notch on his own gun.

Sometimes he heard in imagination the horrible grunt of the policeman whom Basher Tope had shot, the way the man clutched at his stomach and kicked like a wounded rabbit. And then the cold sweat came out on him again . . . He closed his eyes to the vision, and tried to think of it differently. He saw his own eyes behind the sights, his own finger curling steadily and ruthlessly round the trigger, the gun held as firmly as if in a vice—he had read plenty of the literature of his profession, and knew how it ought to be done. Then the crisp smack of the report, the jerk of the barrel, the pride and the confidence that would come . . .

"Hey, you!"

The rasp of a voice that seemed to be aimed straight at his ear made him start.

He looked round with his heart pumping ridiculously. He was almost opposite the range, down at the bottom of Villiers Street, and he had not noticed the approach of the car that had slipped silently down the street and pulled up so close to him that the running-board brushed his trousers.

The man at the wheel had a hard sunburnt face that seemed faintly familiar, but the yellow-tinted tortoiseshell glasses over his eyes and the unlighted cigar in his mouth reassured him. Moreover he spoke with a strong American accent.

"Get in. Goldman wants you—quick."

Clem leaned over, opening the door. The hope that never slept in his narrow bosom roused up and palpitated.

"Any idea wot it is?"

"I can't tell you, but I know there's shooting in it. Got your heater? . . . Good boy. Let's keep moving." Clem Enright leaned back and let himself relax in contemplation of the roseate dawn of his apotheosis. So it had come at last, the chance that he had been praying for. It followed so closely on the trend of his daydream that he could scarcely believe it was true. Now if only luck was with him—if the sudden fit of trembling that had seized his limbs wore off and left him as cool and steady-nerved as he had been in his dreams . . .

He did not notice the way they went, or give another thought or glance to the man who drove him. Again and again he lived over, in visions, a score of shootings in which he was the only surviving hero . . . And then, in what seemed only a few minutes, he became aware that the car had stopped and the engine was switched off. They were in one of the small side streets of Chelsea—he could identify the district by the shops he could see in the King's Road at the end.

"Wot's up?" he demanded. "This ain't the place."

"This is a special secret headquarters," said the driver, with a scrappy smile. "You haven't been here before."

Clem Enright's chest swelled as he followed his guide through the street door, along a narrow passage, and up a long flight of stairs. Special secret headquarters! He had had no notion that there was such a place. He would swear that Ted Orping had never seen it. And he was the privileged one who had been chosen for what must be an extraordinarily important mission. All at once his opinions of Ted Orping underwent a catastrophic change. They became almost pitying. A nice chap, Ted, but a bit full of himself. Liked to pretend he was bigger than he was. Plenty of muscle, of course, but you wanted more than that. Brains. Personality . . .

They went through a miniature hall, and passed into a spacious studio that lofted right up into the roof. It was impossible to see out for all the light came from two large skylights high up in the rafters. And then Clem heard the unmistakable click of a lock, and spun round.

His guide was leaning against the door, detaching the key from the lock and dropping it into his pocket. While Enright stared at him, fascinated, he pitched away the cigar and removed the tinted glasses which had so effectively disguised him.

"What d'you think you could pose as, Clem?" inquired the Saint chattily. "Ajax defying the lightning?"

7

Enright crouched back against a divan, with his eyes distending as if they were being inflated by a couple of power pumps.

"Wot's the idea?" he croaked.

"Just words," answered Simon urbanely. "Words, words, words, as the Swan of Avon used to tell his pals when Ann Hathaway had one of her off days."

He took out his cigarette case and selected a cigarette sauntering across the room with his level gaze fixed on Clem Enright all the time. There was something terrifying to the Cockney about that unswerving and passionless stare. In a flash of unspeakable fear, Clem remembered his gun and reached for it, and his stomach seemed to turn to water when he found that it was no longer at his hip.

Simon produced it from his own pocket.

"I borrowed it, Clem," he explained easily. "You haven't got a licence for it, and that's a serious offence. Besides, it might have chipped the wallpaper if you missed me."

He was right in front of Enright then, and the edge of the divan was directly behind the man's knees. Simon gave him a gentle push, and the Cockney sat down with a bump.

"Now we can talk," said the Saint.

He lighted his cigarette deliberately while Clem watched him with scared and shrinking eyes. And then that very clear and level gaze found Enright's face again.

"This racket of yours is over, Clem," said the Saint quietly. "I'm cleaning it up today. As far as you're concerned, it's just a question whether we should hand you over to the police or give you a run for it."

"I ain't never done nuffink guv'nor!" Enright whined. "Strite I ain't—"

"Straight you certainly aren't," answered the Saint calmly. "But we didn't bring you here to discuss that. We brought you here because there's something we want you to do, and the only interesting point is how long it's going to take to persuade you to do it. Have you ever heard of the Third Degree?"

Enright cringed away with his face going white.

"Yer can't do that to me!" he yelped. "Yer can't—"

"We can only try," said the Saint mildly.

He opened a cupboard and proceeded to lay out on the table a life-preserver, a short length of rubber hose, a large pair of pincers, and an instrument that looked very like a thumbscrew but was actually a patent tin-opener. As he produced each item he weighed it in his hand, tested it meditatively, and gave Enright every chance to visualise its employment before he put it down.

Then he turned again to the shaking man.

"That flat underneath is empty," he remarked pleasantly, "so you can yell as much as you like. What would you like to have done to you first?"

Enright swallowed a lump in his throat. The stimulating effects of the whisky he had drunk had vanished altogether, leaving him at the stage where he would have burst into tears on the slightest provocation. Nobody loved him, and he was going to be tortured till he talked.

"They'd kill me," he said huskily. "Joe Corrigan squealed, and 'e was killed."

"No one will kill you if you behave," said the Saint. "You can lie low here till the gang's broken up, and I'll see you out of the country if you want to go abroad. Also I'll say nothing about you to the police, and I'll let you keep all your money."

Clem Enright tried to lick the saliva round a mouth that had gone unaccountably arid. All his dreams of glory had gone west, and yet he felt lucky. There was that in the Saint's eye which told him that Ted Orping's lurid description paled into fairy-tales beside what that lean soft-spoken man was capable of doing.

"Wot d'yer want to know?"

"How much have you been getting from Goldman?"

"Fifty quid a week, wiv extra pickings when we did somethink good."

"How much did Ted get?"

"I dunno, guv'nor. P'raps 'e got a bit more—'e did more than they let me."

"Didn't it ever occur to you that there was a lot more money than that in what you were doing?"

"Goldman said 'e better bank for us, guv'nor. We 'ad plenty o' dough to spend, and 'e said where we used to go wrong was by spending everythink when we was flush and then 'aving nothink to see us through rainy days. 'E said you 'ad to 'ave capital so's you could wait for the right job, instead of 'aving to do somethink in a hurry."

Simon nodded.

"Where does Goldman keep his money?"

"'E's got a safe in 'is bedroom—in a wall. Some of it's there, anyway. I seen 'im take money out of it to give me, and it was full of dough."

The Saint smoothed his hair and indicated a telephone which stood on a small table beside the divan.

"Now there's just one other little thing you can do for me," he said. "Do you know a man called Ronald Nilder?"

"Yus—I seen 'im once."

"You can ring him up and say what I tell you to."

Enright looked at the telephone, and then at the Saint again.

"Yer wouldn't fergit yer promise, would yer, guv'nor?—cross yer 'eart and 'ope to die?"

"Cross my heart and hope to die," said the Saint gravely.

Mr Ronald Nilder was completing the packing of his third suitcase when the telephone bell rang in his bedroom. For a few minutes he thought of letting it ring unanswered, but cunning dictated the bolder course. He picked up the receiver.

"'Ullo," said a voice. "Is that Nilder?"

"This is Mr Nilder speaking," he replied primly.

"Goldman wants to know why yer ain't come to see 'im like 'e told yer. 'E says yer to meet 'im at once outside Mark Lane Station. It's very urgent."

Nilder hesitated for a moment. Then:

"All right," he said. "Who's that speaking?"

"Enright 'ere," said the voice. "Go on—'urry. If Goldman ain't there yer to wait for 'im. G'bye."

Nilder replaced the receiver, and paced up and down the room. He had planned to catch the eight-twenty train via Newhaven, and that gave him plenty of time to keep the appointment. After all, Goldman had no reason to suspect that he had given anything away. It was just his bad luck that the Saint had caught him—the same thing had happened to other men, and their integrity had not been questioned. He had the testimony of his engineer to support his story. He knew Enright's name and recognised his voice after the name was given him—there was no trap about it. It would be quite safe to hear what Goldman had to say—it might even have a valuable bearing on his own getaway—whereas to evade it would immediately arouse suspicion. And already he was feeling a little ashamed of the panic that had made him draw all his money from the bank and pack up to leave London in such haste.

Thus Ronald Nilder worked it out, as the Saint had expected him to, and left his flat five minutes later. But just in case of accidents he removed the bulging wallet from his pocket and hid it behind a row of books—his pocket would have been well worth picking that afternoon.

He had a long wait at Mark Lane, but with that we are not yet concerned.

It was half-past four when Simon Templar arrived at Tex Goldman's apartment by way of the fire escape and let himself in through the bathroom window. A call from the nearest telephone booth had ascertained that Goldman was not at home, and the Saint was not looking quite like his normal self. He had a suit of workman's overalls over his clothes and a leather bag of tools in his hand, in which outfit he was not likely to arouse so much curiosity on fire escapes as he would have done in one of the light grey fresco suits of Anderson & Sheppard. But the gun which he had taken from Clem Enright was in his pocket, and it was fully loaded. Simon Templar was cleaning up. And he was making no mistakes.

Tex Goldman came in at five.

He had a girl with him—the girl who had partnered him at the night club. She was a rather beautiful child, with fair hair that was a little too brilliant to be natural, and big serious eyes. She hung on Tex Goldman's arm. It was the visit to his apartment that he had worked for so long, and the way it had happened was one that he had not expected a week ago.

"It's marvellous, Tex," she said.

"It ain't bad," said Tex Goldman. "It just wanted one thing and she's here now."

She sat in the settee. He sat on the arm, looking down at her.

"Gee, baby," he said, "if you told me a week ago I could do this, I'd've burst myself laughin'. Must be old age, I reckon."

"I don't care what it is."

Goldman took out a bulky leather case. With the unconsciousness of habit, he nipped the end off a cigar and stuck it between his teeth.

"I guess you know all about me," he said.

"I don't mind."

"It ain't much to think about. All my life I been a hood. That's the way I was raised. I came out of the gutter—but I came out. Back in St. Louis they call me tough. I killed plenty men, but that don't seem to mean a thing. It's the way you work in the racket—bump a guy before he bumps you. But I never double-crossed a pal, and I never carried a gun for vice. I ain't pullin' any reformation act. I guess I'll go on the same way—till I get mine."

She took a scented cigarette from a lacquer case, and stared straight ahead.

"I'm not such a schoolgirl myself," she said quietly. "I've been around. I don't like killing—any of those things you do. I don't like knowing I'll have to sit around and wait till someone does the same thing to you; I didn't think I could ever face it. Now it seems different, somehow. I've got no choice. I just want you to be good to me."

"I'm on the level, kid. I never been mushy in my life so I can't say any of those pretty things you'd like to hear. But I'll play square with you."

"Always?"

"Say, if I ever give you the runaround, you can put me on the spot with my own gun."

It was at that moment that Tex Goldman's head was hit.

The blow didn't stun him. It wasn't intended to. But he felt the sickening sharp crash of a gun-butt at the base of his hair, and it seemed to rock the brain inside his skull so that for a second or two his sight was blotted out in a dizzy sea of blackness filled with whirling red sparks. He pitched forward, throwing out his hands and saved himself on the table. He heard the girl beside him cry out, and then a hand snatched at his hip pocket before his wits could struggle back to coherent functioning. When his own hand reached the pocket his gun was gone.

He turned slowly, and saw the weapon being juggled gently round the forefinger of a tall man in grey.

"Hullo, Tex."

Goldman drew himself up rockily under the rake of the tall man's smile.

"What the hell—"

"No bad language, Tex," said the Saint. "I'm sorry I had to dot you a small one, but I thought it'd be safer. You're the kind of guy who wouldn't be stuck up very easily, and if you tried to shoot it out with me the birds in the other apartments might have heart failure."

Goldman's eyes creased up till only the pupils showed, gleaming like frozen chips of jet.

"Mr Simon Templar?"

"Yeah. And breaking up your racket. This country can get along without your kind of crime. Maybe America can show us lots of things, but you've come over with one kind of thing we don't want to be shown. It upsets all the dear old ladies who make our laws." The Saint was not smiling. "Too many men have been killed since you set up shop. I came here to kill you, Tex."

The girl clutched at Tex Goldman's hand, staring at the Saint with wide pitiful eyes.

"You can't!" she sobbed. "You can't! We were only married today—"

Not a muscle of the Saint's face moved.

"I'm taking the girl, too," he said. "For another reason. You get it together."

She shrank against Tex Goldman's shoulder with horror added to the tragedy of her eyes.

"Why d'you want to kill me?" she whispered. "I've done nothing, I've never killed anyone . . . But I don't care! I don't care! I love him! Go on, you coward—"

"Never mind that." Tex Goldman's voice cut very quietly and tremorlessly through hers. "Never mind what you think she's done, Templar, I guess you're wrong about her. She's on the level. You can't burn down a woman. You got me all right. Give me what's coming to me. But let the kid get the hell out of here first. I can take it for both of us."

He looked at the Saint without flinching. That was the racket. You took it when your turn came, without whining. You didn't show yellow.

And then he saw that the Saint was smiling.

"Thanks, Tex," said the Saint. "You've got the guts. I guess that lets you out."

8

Goldman didn't understand.

"I told you I came here to kill you," said the Saint. "That's about true—anyway, it's one reason. Then I heard your conversation. I just wondered. The girl told me you were married today. I put up the rest of it just to prove to myself whether you were really on the level, and it seems as if you are. It breaks my heart but I suppose we'll have to go home now without killing you. Even I can't spoil a honeymoon . . . It's rather a charming thought, Tex—that after all you may be a white-haired old daddy one day, sitting by the fire with a dozen kiddies perched on your knee, telling them fairy stories about the Little Red Riding Hood, and Goldmanlocks and The Three Bears, and Wicked Uncle Al."

Goldman drew a deep breath, but he did not speak. The cold winds of death had blown too close to him, and when that clammy breath is still in a man's throat he has very little to say.

"But the part about breaking up your racket has got to stand," said the Saint, and his blue eyes were steady steel again as he spoke. "We don't like it—it makes life just a little too strenuous. I've emptied your safe already this afternoon, and I expect you'll find that rather discouraging."

He indicated the open door of the bedroom through which he had come. Smiling momentarily, he dipped into a side pocket and dug out half a dozen large notes which he dropped on to the settee.

"I'll give you these back as a wedding present. You wouldn't want to arrive back in St. Louis broke."

Goldman moistened his lips.

"Still hijacking, huh?"

"Still hijacking. All this is to be divided up among the poor devils who got shot in the course of your campaign, except what I keep myself. I take a rather larger share, because I was getting shot at all the time. You won't see it back, Tex." The Saint's voice was grim and purposeful. "You won't even get me bumped before you go, because you don't know where I'm staying and you won't have time to find me. You're taking a train to France at eight-twenty and you can make your sailing arrangements from Cherbourg. You needn't tell Ted Orping and all the boys, but that's what you're going to do. Because at ten o'clock tonight, whether I'm alive or dead, a message will go to Chief Inspector Teal at Scotland Yard and tell him all about the deportation order that still holds good against William Gold, alias Tex Goldman, cheap stick-up man of six years back. You won't find it so easy to slip into the country again."

Tex Goldman stared at him.

"How did you find out about that?"

"Comrade Nilder told me," said the Saint easily. "He falls apart with a very little shaking."

Goldman showed his teeth.

"I might have known it. That lousy, double-crossing little heel—"

"I should speak to him quite severely about it if I were you," said the Saint, very softly. "Unless I'm mistaken, he'll be calling in here before you go to tell you his troubles . . . And now I must leave you. Have a jolly honeymoon—and when you give my love to the boys in St. Louis, say it with ukuleles. Fare thee well, fair lady."

He retreated smartly to the door and let himself out. In another moment he was flying down the stairs.

On the street corner he came up behind Mr Teal.

"Well, what is it?" demanded the detective. "I got your message and came straight along, but why all the mystery?"

"I don't want to speak too soon," said the Saint, "but I think we may see some fun. A certain gentleman is very annoyed."

"Who do you mean?"

The Saint was smilingly uncommunicative. He took Teal's arm and guided him into a convenient tea-shop, choosing a table near the window from which he could keep the entrance of Tex Goldman's apartment block under observation.

They sat there for two hours, and Mr Teal grew restive.

"If you can't show me any more than a plate of toasted scones," he said, "I'll have to be going. I've got work to do. What's on your mind?"

"Don't go yet, Claud," said the Saint. "I've done more work today than you've done in the last week. I've been cleaning up. Things are happening now."

This was just five minutes after he had seen Ted Orping pass in through the door he was watching.

Tex Goldman answered the bell.

"What is it, Ted?" he asked briefly.

He was impatient, but he did not want Orping to see it. In the bedroom, three suit-cases were packed and ready for his departure.

"That bus depot hold-up tonight, boss—"

"It's postponed—indefinitely."

Ted Orping's eyebrows went up.

"What for, boss?"

"It's poppycock—that's why. It's a waste of time. It's a risk for nothing." Goldman tapped him on the shoulder. "I'll tell you why I'm passing it up, Ted. I've got on to something that'll make you wonder why you ever wasted your time holding up a bank. It's something so big, it'll make your mouth water till you have to tie a bucket round your neck. And it's fool-proof. One grand raid—and finish. There'll be ten thousand pounds in it for every man who doesn't go soft. Have a cigar."

Orping's eyes opened.

"What is it, boss?"

"I can't tell you now." Goldman glanced round him. He lowered his voice. "There's a squealer somewhere—and I got a hunch I could lay my finger on him. Nothing's safe while there's squealers around."

Orping's mouth hardened. He bit off the end of a cigar, and spat it into the fireplace.

"Let me see him!"

The front door bell rang again. Goldman's cold eyes bored into Ted's like the eyes of a statue. He spoke out of the side of his mouth, viciously.

"Let him in."

Orping went to the door.

It was Ronald Nilder— hatless, ashen grey of face, loose mouth quivering. A soiled scrap of paper was clutched in one trembling hand. He rushed half-way across the room towards Goldman and pulled up, his fists clenched and his pasty features jerking.

"What's this mean?" he almost screamed. "Tell me what it means, damn you!"

"What does what mean?" asked Goldman coldly.

Nilder thrust out the scrap of paper. Unhurriedly Goldman flattened it out and read what was written on it.

See me before you take all your money abroad.

T. G.

"I took all my money out of the bank," Nilder was babbling. "I put it in my wallet. When you telephoned for me to meet you at Mark Lane I hid it behind some books in my flat. I waited an hour for you. When I got back, the door had been broken in and my wallet was empty. That's all there was in it. What d'you mean by taking my money, you—"

With three more unhurried movements Goldman tore the paper across, across, and across again, and trickled the pieces into his wastepaper basket. Then he looked at Nilder again, and there was such an inexorable malignity in his gaze that the other's babbling died away into a strangled silence.

"I didn't send for you to meet me at Mark Lane," he said; "I didn't write that note, and I don't know anything about your money. Now tell me why you squealed to the Saint."

Nilder's mouth seemed to go whiter. He took breath in two quick frantic gasps. His mouth was sagging open in a horrible limpness of fear.

"You needn't answer," Goldman said, with that same slow frozen venom. "I can read it in your face. You squealed because you're yellow. He slapped your wrist once, and you fell to pieces. That's what a rat like you does. And then you come here with some lily-livered gold-bricking alibi, and hope I'll eat it. What d'you think this is—a kindergarten? What do I do—fall on your neck and kiss you? You louse!"

"I didn't!" Nilder gibbered throatily. "Don't look at me like that, Goldman. I wouldn't squeal on you. I wouldn't give you away. I can explain everything, I tell you. Listen to me—"

"Get out!" rasped Goldman, in a sudden hiss of icy savagery. "Get out of my sight—before I smash that snivelling face of yours into jelly!"

Nilder backed away with a choking gulp. Never in his life had he seen such a bitter malevolence blazing at him out of a pair of human eyes.

"Don't hit me!" he gabbled. "Don't hit me. I didn't tell anything. I wouldn't double-cross you. Listen, Goldman—"

Ted Orping grasped him by the collar and hurled him back to the door.

"You heard what the boss said," he snarled. "Scram!"

Mr Ronald Nilder had never done anything so undignified. He did not even know what the word meant, but the tone in which it was uttered was sufficient explanation. Shaking with a sick terror of what he had seen in Tex Goldman's eyes, he scrammed.

Ted Orping listened to the front door closing. He looked at the man from St. Louis.

"Do I give him the works, boss?"

Tex Goldman lighted his cigar before replying. It was a long time since he had felt any satisfaction in pronouncing sentence of death. In the racket, death was meted out simply as an operation of expediency— without hate, often even with regret. But for this time at least he felt a vindictive sense of justice.

"Yeah," he said. 'Put him out."

Simon Templar saw Nilder walking blindly away from the block, and stood up, plunking a half-crown down on his bill. Teal followed him. As they reached the pavement, Ted Orping came out and slipped into the footsteps of the Cosmolite Vaudeville Agent.

"What's happening?" asked Teal.

"Something good and fast," answered the Saint, "or I'm no psychologist."

He led Teal on to join the procession of two. Suddenly Nilder stopped and hailed a taxi that came crawling past. Orping spun round and gazed into a shop window just quickly enough to escape notice.

As soon as Nilder had climbed in, Orping dashed across the road and entered another cab. Simon pulled his hat down over his eyes and sprinted for the nearest rank, dragging the detective after him. They sank on to the cushions breathlessly.

"This is a game of follow-my-leader," said the Saint, almost merrily.

The three taxis speeded in procession along the Marylebone Road, worked down to Portland Place, crossed Oxford Street, and went down Regent Street. One tour of the Piccadilly Circus merry-go-round, and they cut down into Jermyn Street.

Simon leaned forward and spoke through the telephone to the driver.

"Take it easy here."

The cab in front stopped, and they were stuck behind it. Sitting well back to keep out of sight, the Saint saw Ted Orping pay off the driver and walk on. The cab in front moved on, and they followed slowly after it. Simon saw Nilder's back in the doorway of the house of service flats where he lived: Orping caught up with him in the entrance and gripped his arm. The Saint could only guess what was said, but the two men passed out of sight together.

Simon stopped the taxi, and they got out. He led Teal to the other side of the street.

"This is another wait," he said, "but it won't be a long one."

He lighted a cigarette, though he was not expecting to get more than a few puffs.

Presently he raised his head sharply.

"Did you hear that?"

It had been a sound like two very distant back-fires in quick succession, but he knew they were not back-fires.

Then he saw Ted Orping coming out, and crossed the road suddenly. Orping did not see him till they were face to face.

"A word with you, Ted," said the Saint affably. "Did you make quite sure Ronald wouldn't talk?"

The other gaped at him with a wild, almost superstitious dread. And then, with a kind of slavering gulp he turned and ran.

Simon ran faster. Looking back, Orping saw him only a yard behind, running easily, and groped for his gun. But he had thought of that too late. Simon clipped his heels together and dropped on him heavily. He twisted Orping's right wrist up between his shoulder blades, and kept one bony knee in the small of the man's back.

"Lemme up," Orping whimpered. "You can't hold me for nothing."

"Only for wilful murder," said the Saint unctuously, and watched Chief Inspector Teal lumbering ponderously across the road towards them.

.

THE DEATH PENALTY

INTRODUCTION

Most of this story takes place in the Scilly Isles, and as you might expect, it is partly the result of a stay which I myself made one summer in that half-forgotten little archipelago off the western tip of Cornwall.

Some of the things I felt about the place are written into the story. The attempt may have fallen far short of what I intended, and I think it was rather rapidly obscured by the exigencies of an unusually melodramatic plot, but I hope that the lovable and friendly islanders whom I knew there will understand from a few lines what I was trying to say.

I have never been back there. But I am happily reminded of that one visit on every Atlantic crossing. Before then, when I saw the first blink of Bishop's Light far down on the dark horizon, it was merely the first landfall of the Old World and a promise that we should be in England in the morning. But now I remember that Bishop's Rock is only one of the farthest outposts of the Scilly Isles, and I have a sentimental feeling that the light is flashing especially for my benefit, because friends have come out to meet me.

But this was not the final reason that made me choose this—I must be candid—not very distinguished story to be reprinted here. It was because, when I read it over to consider it for inclusion in this volume, it brought back one other glimpse that I had of the Scilly Isles.

It was on a westbound trip, that time. They swam out of a grey and hazy dawn, closer than I had ever seen them before on an ocean crossing. The morning mists parted like a drawn veil, and there were the islands suddenly, grey humps of rock breaking the calm of a leaden sea. I could identify them all, as if I saw them on a chart: I fancied that I could even pick out different places in St Mary's where I had been. They fell behind very quickly, and then only the empty Atlantic was ahead of us. But it seemed less empty for that last passing of familiar scenes.

I shall never see the Scilly Isles in exactly that way again. For that was on the first flight to New York of the late Zeppelin *Hindenburg*.

—Leslie Charteris (1939)

1

They hanged Galbraith Stride at eight o'clock on the morning of the 22nd of November.

They came in and strapped his hands together, and led him out to the narrow whitewashed shed that was to be his last glimpse of the world—walking very fast, like a man who has made up his mind to see an unpleasant appointment through as quickly as possible. They stood him on the chalked T in the centre of the trap, and drew the white cap down over his bald head and his pale frightened eyes, till the only feature of his face that could be seen was the thin twitching mouth under his little grey moustache. They settled the rope round his neck, with the knot just under his left ear, and the executioner stepped back to the lever that would send him into eternity.

They asked him if he had anything to say before he paid the extreme penalty of the law, and the tip of his tongue slipped once over those twitching lips.

"Get it over," he said, and with that they dropped him.

All this was after many other things had happened, and a lady had thanked the Saint for assistance.

2

Laura Berwick came into the Saint's life unasked, uninvited, and unintroduced; which was what one might have expected of her. She had brown hair, brown eyes, and a chin that was afraid of no dragons—not even of an outlaw so notorious and unpopular as Simon Templar. And as far as the Saint was concerned, any girl with her face and figure could have come into his life unasked, uninvited, and unintroduced every day of the week, and he would have had nothing but praise for the beneficence of a Providence that provided surprises of such quality. He was able to frame that appraisement of her physical perfections within a bare few minutes of meeting her for the first time—which in this case happens to be a far more respectable statement than it sounds.

Simon Templar had left London. The wanderlust that would never let him be still for long had filled him again with dreams of wild adventurous voyaging after an exceptionally short rest in the city that was as near home to him as anywhere else in the world. Partly because his rest had been so extraordinarily unrestful. In a very few months, London had loaded down his life with such a plentiful supply of excitement that he had made up his mind to take wing again promptly, before the standard of lawlessness and unrest depreciated. The house that he had chosen when he first returned was still in the hands of interior decorators who were struggling to repair the damage that can only be done by a powerful bomb exploded in a small room, and after viewing the progress of their efforts he had decided to terminate his lease and take up residence at the Dorchester for the remainder of his stay. An expensive luxury, but one which he considered he had earned. Or, if he hadn't earned it, he would doubtless contrive to do so before he left . . . And then—since this was in that memorable year when the sun shone upon England—the thermometer hopped back on top of the ninety mark, and after two days of it the Saint tore off his coat and tie and went forth into the West End swearing a quiet sirocco of wrath whose repercussions were recorded at Kew.

"Civilisation be damned," said the Saint, in one of his few lucid moments. "I saw an English Gentleman in Piccadilly yesterday. With great daring he had removed his coat, waistcoat, collar and tie, and he was walking about in a flannel shirt and a hideous pair of braces striped with his old school colours. Under the neck of his shirt and the roll-up of his sleeves you could see the edges of his abominable woollen vest. I refuse to discuss in detail the occult reasonings which may have made him even put on the superfluous garments that he was carrying over his arm. But when you consider the abysmal chasms of imbecility personified in that perspiring oaf, and then realise that he was only a pale pink renegade—that a real English Gentleman and Public School Man would have died before he removed a single garment—then you know that the next deluge is long overdue."

He had a lot more to say, much of which would have made certain seaside Borough Councillors who spend most of their time deliberating on the minimum length of sleeve that may without peril to the public morality be permitted on bathing costumes foam at the mouth with indignation. He said it all very forcefully, using much of the language which by similarly coherent standards is judged to be harmless to an audience of three thousand men, women, and children congregated in a theatre, but definitely corrupting to the same audience if they happen to be congregated in a cinema. Also he travelled—as fast and far as he possibly could on the strength of it, which perhaps has more to do with this story.

The Scilly Islands are not quite at the end of the world, but Simon Templar went there because a letter came to him which quite innocently told him something that he could scarcely ignore.

"We have about the usual number of visitors for the time of year," wrote Mr Smithson-Smith. "They disappear just as they always do, and St Mary's still seems uncrowded . . . The *Scillonian* went aground in a fog the other day, but they got her off quite safely at high tide . . . They caught some Frenchmen picking up their pots inside the three-mile limit on Sunday, and fined them eighty pounds . . . There are a couple of fine yachts anchored over at Tresco—one of them belongs to an Egyptian, a man called Abdul Osman. I've been wondering if he's the man I heard about once when I was in Assuan . . ."

There were six pages of local gossip and general reminiscence, of the kind that Mr Smithson-Smith felt moved to write about three times a year. They had met in a dispute about a camel many years ago outside Ismailia, and the Saint, who was no letter-writer, responded at equally vague intervals. But the name of Abdul Osman was not strange to him, and he had no doubts about its associations.

There was a glint in his eye when he had finished reading.

"We're going to the Isles of Scilly, where the puffins go to breed," he said poetically and Patricia Holm looked at him with an air of caution.

"I'm not a puffin," she said.

"Nevertheless, we'll go," said the Saint.

It may sound flippant to say that if Simon Templar had not shared some of the dim instincts of the puffin Laura Berwick would undoubtedly have been drowned, but that is nothing but the truth.

She was sailing much too close to the wind—quite literally. Simon Templar saw it from the beginning, and had wondered whether it was pure daring or sheer foolishness. He was perched up on a comparatively smooth ledge of rock, sunning himself in a sublime vacancy of relaxation, and thinking of nothing in particular. The cool waters of the Atlantic were swishing and gurgling among the boulders a dozen feet below him, countering the pale brazen blue of the sky with a translucent intensity of colour that was as rich as anything in the Mediterranean; he had bathed in them for a few minutes, feeling the sticky heat of his walk dissolving under their icy impact with a gratitude that touched the foundations of utter physical contentment; then he had climbed up to his chosen ledge to let the sun dry his body. He wondered lazily, whether the RSPCA would have its views about the corruptive influence of his costume on the morals of a score of seagulls that were squabbling raucously over a scrap of food that had been left in a rocky pool by the falling tide, and he wondered also, with the same peaceful laziness, what strange discontent it was that had made Man of his own free will turn his back on the life that was always his, and take himself with his futile insatiable ambitions to the stifling cities from which the escape to his own inheritance seemed so fantastic and impossible. And out of lazily half-closed eyes he watched the white sailing dinghy dancing over the swell. Too close to the wind—much too close . . .

It all happened in a flash, with the suddenness that every experienced yachtsman knows and labours to avoid. The breeze was baffling, switching around six points of the compass in strong gusts that scraped little raw patches of white foam off the tops of the ponderous rollers. The girl stood up and tried to reach something forward, steadying the tiller with one hand as she leaned away from it. The wind shifted round another point and blew a vicious puff at the flapping canvas, and the mainsail swung across with a sharp crack. The boom seemed to catch the girl on the side of the head, and she went over the side with a splash.

Simon stood up, watching for her to come up and swim back to the boat, but she didn't rise again.

It was not a particularly sensational rescue as rescues go. The dinghy was only about thirty yards from the shore, and the Saint was a fast swimmer. He found her in a few moments, and towed her after the boat. The fitful breeze had broken down short-windedly, and it was fairly easy. Simon was able to haul her on board and slacken the sheet before it blew again; then the girl moved, coughing and choking, and the Saint slipped hurriedly over the side again.

She rubbed the side of her head tenderly, and then she opened her eyes and saw his tanned face smiling down at her, with a pair of brown forearms braced over the gunwale.

"What happened?" she asked dizzily.

"You jibed," answered a dispassionate Saint. "A bad show—and not to be encouraged in a real wind."

It was obvious that the power of resenting criticism had been temporarily bumped and soaked out of her—an indicative symptom which might profitably be remembered by harassed husbands who take their spouses for holidays by the sea.

"Where did you come from?"

"Off a rock," said the Saint.

She coughed, and choked again with a grimace.

"Excuse me if I spit," she said.

The Saint excused her. She did it to windward, which was not too successful. Simon regarded her sadly.

"You're new to this, aren't you?" he said mildly.

"You've got to begin sometime," she said defiantly. "I've had a few lessons from one of the men, and I thought I'd like to try it by myself. Nobody was using the dinghy, so I just took it."

"There's only one policeman in the Scilly Isles," murmured Simon, "so if you lie low you may get away with it."

"Oh, I didn't steal it. It belongs to the yacht."

Simon raised his eyebrows.

"Have you got a yacht?"

"My stepfather has. The *Claudette*. We're lying over at Tresco."

The line of black-etched eyebrows seemed to harden fractionally.

"Near Abdul Osman's?"

"Why—how did you know?"

"Sort of bush telegraph," said the Saint "It's amazing how the news travels in these wild parts."

It was during some of this conversation that he was able to review the artistic proportions of her body; for she was dressed in nothing more than a bathing costume in the modern style, consisting largely of entrances for the priceless ultra-violet ray.

"Are you determined to stay where you are?" she inquired presently and the Saint smiled.

"Not permanently," he said. "But my bathing costume is even more modern than yours. You interrupted a lovely sun-bath *à l'allemande*. However, if you like to stay here for a minute I'll swim back and fetch some clothes."

He slid down into the water without waiting for his suggestion to be accepted, and made for the shore again, cutting a clean line through the water and leaving a wake behind. He returned on his back, one hand holding a bundle of shirt, trousers, and shoes high and dry in the air.

"I was born without shame," he said, heaving the bundle over the stern. "But if you feel bashful you can go forward and talk to the fish while I use your towel."

"I suppose you saved my life," said the girl, staring with intense concentration at a completely empty horizon, while the boat rocked under her as he pulled himself on board.

"There is no charge," said the Saint.

"He towelled himself rapidly, and pulled on his trousers; then he set himself to bring the dinghy round and trim her on a straight course back towards Tresco. The girl turned round and watched his easy manoeuvres enviously. It was done with an effortless confidence that seemed no trouble at all, and he settled himself at the tiller and smiled at her again out of that rather reckless brown face. She saw challenging blue eyes gleaming with a ready mockery, wiry muscles that rippled under a skin like brown satin; sensed a personality that had no respect for polite conventions. She knew that the hint of antagonism that had infected her was due to nothing but her own feeling of foolishness, and knew that he knew she knew.

"I shan't tell," he said, and his words fitted in with her thoughts so uncannily that for a moment longer she had to continue looking at him.

"My stepfather might want to know where I picked you up," she said.

"That's true," Simon admitted, and said no more until he had run the dinghy neatly alongside the rather excessively magnificent-looking yacht that was riding in the New Grimsby channel.

He made the boat fast to the gangway, and helped the girl out. One of the hands had noticed their arrival, and there was a middle-aged gentleman in white flannels waiting for them on the deck. He wore a yachting cap and a blue reefer jacket with a vague air of uneasiness, as if every moment he was expecting some rude urchin to utter shrill comments on his pretensions to the uniform.

"Where have you been, Laura?" he demanded unnecessarily.

"Out in the dinghy," said the girl no less unnecessarily, but with a certain impish satisfaction.

The man looked round at the Saint with a kind of restrained impatience, as though his presence had been imposed as a deliberate obstacle to the development of some plain speaking that was definitely called for.

"This hero has just saved my life," said Laura, also looking at the Saint "Hero, this is my stepfather, Mr Stride."

"Ha!" said Mr Stride, intelligently. "Hum!"

His eyes absorbed the Saint's appearance dubiously—they were small eyes, rather surprisingly sharp when they looked at you. Simon was still only wearing his shirt in a haphazard way—he had flung it carelessly over his shoulders and knotted the sleeves loosely under his chin—and he looked quite disreputable and quite happy about it. Mr Stride groped hesitantly for his note-case.

"I got knocked overboard," said the girl. "I did something silly with the sail, and the boom hit me on the head—"

"It might have happened to anyone," said the Saint airily—he had never blushed over a lie in his life. "A sudden squall can make a lot of trouble for any boat, and you get plenty of them around here."

"Ha," said Mr Stride. His sharp eyes ran once up the Saint's lean poiseful length, thoughtfully, but at the sound of the Saint's voice he had let go his wallet as if it had grown red-hot in his fingers. "Ha," said Mr Stride. He tugged at his grey moustache, "Very lucky that you saw the accident, Mr—"

Simon elegantly ignored the invitation to supply his name.

"We were just going to have lunch, Mr—" said Stride, dangling the bait again. "Won't you stay?"

"That's awfully kind of you," murmured the Saint, and thought that Mr Stride would have been more cordial if he had refused.

He proceeded to put on his shirt, with a calm indifference to his host's emotions that would have been boorish if it had been a shade less transparently innocent, and as he did so he was glancing over the other ships that were anchored within a hundred yards of the *Claudette*. There was a couple of French fishing smacks, broad-beamed sea boats, with high bows and low sterns, held idly into the wind by their great rust-red sails. Beyond them was a superb 200-ton Diesel yacht with a sweet line of clipper bow: Simon could read the name painted there— *Luxor*. Beside the wheel-house Simon could see a man focusing a pair of binoculars, and he knew that it was the *Claudette* that was the object of his attention.

"A lovely boat," said Stride, purringly.

"Lovely," agreed the Saint. "You have to be a very successful man to own a ship like that—or even a ship like yours, Mr Stride."

The other shot one of his surprisingly sharp glances at the unruffled young man beside him.

"Hum," he assented mechanically, but he was spared the necessity of finding some suitable amplification of his answer by the arrival of a white-coated steward with a tray of glasses, followed by what appeared to be the remainder of his guests.

These consisted of a pleasant-faced youngster of about twenty-five, with a diligently suppressed crinkle in his fair hair, and a sleek and saturnine man of indeterminate age whose coat fitted very tightly to his waist and whose hair waved unashamed in faultless undulations that Nature unaided could scarcely have made so symmetrical. The fair-haired youngster's name was Toby Halidom, and his solicitude for Laura Berwick's complete recovery from the effects of her adventure seemed to account satisfactorily for the engagement ring which appeared on her finger when she had powdered her nose and changed for lunch. The sleek and saturnine one was introduced as Mr Almido, private secretary to Mr Stride; he spoke little, and when he did so it was with a lisping accent that was certainly no more English than his clothes.

Mr Stride swallowed his cocktail in silence, and led the way below almost abruptly. His lack of festive geniality, remarkable in a man whose stepdaughter had so recently been saved from a watery grave, continued for fully half the meal, but the Saint was unabashed. And then, just as surprisingly for anyone who had begun to accept his taciturnity, he began to thaw. He thawed so much that by the time the dessert was placed on the table he was inquiring into the Saint's plans with something approaching affability.

"Are you staying long?" he asked.

"Until I'm tired of absorbing Vitamin D, probably," said the Saint. "I have no plans."

"I always thought the South of France was the favourite resort of sunbathers," remarked Mr Stride, with a show of interest in which only an ear that was listening for it could have discerned the veiled point. "I think, if that were my object, I should be inclined to go there rather than risk the uncertainties of the British climate. I'm sure that would be wiser."

"Ah, but even there they make you wear some clothes," said the Saint ingenuously. "It always annoys me to see myself in my bath looking as if I was wearing a ridiculous pair of transparent white pants. Here I can find a nice piece of coast all to myself, and acquire the same beautiful colour all over."

Mr Toby Halidom, who was wearing an Old Harrovian tie, looked faintly shocked, but Mr Stride was unmoved.

He accompanied Simon on to the deck, with Laura Berwick, when the Saint excused himself as soon as coffee had been served. One of the men, he said, would take Mr Hum Ha back to St Mary's in the motor dinghy, and while the boat was being brought round Simon glanced across again to the *Luxor*. A seaman was standing on the deck, looking towards them, and as Simon came into view the man turned and spoke through a hatch to someone below. A moment later the man who had watched the Saint before came up with the companion and adjusted his binoculars again.

"I hope we shall see some more of you," said Mr Stride, standing by the gangway. "Come and pay us a call whenever you like."

"I should love to," murmured the Saint, just as politely, and then, with such a smooth transition that the effect of it was like a gunshot, he said, "I didn't know Abdul Osman was short-sighted."

Galbraith Stride went white, as if the blood had been drained from his face by a vacuum pump.

"Do you know Mr Osman?" he asked, with an effort.

"Fairly well," said the Saint casually. "I branded him on both cheeks five years ago, and it must have cost him no end of money in plastic surgeons to put his face right again. If anyone had done that to me I shouldn't have to look at him twice through field-glasses to be sure who it was."

"Very interesting," said Galbraith Stride slowly. "Very interesting." He held out his hand. "Well, good-bye, Mr . . . er . . . hum."

"Templar," said the Saint. "Simon Templar. And thanks so much for the lunch."

He shook the proffered hand cordially and went down to the boat, and he was so happy that he wanted to sing to himself all the way back to St Mary's.

3

"If," said Patricia Holm, "that was supposed to be another of your famous Exercises in Tact—"

"But what else could it have been?" protested the Saint. "If I hadn't used extraordinary tact, I shouldn't have been invited to lunch, and that would have meant I'd have missed a display of caviar, lobster mayonnaise, and dry champagne that no man with a decent respect for his stomach could resist—not to mention a first-hand knowledge of the geography of Stride's boat—"

"And by dinner-time," said Patricia, "she'll be fifty miles away, with the *Luxor* racing her."

Simon shook his head.

"Not if I know Abdul Osman. The surgeons may have refashioned his face, but there are scars inside him that he will never forget . . . I should have had to scrape an acquaintance with Laura some time, and that accident made it so beautifully easy."

"I thought we were coming here for a holiday," said Patricia, and the Saint grinned, and went in search of Mr Smithson-Smith.

Mr Smithson-Smith was the manager of Tregarthen's, which is one of the three hotels with which the island of St Mary's is provided. Simon Templar, whose taste in hotels could be satisfied by nothing less lavish than palaces like the Dorchester, failing which he usually plunged to the opposite extreme, had declined an invitation to stay there, and had billeted himself in a house in the village, where he had a private sitting-room thrown in with the best of home-cooked meals for a weekly charge that would have maintained him in an attic at the Dorchester for about five minutes. At Tregarthen's, however, he could stay himself with draught Bass drawn from the wood, and this was one of the things of which he felt in need.

The other thing was a few more details of local gossip, with which Mr Smithson-Smith might also be able to provide him.

It was then half-past three in the afternoon, but by a notable oversight on the part of the efficient legislators who framed that unforgettable Defence of the Realm Act which has for so long been Britain's bulwark against the horrors of an invasion of foreign tourists, the Scilly Islands were omitted from the broad embrace of that protection, and it is still lawful to drink beer at almost any hour at which a man can reasonably raise a thirst. As Simon entered the long glass-fronted verandah overlooking the bay, he naturally expected to find it packed to suffocation with sodden islanders wallowing in the decadent excesses from which a beneficent Government had not been thoughtful enough to protect them, but such (as the unspeakable newspapers say, in what they apparently believe to be the English language) was not the case. In fact, the only occupant of the bar was Mr Smithson-Smith himself, who was making out bills beside an open window.

"Why—good afternoon, Templar. What can I do for you?"

"A pint of beer," murmured the Saint, sinking into a chair. "Possibly, if my thirst holds, two pints. And one for yourself if you feel like it."

Mr Smithson-Smith disappeared into his serving cubicle and returned with a brimming glass. He excused himself from joining in the performance.

"I'd rather leave it till the evening, if you don't mind," he said with a smile. "What have you been doing today?"

He was a thin mild-mannered man with sandy-grey hair, a tiny moustache, and an extraordinary gentle voice, and it was a strange thing that he was only one of many men in those islands who were more familiar with the romantic cities of the East than they were with the capital of their own country. Simon had been struck by that odd fact on his first call at Tregarthen's and subsequent visits had confirmed it. There, on those lonely clusters of rock breaking out of the sea forty miles from Land's End, where you would expect to find men who had seen scarcely anything of the world outside the other rocky islands around their own homes, you found instead simple men whose turns of reminiscence recalled the streets of Damascus and Baghdad by their names. And whenever reminiscence turned that way, Mr Smithson-Smith would call on his own memories, with a far-away look in his eyes, and the same far-away sound in that very gentle voice, as if his dreams saw the deserts of Arabia more vividly than the blue bay beyond his windows. "I mind a time when I was in Capernaum . . ." Simon had heard him say it, and felt that for that man at least all the best days lay in the past. It was the War, of course that had picked men out of every sleepy hamlet in England and hurled them into the familiarity of strange sights and places as well as the flaming shadows of death, and in the end sent some of them back to those same sleepy hamlets to remember, but there was in that quiet man a mystic sensitiveness, a tenseness of poetry struggling rather puzzledly for the expression he could not give it, that made his memories more dreamy with a quaint kind of reverence than most others.

"I've been over by Tresco," said the Saint, lifting his face presently from the beer.

"Oh. Did you see those yachts—are they still there?"

Simon nodded.

"As a matter of fact, I managed to scrounge lunch on one of them."

"Was it Abdul Osman's?"

"No—Galbraith Stride's. I saw Osman's though. It's a long way for him to come all the way over here."

He knew that the other would need the least possible encouragement to delve into the past, and his expectations were founded on the soundest psychology. Mr Smithson-Smith sat down and accepted a cigarette.

"I think I said in my letter that I thought I'd heard his name before. I was thinking about it only yesterday, and the story came back to me. He hasn't visited St Mary's—at least, if he has, I don't think I've seen him—but I should know this Abdul Osman if he was the same man, because he was branded on both cheeks."

The Saint's eyebrows rose in innocent surprise.

"Really?"

The other nodded.

"It's quite a story—you could almost put it in a book. An Englishman did it—at least, the rumour said he was an Englishman, although they never caught him. This Abdul Osman was supposed to have a monopoly of various unpleasant things in the East—brothels and gambling dens and drug trafficking, all that sort of thing. I don't know if it was true, but that was what they told me. He had a fine house in Cairo, anyway, so he must have made plenty of money out of it. I remember what happened distinctly. It was a local sensation at the time . . . I hope I'm not boring you?"

Mr Smithson-Smith was oddly afraid of being boring, as if he felt that any mundane restlessness in his audience would break the fragile glamour of those wonderful things he could remember.

"Not a bit," said the Saint. "What happened?"

"Well apparently this Abdul Osman disappeared one night. He was supposed to be driving back to Cairo from Alexandria, just himself and his chauffeur. It was a beautiful car he had. I've often seen it driving past Shepheard's Hotel. Well, he didn't arrive when they were expecting him, and as the time went on, and he was three or four hours late and hadn't sent any message to say what had held him up, his household became anxious and went out to look for him. They drove all the way to Alexandria without seeing him, but when they got there they were told by the place where he'd been staying that he'd left about eight hours previously. Then they went to the police, and there was another search. No trace of him was found."

A couple of young men in white open shirts and flannel trousers came in and sat down. Mr Smithson-Smith excused himself to go and take their order, and while he was filling it the Saint lighted a cigarette and glanced at them disinterestedly. They were quiet, very respectable young men, but their faces were sallow and the arms exposed by their rolled-up sleeves were white above the elbows.

"Well," said Mr Smithson-Smith, returning to his chair, "they searched for him half the night, but he seemed to have vanished into thin air. Of course, it wasn't easy to make a thorough search in the dark, so in the morning they tried again. And then they found him. His car was on the road—they found tracks that showed it had been driven off quite a long way into the desert, and brought back again, and out in the desert where it had been turned round there was the remains of a fire. The chauffeur was just recovering consciousness—he'd been knocked on the head and tied up and gagged—and Abdul Osman was in the back of the car with this brand on both his cheeks. Whoever did it had burnt it in almost to the bone with a red-hot iron—it was an Arabic word, and it meant just what this man was."

"Stout piece of work," murmured the Saint, pushing his glass forward for replenishment.

"Probably it was." Mr Smithson-Smith provided another pint of beer, and resumed his seat. "And the only clue they had was a sort of drawing that had been painted on the sides of Osman's beautiful car—the paint was still wet when they found it. It was a sort of figure made out of straight lines, with a round head, like you see kids drawing on walls, only this one had a circle on top like the haloes in those medieval church pictures. I've often wondered what it was meant to be. It couldn't have been a picture of Abdul Osman, because he had no right to a halo. Perhaps it was meant for a picture of the man who did it."

"It sounds possible," murmured the Saint.

One of the respectable young men rose and left the bar; idly, Simon watched him going slowly down the sloping path to the gate.

"Yes," said Mr Smithson-Smith thoughtfully . . . "I mind another time when I heard of him. This was in Beirut. A friend of mine met a girl there in a dance place—it was the sort of dance place that wouldn't be allowed at all in England. She told him a story about Abdul Osman—I don't think I should like to repeat the details to anyone, but if it was true he couldn't be painted any blacker than he is. As a matter of fact, I did tell this story to a man I met on a boat going across to Marseilles, who had just retired from the Egyptian Police, and he said it was probably true. It was—"

"Hullo," said the Saint. "Bloke seems to have fallen down."

The respectable young man who had gone out had stumbled as he stepped down to the road, and at that moment he was sprawled in the dust just beyond the gate. He was clutching one ankle, and his face was turned back towards the verandah with a twisted expression of agony.

Mr Smithson-Smith looked out, then round to the respectable young man's companion.

"Your friend seems to have hurt himself," he said. "It looks as if he has sprained his ankle."

The respectable young man came over to their table and also looked out.

"I'll go and see," he said.

Simon watched him go, inhaling speculatively.

"Staying in the hotel?" he queried.

"Yes," said Mr Smithson-Smith, with his eyes on the developments below. "They're staying here."

"Have they been here long?"

The question was put with perfect casualness.

"About a fortnight," said Mr Smithson-Smith. "I don't know much about them. They're out most of the day—I think they go bathing, but by the look of the basket they take with them you'd think they needed towels enough to dry a regiment."

"They aren't very sunburnt," said the Saint softly, almost as if he was speaking to himself.

He picked up his glass mechanically—and put it down again.

The young man with the injured ankle was coming back, limping painfully and leaning on his companion's arm.

"Silly thing to do, wasn't it?" he said, and Mr Smithson-Smith nodded with some concern.

"Would you like me to get you a doctor?"

The young man shook his head.

"I'll just go and bathe it with cold water and rest it for a bit. I don't think it's anything serious."

The three-legged party went on through into the hotel premises, and Simon sat down again and lighted another cigarette. Mr Smithson-Smith's gentle voice was continuing his interrupted anecdote, but the Saint scarcely heard a word. The narrative formed no more than a vague undercurrent of sound in his senses, a restful background to his working thoughts. In a life like the Saint's, a man's existence is prolonged from day to day by nothing but that ceaseless vigilance, that unsleeping activity of a system of question marks in the mind which are never satisfied with the obvious explanations that pass through the torpid consciousness of the average man. To him, anything out of the ordinary was a red light of possible danger, never to be dismissed as mere harmless eccentricity: nine times out of ten the alarm might be proved false, but it could never be ignored. And it seemed odd that two very respectable young men should have attracted attention by carrying an outsize basket of towels; odd, too, that after bathing every day for a fortnight they should still have the soft white bodies of men who have not been free of the muffling protection of clothes for many years . . . And then the Saint's probing suspicions came to a head in a sudden flash of inspiration, and he pulled himself swiftly out of his chair. He was across the bar in a flash, over to the closed door through which the two respectable young men had disappeared, and Mr Smithson-Smith, startled to silence by his abrupt movement, noticed in an eerie moment of perplexity that the Saint's feet made no sound as they swung over the floor. It was like the charge of a leopard in its smooth powerful noiselessness, and then Simon Templar had his hand on the handle of the door, jerking it open, and the young man who had assisted the injured one stumbled and almost fell into the room.

"Come in, brother," said the Saint heartily. "Come in and have a drink."

The young man's face went red, and his mouth opened in a weak grin.

"I-I'm sorry," he stammered, "I must have tripped or something—"

A thin smile cut into the corners of the Saint's mouth.

"Sure you must, brother."

"I'll-I'll have a whisky and soda."

"You'll have beer!"

The Saint caught up his own glass from the table and thrust it out. He was only a yard from the other, on his toes, indefinably dangerous.

"Drink this," he said, and the young man went white.

"I-I don't—"

Simon's free fist caught him on the mouth and knocked him backwards.

"I'll have the police on you for this," blustered the other, and the Saint smiled again.

"Go get him. And don't be too lavish with your plurals, because there is only one. But ask Abdul what he thinks of the idea first, or you may find yourself unpopular. Now amscray—and if you value your beauty, don't damage my beer again!"

He seized the respectable young man by the ear and propelled him deftly and vigorously out of the bar; then he turned back to face the outraged stare of Mr Smithson-Smith. The course of events had been so violently sudden and incomprehensible that the manager had been pardonably nonplussed, but by this point at least his path of duty seemed unmistakable.

"Why—really, Templar," he said, with his quiet voice shaking. "You can't behave like that here, I shall have to apologise to my guest. I'm afraid you'll have to leave this bar—"

Simon took his arm calmly, and pointed.

A fly was crawling down the inside of the half emptied glass of beer which he had just replaced on the table. It was quite unhurried about the journey, after the impudent fashion of flies; perhaps its thirst was of no great dimensions, or perhaps it had been reared in scrupulously well-mannered circumstances. It moved downwards in little short runs, pausing once to wash its hands and once to rub its feet together, in a genteel ecstasy of anticipation. Mr Smithson-Smith's eye followed it because it was the only moving object in the direction which the Saint had indicated, and there seemed to be nothing else to look at.

Even so, it seemed an extremely trivial spectacle and he moved his arm restlessly in the Saint's grasp. But Simon Templar continued to point at it, and there was something dynamic about the immobility of that extended finger. Mr Smithson-Smith watched, and saw the fly reach the level of the beer. It looked around cautiously, and lowered his proboscis delicately into the liquid. For two or three seconds after that it was motionless. And then, without any kind of struggle, it pitched over in a limp somersault and floated quietly on its back, with its legs stretched stiffly upwards . . .

4

Mr Smithson-Smith blinked, and wiped his forehead. His arm relaxed slowly, as if it required a conscious effort to loosen the involuntary contraction of his muscles. He had no idea why the miniature drama that he had seen enacted should have had such an effect on him. It might have been the utter stillness in which it was played out, the unexplanatory silence of the man beside him—anything. But it seemed as if for the last few seconds he had forgotten to breathe, and when it was finished he expanded his chest with an inaudible sigh.

Then the Saint spoke, and his voice jarred the other's ears by sheer contrast with the silence.

"Don't tell me your beer's as potent as all that!"

The manager stared at him.

"Do you mean—do you mean it was drugged?"

"No less, and possibly even some more. We'll soon see." With unruffled calm, the Saint fished out the fly with a match-stick and laid it in an ash-tray to cool off. "But I don't somehow think it was sudden death—that would probably be considered too good for me."

"But . . . but . . . damn it!" Mr Smithson-Smith felt queerly shaken under his instinctive incredulity. "You can't tell me that Mr Trape—"

"Is that his name?" The Saint was as cool as an ice-pack. "I can't tell you much about him, but I can tell you that. My dear chap"— he put his hand on the manager's shoulder for a moment—"can you be expected to guarantee the morals of everyone who stays at your hotel? Can you demand a budget of references from anyone who asks for a room? Of course you can't. You have to take them at their face value, and so long as they behave themselves while they're here you aren't expected to ask them whether their finger-prints are registered at Scotland Yard. No—they just had to find somewhere to stay, and you were unlucky."

The manager frowned.

"If what you say is true, Templar, I shall have to ask for their room," he said, and the Saint had to laugh.

"You've got your room now, old lad. But whether they've left money to pay the bill is another matter."

He sat on the table with a glance at the fly, which was still sunken in its coma. He found it difficult to think that it could be dead— although, of course, a drug that a man would survive might be fatal to an insect. But his summary of Abdul Osman's character didn't fit in with such a clean conclusion. The hot irons that had scored their insult on the Egyptian's face would call for something much more messy in the way of vengeance—Abdul Osman would not forget, nor would he be so easily satisfied when his chance came. Then why the drug? And why, anyway, the very presence of those two respectable young men who on Smithson-Smith's own statement had been staying at the hotel for the past fortnight? It seemed improbable that Abdul Osman claimed any of the gifts of necromantic clairvoyance which popular novelists attribute to the "mysterious East." And yet—

All at once he recognised a slim figure in wide blue trousers walking up from the harbour towards the hotel, and waved to it joyfully out of the window. He was in a state of puzzlement in which he wanted to think aloud, and he could not have hoped for a better audience. But it struck him, while he was waiting for her to arrive, that it was a remarkable thing that he had not seen the two respectable young men making their way hastily towards the harbour, even as he had seen her coming in the opposite direction.

"Look here, Templar," began Mr Smithson-Smith worriedly, but the Saint interrupted him with a smile of seraphic blandness.

"Excuse me—I'll be back in a sec."

He went out and met Patricia at the gate.

"What about a spot of tea, boy?" she suggested, and then the electric gaiety of him opened her eyes, and she stopped.

"Sit down here—this is a conference, but since we aren't politicians we can't fix a date for it next year on the other side of the world." The Saint pulled open the gate, seated himself on the step, and drew her down beside him. "Pat, a very respectable-looking young man, name of Trape, has just put a sleeping-draught in my beer."

"Good Lord—you haven't drunk it, have you?"

The Saint laughed.

"I certainly haven't. In fact, I punched the face of Mr Trape, just to learn him, and kicked him out of the bar—to the pardonable indignation of our friend Mr Smith. But I think he's beginning to understand—probably more than I wanted him to. I dropped a line about Abdul Osman while interviewing Mr Trape that must have made Smith think a bit . . . I'll tell you how it happened. I was having my drink, and these two harmless-looking birds rolled in. They ordered lemonade, or something, and then one of them went out. He walked down the path, tripped on this very spot where we're sitting, and appeared to sprain his ankle. I saw it happen, and Smith called his pal over to the window.

That was when he did it, of course. He wanted an excuse to come over to our table, with both of us looking outside, so he could slip in the dope. That's what the whole plant was for—and damned well done it was, too. I didn't see it at all until the injured warrior had been helped back to the hotel and away to his room, and then only because I'm naturally suspicious. I'll tell you the things that struck me as odd later—never mind them now. But all at once it dawned on me that there was something in my beer that hadn't been there when I started it, and also that Mr Trape might be listening outside the door to see what happened. I opened the door, and there he was—so I pushed his teeth in. Episode over."

"But what was the idea?"

"That's just what I want to get—and I want it quick." He was speaking so rapidly that it wasn't easy for her to pick the facts and deductions out of that vital rush of vivid sentences. "I want to reconstruct what might have happened if I'd drunk the beer. Make holes in it anywhere you can."

"Go ahead."

"Right. I drink the beer. I appear to go groggy. Smith registers alarm. Trape hears, and walks innocently in—probably requesting brandy for wounded comrade. Apparently I've fainted. Cold water, keys, feathers, smelling-salts—all tried and found wanting. Smith departs to summon doctor, leaving me with Trape. Whereupon I'm rushed out of the place—?"

"But what happens when Smith comes back?"

"Exactly . . . No, that's easy enough. Trape returns to bewildered Smith, explains that I revived and pushed off. Maybe I saw a man I had to talk to about a dog, or anything like that. Apologies, thanks, and so forth . . . Well, where do they take me? Answer, the *Luxor*, of course—Abdul was watching me through field glasses all the time I was on Stride's deck. That's all right till—"

"But there are holes everywhere!" she protested. "Suppose anyone saw him carrying you away?"

The Saint's keen blue eyes flicked round the scene.

"Abdul's a clever man—he doesn't forget much. There's a donkey and jingle two yards away, isn't there? And probably Trape hired it for the occasion. He could also have a cask—and I become cold potatoes. Down to the harbour—into a boat—there'd be no hurry. Once he had me in the cart he could leave me there for hours if it was good dope. And even when I was missing for good, his alibi would hold water. I don't say there was no risk, but it could have been done. And Abdul would be the man to do it. What I want to know is what the scheme is now that I haven't drunk the beer. Those two birds have been here a fortnight so they were put here for some other job. Have they finished that job, and are they free to get away? I expect they'd have to consult Abdul, and Abdul wouldn't approve of bungling. I haven't seen them come out of the hotel, though I expect they could work round the back of the town—"

He was still trying to frame his thoughts aloud, but actually the thread of them was racing away ahead of his voice. And a new light dawned on him at the same moment. His fingers clamped on Patricia's wrist.

"Organisation—that's what it is! Gee, I'm as slow as a village concert today!"

In another second he was on his feet and sprinting back to the bar. He entered it from the path as Mr Smithson-Smith came in at the other end.

"What have you decided to do about all this unpleasantness?" asked the Saint, and the manager put his hands on his hips.

"Well, I've just seen the young fellow with the sprained ankle—"

The Saint's smile was fast and thin.

"I thought you would. And if you hadn't gone to see him, he'd have sent for you. Meanwhile the most extraordinary things go on happening to my beer. First a sleeping-draught—then it grows legs!"

Mr Smithson-Smith looked down at the table rather blankly. The fly still reclined in the ash-tray, oblivious of all excitement in its rigid stupor, but the glass of beer from which oblivion had overtaken it was gone.

"Someone may have been in here and moved it," began Mr Smithson-Smith hazily, and Simon showed his teeth.

"Someone has been in here and moved it—you can write that down in the family Bible. That sprained ankle was good enough for another stall. Did you go up and see the bloke off your own bat?"

"As a matter of fact, he asked me to go up—"

"And naturally you had to go. Organisation, that's what it is. What did he say?"

"He said that his friend had told him what happened, and he couldn't understand it. He wanted to know if I should be asking them to leave."

"Did you say anything about doped beer?"

"No."

"Or flies?"

"No."

"Then that lets you out," said the Saint, with some relief. "If they think you don't know anything they won't worry about you. What did you say?"

"I said I should have to consider the matter."

"That," said the Saint grimly, "will be all right so long as you don't consider it too deeply."

Mr Smithson-Smith looked at him. The events he had witnessed, and that rattle of cross-examination, had left that gentle-voiced man utterly bewildered without shifting the foundations of his practical standpoint.

"Look here, Templar," he said directly. "I don't know what you or these two young men are playing at, but I'm in a responsible position. I can't take any risks with this hotel. Unless one of you can give me a satisfactory explanation, I think I shall have to tell the Sergeant as much as I know, and leave him to deal with it."

Simon pondered for a moment, and then he nodded.

"That's obviously your duty, and I think it would be better from every point of view if you did it. May I go up to Trape's room and see if he'll speak to me? I don't know if he'll accept an apology, but if he did it might save a little scandal."

He knew that he was taking rather an unfair advantage, but the idea was one that he had to follow. The bait was tempting, and Mr Smithson-Smith, with the interest of his employers at heart and no conception of the depth of duplicity to which Simon Templar could sink when it was necessary, could scarcely refuse it. Simon obtained permission, and the number of the room which the two respectable-looking young men were sharing, and went upstairs with as much consolation as he could derive from the knowledge that if his plan went through successfully the victims would be most unlikely to complain to the management. If he were caught in the act, of course he would find himself ten times more unpopular with the controlling powers of that respectable hotel than he was already, but the Saint had an unshakable faith in his guardian angels.

He knocked on the door, and went in with the forefinger of his right hand prodding out the shape of his trouser pocket in an ostentatious untruth. Both the respectable-looking young men were there.

"Put your hands up, and don't even think of shouting," he said genially. "You'd only give the chambermaids hysterics."

For a moment the two young men were speechless.

"Sorry to arrive so late, boys," Simon went in the same friendly tone. "I should have been here long ago, but your organisation was so slick it took me a little while to catch up with. I congratulate you on getting rid of the evidence of that doped beer so smartly. We gather that you haven't yet told Abdul about our mutual misunderstanding. I guess you were wise—he wouldn't have been very sympathetic, and you had lots of time to take a second shot at me."

Their faces gave him confirmation. And then Mr Trape, who was nearest, brought himself a couple of paces nearer, with his head twisted viciously on one side.

"Why not, Templar?" he said. "You wouldn't dare to shoot here."

"Maybe you're right, Eric," admitted the Saint, with astonishing meekness, and removed his hand from his empty pocket. "But then it mightn't be necessary—considering the evidence you've got on your ceiling."

He glanced upwards as he spoke, and Mr Trape would not have been human if he had not followed that compelling gaze. He also glanced upwards, and in so doing he arranged his chin at an angle that could not have been posed better. Simon's fist shot up to the inviting mark, and impacted with a crisp click . . .

The Saint had been long enough in the game to know that even a modest two to one is bigger odds than any sane man takes on for his health, and at that moment he was feeling more hurried than heroic. Mr Trape was sinking limply towards the carpet before his companion realised that he was left to carry the banner alone, and by that time it was a bit late for realisations. The second respectable-looking young man was only beginning to scramble up off the bed when the Saint's flying leap caught him irresistibly round the shoulders and hurled his face mufflingly back into the pillow; then Simon aimed his fist in a scientifically merciless jolt to the nape of the exposed neck.

The Saint returned coolly to the floor, and smoothed his hair. The second respectable-looking young man would not recover from the effects of that blow for several minutes, but it was the aggressive Mr Trape whom Simon selected automatically for his experiment. There was a large gunny sack and a coil of manila under the bed—Simon could not have deduced the plans for his own transportation better if he had been in the know from the beginning like any story-book detective—and in a few seconds he had Mr Trape inside the sack and the sack fastened. Then he went to the window and looked out. It was only a short drop to a small garden at the rear of the hotel, which was built on a steep slope, and Simon dumped Mr Trape over the sill unceremoniously. That was the greatest risk he took, but a searching glance round before he did it revealed a landscape apparently bare of watchers. Then he followed himself and went back to Patricia.

"Let's exercise the donkey," he said.

The ensacked Mr Trape was loaded into the cart, and they were moving passively down towards the harbour, before Patricia asked the inevitable question.

"I'm giving Abdul a visitor," said the Saint cheerfully. "He's expecting one, and why should he be disappointed? If you want another reason, write it down as my everlasting love of exasperating the ungodly. I have no other mission in life . . . You'd better stay back here—I'm banking on the sea gang not knowing the land operators, but they'd certainly ask questions about you."

The girl fell back, and Simon led the donkey out on to the jetty. For a very brief space he wondered if he would be able to locate the tender that awaited him, and then he saw a glistening white speedboat moored by some steps running down to the water. Its crew was dark-complexioned and swarthy, and to remove all doubt it flew a red burgee with the name *Luxor* woven into it.

Simon hitched the sack on to his shoulder, and walked brazenly down the steps.

"Here he is," he said.

Not one of the crew raised an eyebrow. Simon lowered his burden into the boat, saw the engine started, and went back along the causeway in an anguish of noiseless laughter.

5

It had been a simple gesture of a kind that Simon Templar could never resist, and it gave him exactly the same unfathomably primitive satisfaction that an urchin derives from putting his thumb to his nose and extending his fingers outwards. It was a moral catharsis that touched the well-springs of all unsophisticated human bliss. And if he could have witnessed the reception of his jest his pleasure would have been almost too ecstatic to be borne.

Abdul Osman himself came out on deck to supervise the hoisting up of the sack, and the leer on his face did not improve his beauty. Mr Trape was beginning to recover by that time, and the sack was squirming vigorously to an accompaniment of hoarse grunts and indistinguishable words.

"He must have a head of iron, that Englishman," muttered Osman. "He should have slept for many hours."

The thought crossed his mind that a man with a constitution like that would stand much torture, and his mouth watered at the prospect. He lifted his foot and kicked the sack cold-bloodedly, and it yelped at each thump of his shoe.

"Before you die you shall have much more to shout for," said Osman gloatingly. "Take him to the saloon."

Rough hands dragged the sack below, and Abdul Osman followed. Then it was cut open, and the storm broke.

Osman, it must be admitted, had never been considered even attractively ugly. He was a short pot-bellied man with a fat sallow face and black hair that covered his head in tight curls; out of his own hearing, it was said that much of his family tree was as black as his hair, and certainly he had a squat nose and a yellowish tinge in the whites of his pig-like eyes that supported the theory. A closely-clipped black moustache curved in a broad arch over his thick pouting lips and gave his face, even in repose, an expression of sensual bestiality that was nauseating.

And his rage at the sight of Mr Trape emerging from the sack put him right out of comparison with anything human. His face resembled nothing so much as the fat end of a bloated and malignant slug. His eyes almost disappeared in the rolls of unhealthy looking fat that creased down on them. Clearly marked circles of bright red sprang up and burned on his cheeks, plainly revealing the edges of the skin-grafting operations that had obliterated the Saint's brands; the rest of his jowl was blotched yellow and grey. And out of his distorted mouth flowed a stream of shrill profanity that was horrible to hear.

Nor was his wrath purely vocal. He kicked Trape again, and kicked and tore at the men who had carried in the sack until they fled from the room. And then, with the most lasting and concentrated malignance he kicked his secretary, who had played no part in the proceedings at all.

But that was nothing unusual. Mr Clements was there to be kicked. He was kicked whenever anything went wrong, and just as impartially when everything went right. Abdul Osman kicked him, cuffed him, and spat in his face, and his secretary cringed. There was something hideous about his quivering submission.

For Clements was a white man. His hair was almost ash-blonde, his shrinking eyes grey.

"Swine!" Osman hissed.

His sunken eyes glittered with the vindictive pleasure that soothed his senses whenever he heaped humiliations on that cowering travesty of a man. Even in that paroxysm of fury the sensation was like balm to his uncontrolled nerves—perhaps it was the very thing that finally turned the tide of his unleashed savagery and began to restore him to reason. For that crawling servile thing that had once been a man was the most permanently soothing monument to Abdul Osman's vanity in the world. Simon Templar, as a helpless prisoner, might supplant him, but until the day came when Osman could look down and spit in the face of that ultimate triumph the degradation of Clements reigned as his supreme achievement.

Less hastily, ten times more malignantly, Osman reached out a hand, grasped his secretary by the nose, and forced him to his knees. He stared at him contemptuously for a moment; then he put a foot in his face and sprawled him over.

"Get up, pig."

Clements obeyed.

"Look at me."

The white man raised his eyes slowly. Abdul Osman saw the red sparks of futile hate glowing in their depths like hot embers, and laughed.

"You know that I always have my revenge, don't you?" His almost perfect English had a sibilant accent, as if a snake had spoken. "How unfortunate it was that my misguided parents should have sent me to an English school! Unpleasant for me, perhaps, but how much more enduringly regrettable for you! I was a dirty nigger then, wasn't I? And it seemed so humorous to you to humiliate me. I trust you look back on those days with satisfaction, Clements?"

The man did not answer.

"It was such a pity that you began to try the needle, and then found you couldn't live without it. And then that you committed that indiscretion which finally put you at my mercy . . . You were so strong and healthy once, weren't you?—so proud and brave! You would never have let me strike you. You would have struck me yourself, like this."

His flat hand smacked the other's face from side to side—once, twice.

"You would like to strike me again, wouldn't you? But then there is always the certainty that you would have to bare your back to my little whip. It's wonderful how hunger for the needle, and the entertainment of my little whip, have curbed your spirits." He was playing with the man now, drugging his disordered vanity again with the sadistic repetition of a scene that he had played hundreds of times and never tired of. "Pah! I've crushed you so much that now you haven't even the courage to kill yourself and end your misery. You're mine, body and soul—the idol of the school fawning on the dirty nigger. Doesn't that reflection please you, Clements?" He was watching the silent man with a shrewdness in his slow malevolence. "You'll be wanting the needle again about now, won't you? I've a good mind to keep you waiting. It will amuse you to have to come crawling round my feet, licking my shoes, pleading, weeping, slobbering—won't it, Clements?"

The secretary licked his lips. It looked for a moment as if at last the smouldering fires in him would flare up to some reply, and Osman waited for it hopefully. And then came voices and footsteps on the deck over their heads, feet clattering down the companion, and the door was opened by a smart uniformed Arab seaman to admit a visitor.

It was Galbraith Stride.

"Did you get him?" he demanded huskily.

There were beads of perspiration on his face, and not all of them were due to the heat of the day. Osman's puffy lips curled at the sight of him.

"No, I didn't," he said shortly. "A fool bungled it. I have no time for fools."

Stride mopped his forehead.

"It's on my nerves, Osman. He's been on the *Claudette*, admitted who he was—who knows what he'll do next? I tell you—"

"You may tell me all you want to in a few minutes," said Osman suavely. "I have some business to attend to first—if you will excuse me." He turned to the seaman. "Ali, send Trape to me."

The Arab touched his forehead and disappeared, and Osman elbowed his secretary aside and helped himself from an inlaid brass cigarette box on the table. All his self-possession had returned, and somehow his heavy tranquillity was more inhuman than his raving anger.

Presently the Arab came back with Trape. Osman gazed at him unwinkingly for some seconds, and then he spoke.

"I have no time for fools," he repeated.

Young Harry Trape was sullen and frightened. The ways of violence were not new to him—he had been in prison three times, and once they would have flogged him with a nine-thonged lash if the doctors had not said he was too weak to endure the punishment. Young Harry had a grievance: he had not only been knocked out by the Saint and tied up in a stuffy sack, but he had been viciously kicked both unknowingly and knowingly by the man he had tried to serve, and he felt he had much to complain about. He had come to the saloon prepared to complain, but the snake-like impassiveness of the unblinking stare that fastened on his face held him mute and strangely terrified.

"You are a fool, Trape," said Osman, almost benevolently, "and I don't think I require your services any longer. Ali will take you back to

St Mary's in the speed-boat. You will give up your room at Tregarthen's, make a parcel of all the cocaine you have and post it to the usual address, and then you will take yourself, your friend, and your luggage back to the speed-boat, which will take you both to Penzance immediately. Your money will be waiting for you in London. You may go."

"Yes, sir," said Trape throatily.

He left the saloon quickly. The seaman was about to follow him, but Osman stayed him with a gesture.

"It will not really be necessary to go to Penzance, Ali," he remarked deliberately, and the man nodded and went out.

Stride's bloodshot eyes stared at the Egyptian.

"My God—you're a cold-blooded devil!" he half-gasped.

Osman chuckled wheezily.

"Oh, no, not cold-blooded, my dear Stride! You ought to know that. Far from it. But a dead fool is a safe fool, and I believe in safety first. But not cold-blooded. There are times when my flesh burns like fire—have I not told you?"

Galbraith Stride shuddered in spite of himself, for he knew what Osman meant.

"I came to see you about that," he said jerkily.

"Ah! You have decided?"

Stride nodded. He sat down at the table, helped himself with nervous fingers from the inlaid cigarette box. The secretary stood by, ignored by both.

It was a strange venue for a peace conference, but that was what it was—and it explained also the terror which had come to Galbraith Stride that afternoon on the sunny deck of his yacht, the terror that had looked at him out of two cold reckless eyes that were as blue as the sea. Each of those two men was a power in an underground world of ugly happenings, though in their personal contact there was no question about which was the dominating personality. Even as Abdul

Osman's tentacles of vice reached from Shanghai to Constantinople, so did Galbraith Stride's stretch from London south to the borders of the Adriatic and out west across the ocean to Rio.

Looking at Abdul Osman, one could build about him just such a mastery, but there was nothing about Galbraith Stride to show the truth. And yet it was true. Somehow, out of the restless cunning that evolved from the cowardice of his ineffectual physique, Stride had built up that subterranean kingdom and held it together, unknown to his step-daughter, unknown to the police, unknown even to the princelings of his noisome empire who communicated with him only through that silent Ramon Almido who passed as Stride's secretary. And thus, with the growth of both their dominions, it had come to a conference that must leave one of them supreme. Abdul Osman's insatiable lust for power dictated it, for Stride would have been content with his own boundaries. And with it, in the first meeting between them, had come to Abdul Osman the knowledge that he was Stride's master, that he need not be generous in treating for terms. The spectacle of Stride's uneasiness was another sop to Osman's pride.

"What a different conclusion there might have been if we had not both simultaneously thought of depositing the same letters with our solicitors!" said Osman reflectively. "To think that if either of us died suddenly there would be left instructions to the police to investigate carefully the alibi of the other! Quite a dramatic handicap, isn't it?"

Stride licked his lips.

"That's the only part of the bargain you've kept," he said. "Why, I've just heard you admit that your men have been landing cocaine here."

"I took the liberty of assuming our agreement to be a foregone conclusion," said Osman smoothly. Then his voice took on a harsher tone. "Stride, there's only one way out for you. For the last two years my agents have been steadily accumulating evidence against you—

evidence which would prove absorbing reading to your good friends at Scotland Yard. That is the possibility for which you were not prepared, and it's too late now for you to think of laying the same trap for me. In another month that evidence can be brought to the point where it would certainly send you to prison for the rest of your life. You see, it was so much easier for me than for the police—they did not know whom to suspect, whereas I knew, and only had to prove it."

Stride had heard that before, and he did not take much notice.

"And so," continued Osman, "I make you the very fine offer of your liberty, and in return for that you retire from business and I marry Miss Laura."

Stride started up.

"That's not what you said!" he blurted. "You said if I . . . if I gave you Laura—you'd retire from Turkey and—"

"I changed my mind," said Osman calmly. "Why should I give? I was foolish. I hold all the cards. I am tired of arguing. As soon as this Simon Templar is on board I wish to leave—the year is getting late, and I can't stand your winters. Why should I make concessions?" He spat—straight to the priceless carpet, an inch from his visitor's polished shoes. "Stride, you were a fool to meet me yourself. If you had dealt with me through your clever Mr Almido I might have had some respect for you. You are not sufficiently important to look at—it shows me too plainly which of us is going to get his own way."

He spoke curtly, and, oddly enough for him, with a lack of apparent conceit that made his speech deadly in its emphasis. And Stride knew that Osman spoke only the truth. Yet, even then, if certain things had not happened . . .

"You are afraid of the Saint, Stride," said Osman, reading the other's thoughts. "You are more afraid of him perhaps than you are of prison. You did not know that he knew you, but now that you know you want nothing more than to run away and hide in some place where he can't find you. Well, you can go. I shouldn't stand in your way, my dear Stride."

The other did not answer. Something had broken in the core of his resistance—a thing which only a psychologist who knew the workings of his mind, and the almost superstitious fear which the name of the Saint could still drive into many consciences, could have understood. He sat huddled in a kind of collapse, and Osman looked at him and chuckled again.

"I shall expect a note to tell me that you agree by ten o'clock tonight. You will send it across by hand—and who could be better employed to deliver it than Miss Laura?"

Galbraith Stride stood up and went out without a word.

6

Simon Templar saw Young Harry Trape and his companion carrying their suit-cases down to the quay and thought they were trying to catch the *Scillonian*, which was scheduled to sail for the mainland at 4:15. He watched their descent rather wistfully, from the hillside where he was walking, for it was his impression that they had got off much too lightly. He was not to know that Abdul Osman had himself decided to dispense with their existence according to the laws of a strictly Oriental code by which the penalty of failure was death, but if he had known, the situation would have appealed to his sense of humour even more than the memory of his recent treatment of Young Harry.

At the same time, their departure solved at least one problem, for it definitely relieved Mr Smithson-Smith of further anxiety about the good name of his hotel.

It was past six o'clock when he came back to the village, for the solution of the mystery of an overloaded basket of towels had suddenly dawned on him, and he had set out to visit a few likely spots on the coast in the hope of finding further evidence. He had failed in that, but he remained convinced that his surmise was right.

"It was an ingenious method of smuggling dope," he told Patricia. "Nobody's thinking about anything like that here—if they see a strange ship loafing around their only suspicion is that it may be another French poacher setting lobster-pots in forbidden waters, and if the boat looked ritzy enough they simply wouldn't think at all. The sea party would dump sacks of it somewhere among the rocks, and the Heavenly Twins would fetch it home bit by bit in their basket without attracting any attention. Then they pack it in a suit-case and take it over to Penzance with their other stuff, and there isn't even a Customs officer to ask if they've got a bottle of scent. Which is probably what they're doing now—I wish we could have arranged a sticky farewell for them."

He had been much too far away to think of an attempt to intercept the evacuation and the idea of telegraphing a warning to the Chief of Police at Penzance did not appeal to him. Simon Templar had no high idea of policemen, particularly provincial ones. And as a matter of fact his mind was taken up with a graver decision than the fate of two unimportant intermediaries.

He walked along from the lifeboat station with the details of his plan filling themselves out in his imagination, and they were just about to turn into Holgate's, the hotel at the other end of the town, when his ruminations were interrupted by a figure in uniform that appeared in his path.

"I've been looking for you, sir," said the Law.

The Law on the Scilly Islands was represented by one Sergeant Hancock, a pensioner of the Coldstream Guards, who must have found his rank a very empty honour, for there were no common constables to salute him. In times of need he could call upon a force of eight specials recruited from among the islanders, but in normal times he had nothing to make him swollen-headed about his position. Nor did he show any signs of ever having suffered from a swollen head—a fact which made him one of the very few officers of the law whom Simon had ever been able to regard as even human. Possibly there was something in the air of the Islands, that same something which makes the native islanders themselves the most friendly and hospitable people one could hope to meet, which had mellowed the character of an ex-sergeant-major to the man who had become not only the head, but also the personal body and complete set of limbs of the Scilly Islands Police, but certainly the Saint liked him. Simon had drunk beer with him, borrowed his fishing line and fished with it, and exchanged so many affable salutes with him that the acquaintance was in danger of becoming an historic one in the Saint's life.

"What is it, Sergeant?" asked the Saint cheerfully. "Have I been seen dropping banana-peel in the streets or pulling faces at the mayor?"

"No, it's nothing like that. I want to know what's been going on up at Tregarthen's."

"Mr Smith has seen you, has he?"

"Yes, he came down and told me about it. I went to have a talk with those two young men but they'd just paid their bill and gone. Then I came looking for you."

Simon offered a cigarette.

"What did Smith tell you?"

"Well sir, he told me that you were having a drink in the bar, and one of those fellows put dope in your beer, and you punched his nose. Then one of them came down and threw the beer away, so there was no evidence, except a fly that Smith couldn't find. And Smith said you said something about Abdul Osman, which he said he thought might be a man who has a yacht over by Tresco."

The Sergeant's pleasant face was puzzledly serious, as well it might be. Such things simply did not happen on his well-conducted island.

Simon lighted his cigarette and thought for a moment. Abdul Osman was too big a fish for the net of a police force consisting of one man, and the only result of any interference from that official quarter would most likely be the unhappy decease of a highly amiable sergeant—a curiosity whom Simon definitely felt should be preserved for the Nation. Also he recalled a story that the Sergeant had told him on their first meeting—a story so hilariously incredible that it surpassed any novelist's wildest flights of fantasy.

A previous holder of the office once arrested a man and took him to the village lock-up only to find that he hadn't the keys of the lock-up with him.

"Stay here while I get my keys," said the worthy upholder of the Law sternly, and that was the last they saw of their criminal.

While Simon did not doubt for a moment that Sergeant Hancock would be incapable of such a magnificent performance as that, his faith did not extend to the ability of a village lockup to keep Abdul Osman inside and his ship load of satellites out.

"That's very nearly what happened, Sergeant," he said easily. "I think their idea was to rob the hotel and get away on the boat that afternoon. Smith wasn't drinking, so they couldn't drug him, but with me out of the way they'd have been two to one, and he wouldn't have stood much chance. They'd been staying in the hotel for a fortnight to get the lie of the land. I just happened to notice what they'd done to my beer."

"But what was that about Abdul Osman?"

"I think Smith can't have heard that properly. He was telling me some story about a man of that name and it must have been on his mind. When I punched this bloke's face he threatened to call the police, and what I said was: 'Ask your pal what he thinks of the idea first.' Smith must have thought I said 'Ask Abdul.'"

The Sergeant's face was gloomy.

"And you just punched his nose and let him get away! Why, if you'd only got hold of me—"

"But Smith did get hold of you."

"Oh yes, he got hold of me after they'd gone. I had to go over and see a man over the other end of the island about paying his rates, and Smith couldn't find me till it was too late. I can't be everywhere at once."

The Saint grinned sympathetically.

"Never mind. Come in here and drown it in drink."

"Well, sir, I don't mind if I do have just one. I don't think I'm supposed to be on duty just this minute."

They went into the bar and found the barman enjoying his evening shave—a peculiarity of his which the Saint had observed before, and which struck Simon as being very nearly the perfect illustration for a philosophy of the Futility of Effort.

They carried their drinks over to the window at the bottom end of the bar, which looked across the harbour. The local boats were coming in to their moorings one by one, with their cargoes of holiday fishing parties. Simon studied them as they came in with a speculative eye.

"Whose boat's that—just coming in?" he asked, and the Sergeant looked out.

"What, that nearest one? That's Harry Barrett's. He's a good boatman if you want to go out for the day."

"No—the other one—just coming round the end of Rat Island."

The Sergeant screwed up his eyes.

"I don't know that one, sir." He turned round. "John, what's the name of that boat out there by the pier?"

The barman came down and looked out.

"That? That one's Lame Frankie's boat—the *Puffin*. Built her himself, he did."

Simon watched the boat all the way in to her mooring and marked its position accurately in his memory. He discarded the idea of Barrett's trim-looking yawl reluctantly—he was likely to have his hands full while he was using the craft he proposed to borrow, and the *Puffin*, though she was too broad in the beam for her length, judged by classic standards of design, looked a trifle more comfortable as a single hander for a busy man. And, in making his choice he noted down the name of Lame Frankie for a highly anonymous reward, for the Saint's illicitly contracted obligations were never left unpaid.

But none of his intentions just then were public property. He held up to the light a glass of gin-and-it of astounding size for which he had been charged the sum of ninepence, and sighed.

"How shall I ever be able to bring myself to pay one and six for a drink about one-eighth the size of this in London again, is more than I know," he murmured contentedly, and improved the shining hour by drinking it down rapidly and calling for another.

He strolled back with Patricia to their modest supper as it was beginning to grow dark. Their meal was just being put on the table.

"You poach a wonderful egg, Mrs Nance," he remarked approvingly, and sank into his chair as the door closed behind that excellent landlady. "Pat, darling, you must wish me *bon appétit*, because I've got a lot to do on these vitamins."

She had not liked to question him before but now she gazed at him resignedly.

"We were going away for a holiday," she reminded him.

"I know," said the Saint. "And we still are—away to the south, where there's sunshine and good wine and tomorrow is also a day. But we came by this roundabout way on a hunch and the hunch was right. There is still a little work for us to do."

He finished his plate without speaking again, poured himself out a cup of coffee, and lighted a cigarette. Then he said, "There's more nonsense talked about capital punishment than anything else, and the sentimentalists who organise petitions for the reprieve of every murderer who's ever sentenced are probably less pernicious than the more conventional humanitarians. Murder, in England anyway, is the most accidental of crimes. A human life is such a fragile thing, it's so easily snuffed out, and dozens of respectable men, without a thought of crime in their heads, have lost control of themselves for one second, and have woken up afterwards to the numbing and irrevocable realisation that they have committed murder, and the penalty is death. There are deliberate murders, but there are other crimes no less deliberate and no less damning. The drug trafficker, the white slaver, the blackmailer—not one of them could ever plead that he acted in uncontrollable passion, or gave way to an instant's temptation, or did it because his wife and children were starving. All of those crimes are too deliberate—need too much capital, too much premeditation, too long to work through from beginning to end. And each of them wrecks human lives less mercifully than a sudden bullet. Why should the death penalty stop where it does? . . . That is justice as we have chosen to see it, and even now I believe that the old days were worthwhile."

He sat and smoked until it was quite dark, and, being the man he was, no detail of the future weighed on his mind. He scribbled industriously on a writing pad, with occasional pauses for thought, and presently Patricia came round behind him to see what he had written.

At the top of the sheet he had roughly pinned the scrap of a report from *The Daily Telegraph*, and panelled it in characteristic slashes of the blue pencil.

" . . . He saw his friend in difficulties," said the Coroner, "and although he could not swim himself he went to his assistance. *He did what any Englishman would have done . . .*"

The blue pencil had scored thickly under the last sentence. And underneath it the Saint was writing:

FLOREAT HARROWVIA !

When Adam fell, because of Eve,

Upon that dreadful day,
He did not own up loud and strong,
And take his licking with a song,
In our good English way:
He had so little chivalry,
He said "The Woman tempted me,"
And tried to hide away.

(Chorus)

But in the blaze of brighter days
Britannia yet shall rule,
While English Sportsmen worship God
And bend their bottoms to the rod
For the Honour of the School!

When Joshua strafed Jericho
(N.B.—another Jew)
He did not risk his precious gore
Or take a sporting chance in war
As English soldiers do:
He marched his bandsmen round the walls
And knocked it down with bugle calls—
A trick that is tabu.

(Chorus)

When Roland, at the gates of Spain,
Died beside Oliver,
He must have found it rather hard
To stand his ground and keep the guard,

233

Being a foreigner:
So we can only think he went
There by some kind of accident,
   Or as an arbiter.

(Chorus)

When Louis faced the guillotine,
   That calm the people saw
Flinched to a sickly pallor when
He knew he was an alien,
   A Breed without the Law;
Where one of truly British phlegm,
Of course, would have leapt down at them
   And socked them on the jaw.

(Chorus)

"Is all that necessary?" asked Patricia with a smile.

"Of course it is," said the Saint. "Because I've got an appointment with one kind of excrescence, must I forget all the others? God in Heaven, while there's still a supply of smug fools for me to tear in pieces I shall have everything to live for . . . There are about five hundred and fifty more verses to that song, embracing everything from the massacre of Garigliano, down through Christopher Columbus and Marco Polo to the last Czar of Russia, which I may write some day. I think it will end like this—"

He wrote again, rapidly:

But in our stately tolerance
   We condescend to see

That heroes whose names end in -vitch
Are striving to be something which
We know they cannot be,
But, sweating hard, they make a good
Attempt to do what Britons would
Achieve instinctively.

(Chorus)

So let's give praise through all our days,
Again and yet again,
That we do not eat sauerkraut,
That some storks knew their way about,
And made us Englishmen!

"I can never finish my best songs—my gorge rises too rapidly," said the Saint, and then he looked at his watch, and stood up, stretching himself with his gay smile. "Pat, I must be going. Wish me luck."

She kissed him quickly, and then he was gone, with the cavalier wave of his hand that she knew so well. All the old ageless Saint went with him, that fighting troubadour whom he chose to be who could always find time to turn aside in an adventure to shape one of those wild satires that came from him with such a biting sincerity. In some way he left her happier for that touch of typical bravado.

Her emotion was not shared by Galbraith Stride.

Something had come into the life of that successful man that he felt curiously impotent to fight against, something that had stricken him with a more savage shock because it was the one thing that he had never prepared himself for. It had the inexorable march of a machine. It left him unable to think clearly, with a sense of physical helplessness as if he had been worn down overnight by a fierce fever, struggling with the fore-knowledge of defeat against a kind of paralysis of panic. And that thing was the name of the Saint.

He was a silent man at dinner that night. He knew that Abdul Osman had crushed and beaten him with an ease that seemed fantastically ridiculous, and the knowledge hypnotised him into a sort of horrible nightmare. And yet at the same time he knew that he might still have been fighting, calling on all the resources of guile and duplicity that had brought him to the power that was being stripped from him, if it had not been for the words that had stunned his ears early that afternoon. He was that strange psychological freak, a criminal possessed of an imagination that amounted almost to mania, and when Osman had told him that the Saint was still at large, an overstrained bulwark on the borders of his reason seemed to have crashed inwards. He was still fighting for all he could hope to save from the disaster, but it was a dumb stubborn fight without vitality.

He sent for Laura Berwick at nine o'clock. Her slender young body looked particularly beautiful in the black evening gown she was wearing; in some way its cool sweetness was framed in that sombre setting with an effect that was pulse-quickeningly radiant from the contrast. To do him justice, Galbraith Stride felt a momentary twinge of remorse as he saw her.

"My dear, I want you to take a note over to Mr Osman. It's rather important, and I'd feel relieved if you delivered it yourself."

He had been drinking, but the whisky that reeked on his breath had thickened his voice without making him drunk. It served the purpose of nipping that twinge of remorse in the bud, before he had time to forget his own danger.

"Couldn't one of the crew go?" she asked, in some surprise.

"I'm afraid there are reasons why they can't," he said. "They . . . er . . . hum . . . I may be able to explain later. A matter of business. It's vitally important—"

"But what about Mr Almido?"

"Mr Almido," said Stride, "is a fool. Between ourselves, I don't trust him. Some funny things have been happening to my accounts lately. No, my dear, you must do this for me. I'd go myself, only I . . . I'm not feeling very well. You can take the motor-boat."

He was staring at her with the fixed and glassy eyes of semi-intoxication—she could see that—but there was something besides alcohol in his stare that frightened her. His excuses for requiring her to go over in person seemed absurd, and yet it seemed equally absurd to imagine that there could be anything serious behind them. She was fond of him, in a purely conventional way—chiefly because he was the only relative she had had since she was six years old. She knew nothing of his business, but in his remotely fussy way he had been kind to her.

"All right—I'll go for you. When do you want it done?"

"At once." He pressed a sealed envelope into her hand, and she felt that his own hand was hot and sticky. "Run along right away, will you?"

"Right-ho," she said, and wondered, as she went to the door, why her own words rang in her ears without a trace of the artificial cheerfulness that she had tried to put into them.

She left him sitting at the table, squinting after her with the same glazed stare, and went up on deck to find Toby Halidom.

"Daddy wants me to go over to the *Luxor* and deliver a note," she said, and he was naturally perplexed.

"Why shouldn't one of the crew go—or that Dago secretary with the Marcel wave?"

"I don't know, Toby." Out under the stars, the vague impressions she had received in the saloon seemed even more absurd. "He was rather funny about it, but he seemed to want it particularly badly, so I said I'd go."

"Probably suffering from an attack of liver," hazarded Toby heartily. "All the same, he ought to know better than to ask you to pay calls on a reptile like that at this hour of the night. I'd better come with you, old thing—I don't like you to go and see that ugly nigger alone."

It was not Toby Halidom's fault that he had been brought up to that inscrutable system of English thought in which all coloured men are niggers unless they happen also to be county cricketers, but on this occasion at least his apprehensions were destined to be fully justified. They had both met Abdul Osman once before during their stay, and Laura knew that her fiancé had shared her instinctive revulsion. She felt relieved that he had spontaneously offered to go with her.

"I'd be glad if you would come, Toby."

Galbraith Stride heard the motor-boat chugging away from the side, and listened to it till the sound died away. Then he went over and pressed a bell in the panelling. It was answered by the saturnine Mr Almido.

"We shall be leaving at ten," he said, and his secretary was pardonably surprised.

"Why, sir, I thought—"

"Never mind what you thought," said Stride thickly. "Tell the captain."

Almido retired, and Stride got up and began to pace the saloon. The die was cast. He had abdicated to Abdul Osman. He had saved his liberty—perhaps he could even save himself from the Saint. The reaction was starting to take hold of him like a powerful drug, spurring him with a febrile exhilaration and scouring an unnatural brightness into the glaze of his eyes. He had no compunction about what he had done. Laura Berwick was not his own flesh and blood—that would have been his only excuse, if he had bothered to make any. The thought of her fate had ceased to trouble him. It counted for nothing beside his own safety. For a brief space he even regretted the feebleness of his surrender—wondered if a card like Laura could not have been played to far better effect . . .

It was only another twist in the imponderable thread that had begun to weave itself when the boom of the *Claudette's* dinghy had swung over against Laura Berwick's head that morning, but the twist was a short one. For Fate, masking behind the name which Galbraith Stride feared more than any other name in the world, had taken a full hand in the game that night.

There were two doors into the saloon. One of them opened into a microscopic vestibule, from which a broad companion gave access to the deck and an alley-way led out to other cabins and the crew's quarters forward; the other opened into Stride's own stateroom. In his restless pacing of the saloon, Stride had his back turned to the second door when he heard a sharp swish and thud behind him. He jerked round, raw-nerved and startled, and then he saw what had caused the sound, and his heart missed a beat.

Standing straight out from the polished woodwork of the door was a long thin-bladed knife with a hilt of exquisitely carved ivory, still quivering from the force of the impact that had driven it home.

His lungs seemed to freeze achingly against the walls of his chest, and a parching dryness came into his throat that filled him with a presentiment that if he released the scream which was struggling for outlet just below his wishbone it could only have materialised in a thin croaking whisper. The hand that dragged the automatic from his pocket was shaking so much that he almost dropped it. The sudden appearance of that quivering knife was uncanny, supernatural. The opposite door had been closed all the time, for he had been pacing towards it when the thing happened; the ports and skylights also were fastened. From the angle at which it had driven into the door it should have flashed past his face, barely missing him as he walked, but he had not seen it.

If he had been in any state in which he could think coherently, he might have hit on the explanation in a few moments, but he was not in that state. It never occurred to him that the door behind him might have been opened, the knife driven home, and the door rapidly and silently closed again, with just that very object of misleading his attention which it had achieved.

Which was indubitably very foolish of Mr Galbraith Stride.

Filled with the foreboding that a second attack would almost instantly follow the first unsuccessful one, trembling in the grip of a cold funk that turned his belly to water, he backed slowly and shakily towards the door where the knife had struck, facing in the direction from which he believed the danger threatened. Curiously enough his only idea was that Abdul Osman had decided to take no chance on his regretting his bargain, and had sent one of his men stealthily to eliminate that possibility. If he had thought of anything else, it is possible that the scream which he ached to utter would not have been suppressed.

Back . . . back . . . three paces, four paces . . . And then suddenly he saw the bulkheads on each side of him, and realised with an eerie thrill of horror that he was actually passing through them—that the door which should have come up against his back had been opened noiselessly behind him, and he was stepping backwards over the threshold.

He opened his mouth to cry out, turning his head as he did so, but the cry rattled voicelessly in his throat. A brown shirt-sleeved arm whipped round his neck from behind and strangled him in the crook of its elbow, while fingers like bars of steel fastened on his wrist just behind the gun. His head was dragged back so that he looked up into the inverted vision of twin blue eyes that were as clear and cold as frozen ultramarines, and then the intruder's mouth spoke against his ear.

"Come and pay calls with me, Galbraith," he heard, and then he fainted.

7

Abdul Osman had also been drinking, but with him it had been almost a festive rite. He had put on a dinner suit, with a red tarboosh, and his broad soft stomach, swelling out under the sloping expanse of a snowy shirt-front, gave him the appearance of a flabby pyramid walking about on legs, as if a bloated frog had been dressed up in European clothes. His wide sallow face was freshly shaved, and had a slightly greasy look around the chin. Although he wore Western clothes, cut by the best tailors in London, the saloon of his yacht, in which he was walking about, was decorated entirely in the Oriental style, which was the only one in which he felt truly comfortable. The rugs on the floor were Bokhara and Shiraz, virtually priceless; the tables ebony inlaid with mother-of-pearl; the couches low, covered with dark silk brocades, heavily strewn with cushions. Even the prosaic portholes were framed with embroidered hangings and barred with iron grilles so that they should not clash with the atmosphere and the dim concealed light left corners full of shadows. Osman, in his dinner jacket and white starched shirt-front, fitted into those surroundings with a paradoxical effect, like an ardent nudist clinging to his straw hat and *pince-nez*, but he was incapable of perceiving the incongruity.

He was preening himself before a mirror, a half-emptied glass in one hand, the other smoothing an imperceptible crease out of his bow tie, a thin oval cigarette smouldering between his lips, when he heard the approaching sputter of a motor launch. He listened in immobile expectancy, and heard the engine cut off and the sound of voices. Then the Arab seaman, Ali, knocked on the door and opened it, and Laura Berwick stood in the entrance.

Abdul Osman saw her in the mirror, from which he had not moved, and for a second or two he did not stir. His veins raced with the sudden concrete knowledge of triumph. Cold-blooded? The corners of his mouth lifted fractionally, wrinkling up his eyes. At their very first meeting, the formal touch of her hand had filled him with a hunger like raging furnaces; now seeing her gloriously-modelled face and shoulders standing out brilliantly pale in the dark doorway, his heart pounded molten flame through his body.

He turned slowly, spreading out one arm in a grandiose gesture.

"So you have come—my beautiful white rose!"

Laura Berwick smiled hesitantly. The room was full of the peculiarly dry choky scent of sandalwood. Everything in her recoiled in disgust from its ornately exotic gloom. It seemed unhealthy, suffocating, heavy with an aura of horribly secret indulgence, like the slack puffy body of the man who was feeding his eyes on her. She was glad that Toby had come with her—his clear-cut Spartan cleanness was like an antiseptic.

"Mr Stride asked me to bring a note over to you," she said.

He held out his hand, without taking his eyes from her face. Unhurriedly he ripped open the envelope—it contained nothing but a blank sheet of paper. Deliberately he tore it into four pieces, and laid them on a table.

"Perhaps," he said, "it was more important that a note should bring you over to me."

Then for the first time he saw Toby Halidom, and his face changed.

"What are you doing here?" he inquired coldly.

The young man was faintly taken aback.

"I just buzzed over with Miss Berwick," he said. "Thought she might like some company, and all that."

"You may go."

There was an acid, drawling incisiveness in Osman's voice that was too dispassionate to be rude. It staggered Halidom with the half-sensed menace of it.

"I asked Mr Halidom to come with me," said Laura, striving to keep a sudden breathlessness out of her voice. "We shall be going back together."

"Did . . . er . . . your stepfather suggest that arrangement?"

"No, Toby just thought he'd come."

"Really!" Osman laughed softly, an almost inaudible chuckle that made the girl shiver unaccountably. "Really!" He turned away, a movement that came after his temporary motionlessness with a force that was subtly sinister. "Really!" The joke seemed to amuse him. He strolled away down the room, the cigarette smouldering between his fingers, and turned again at a place where the dim lights left him almost in darkness. The cigarette-end glowed like a hot ruby against the grey smudge of his shirt-front in the gloom—they could not see his thick fingers touching bells that had men always waiting to answer them. "How very romantic, my dear Halidom! The perfect knight-errant!"

Toby Halidom flushed dully at the sneer. Something in the atmosphere of the interview was getting under his skin, in spite of the healthy unimaginativeness of his instincts.

"Well, Laura, let's be getting along," he said, and heard the note of strain in his own assumed heartiness.

Osman's ghostly chuckle whispered again out of the shadows, but he said nothing. Halidom turned abruptly to the door, opened it, and stopped dead. There were three of Osman's crew outside, crowded impassively across the opening.

Toby faced the Egyptian with clenched fists.

"What's the idea, Osman?" he demanded bluntly.

Abdul moved an inch or two from his position, so that his broad fleshy face stood out like a disembodied mask of evil under one of the rose-shaded light globes.

"The idea, Halidom, is that Laura is staying here with me—and you are not."

"You lousy nigger—"

Halidom leapt at the mask like a young tiger-cat, but he was stopped short in less than a foot. Sinewy brown arms caught his arms from behind, twisted and pinioned them expertly.

Osman stepped forward slowly.

"Did you say something, Halidom?"

"I called you a lousy nigger," retorted Toby defiantly. "You heard me all right. Shall I say it again?"

"Do."

Osman's voice was sleek, but his hands were shaking. His face had gone a dead white, save only for the scarred red circles on his cheeks. Toby swallowed, and flung up his head.

"You foul slimy—"

Osman's fist smacked the last word back into his teeth.

"If you had remembered your manners, Halidom, your fate might have been very different," he said, and it was obvious that he was only controlling himself momentarily, by an effort of will that brought beads of perspiration on to the whiteness of his forehead. "But that is one word you cannot use. There was another man who used it many years ago—perhaps you would like to see him?"

He spoke to Ali purringly, in Arabic, and the man disappeared. Halidom was struggling like a maniac.

"You can't get away with this, you ugly swine—"

"No?"

Osman struck him again, and then, after a moment's pause, deliberately spat in his face. Laura cried out and flung herself forward, but one of the men caught her instantly. Osman sauntered over to her and tilted up her chin in his bloated hands.

"You're a spitfire too, are you, my dear? That makes it all the more interesting. I'm good at training spitfires. In a moment I'll show you one of my tamed ones. You shall see me tame Halidom in the same way—and you too."

He looked round as the seamen returned with his secretary. Clements was in a pitiful state—Osman had withheld the needle from him all that day, as he had threatened to do, and the slavering creature that tottered into the room made even Halidom's blood run cold.

The man fell on his knees at Osman's feet, slobbering and moaning unintelligibly, and Osman caught him by the hair and dragged him upright.

"Do you see this, Halidom? This is a man who used to call me a dirty nigger. Once upon a time he was just like you—strong, straight, insolent. He feared nothing, and despised me because I wasn't another stupid Englishman like himself. But then, one day, someone introduced him to the needle—the little prick that brings so much courage and cleverness for a while. Have you ever tried it, Halidom? You haven't even thought of it. You've been too busy playing cricket and being called a fine fellow because you could play it well. But you will try it. Oh, no, not voluntarily perhaps—but the effects will be just the same. You will feel big, strong, clever, a fine fellow, until the drug wears off, and then you will feel very tired. Then I shall give you some more, and again you will feel fine and big and strong. And so we shall go on; you will want a little more each time, but I shall give you just the right amount, until"—in a sudden spasm of savagery he shook Clements by the handful of hair that he was still holding—"until you are bigger and stronger than ever—a finer fellow than you have ever been—like this thing here!"

He thrust the man away, but Clements was back as soon as he had recovered his balance, clutching Osman's hand, kissing it, fawning over it in a trembling abjectness that was nauseating.

"That will be pleasant for you, Halidom, won't it?"

Toby was staring at Clements with an incredulous loathing that turned his stomach sick.

"You filthy swine—"

"I have found, Halidom," said Osman, staring at him steadily, "that the needle is an excellent help for taming your kind. But my little whip also does its share—especially in the beginning when there are moments of open rebellion. Would you like to see that as well?"

He touched a concealed spring, and a section of the panelling sprang open. Clements darted forward as he saw it, but Osman pushed the enfeebled body away easily with one hand and sent it sprawling. Inside the cupboard that was disclosed they could see a couple of hypodermic syringes set in gleaming nickelled racks, with a row of tiny glass phials beside them, but Osman left those alone. He took out a short leather whip, so thick at the base that it was difficult to see where it joined the handle, and tapering to a point in which there was a thin hard knot.

"An excellent instrument," Osman said, "which has helped to drive a proper sense of respect into the man you see."

He ran the lash through his fingers thoughtfully, gazing down at the grovelling creature by his feet. Something in the sight of that last triumph of his, that living completeness of humiliation, seemed to snap the thread of his gloating self-control. With his thick lips twisting back wolfishly, he leapt at Halidom and slashed twice at his face; then he turned and dragged Clements up again, holding him pinned against the wall with a hand grasping his throat.

"Look at them, Clements!" he screamed. "Look at them!" He forced the man's livid face round towards Toby and Laura. "Can you see them—or are you too hungry for the needle? They're white—white—the colour you were so proud of! And you're not ashamed, are you? I've thrashed you often enough before my blacks—you're used to that—but how do you like your own people to see what you've sunk to? Look at them, I tell you.

"A white man and a white girl—staring at you—despising you—and even that doesn't give you enough self-respect to stand up for yourself. Bah!"

He stepped back and sent the whip hissing about the man's thin shoulders, and then he came close to Halidom again.

"And that," he said hoarsely, "that is what you will be like, Halidom."

His mouth was drooling at the corners, his fingers twitching with the intensity of his passion. Toby looked him in the eyes.

"You'll never get away with this," he said, as quietly as he could. "Stride knows we're here, and as soon as he gets worried about Laura—"

Abdul Osman laughed harshly.

"My dear Halidom, you're mistaken. Stride sent Laura to me—to stay! He did not send you, but I imagine your disappearance will be a relief to him—if you had been left on his hands he might not have known what to do with you. By this time he is making his preparations to leave."

"I don't believe it!" cried the girl. "Toby . . . it can't be true . . . he's lying—"

Osman looked at her.

"It doesn't matter to me what you believe," he said silkily. "Doubtless you will be convinced in course of time."

"It's a lie!" she protested again, but a chill fear had closed on her heart. "He'd go straight to the police—"

"The police?" Osman's sinister chuckle whispered through the room. "They would be delighted to see him. You little fool! Didn't you know where his money came from? Didn't you know that all his life he's done nothing but trade in women and drugs—that I hold enough evidence to send him to prison for twenty years? You, my dear Laura, are the price of his liberty: you and . . . er . . . his retirement from business. A price that he was glad to offer, and that I was very happy to accept."

She could not think properly, could not comprehend the whole hideous significance of what he was saying. She could not believe it, and yet from the manner in which he said it, either it must be true or he must be mad. And neither alternative opened out a gleam of hope. But she remembered the strangeness that she had seen in Galbraith Stride's eyes when he insisted that she must deliver his message herself and she was frozen with dread before that unspeakable explanation.

Beside her, Toby Halidom was struggling again in a blind fury of helplessness, and Osman looked at him again.

"I shall commence your treatment very soon, my friend," he said, and then he spoke again to Ali. "Take him away and bind him carefully—I shall ring when I wish to see him again."

Almost before he could speak Halidom was hustled out of the room, with the girl's wild pitiful crying ringing in his ears. Rough brown hands forced him down a dark alley-way, tightened ropes round his wrists and ankles, and hurled him into an evil-smelling unlighted cabin. He heard the door locked on the outside, and was alone with a despair such as he had never dreamed of in his life, a despair haunted with visions that verged on sheer shrieking madness. There was only one hope left for him—a hope so small that it was almost worse than no hope at all. They had not troubled to search him, and there was a penknife in his pocket. If he could reach that, saw at the ropes on his wrist . . . then there would still be the locked door, and a hostile crew to break through unarmed . . . But he was trying to get at that knife, with strange futile tears burning under his eyelids.

Laura Berwick thought that her reason would break. The last of the swarthy seamen had released her and gone out with Toby—there was no one in the saloon but herself and Abdul Osman, and that ghastly relic of a man cowering in a corner and watching Osman's movements with blubbering hate-filled eyes. Osman did not even seem to be aware of his existence—perhaps he had grown so used to having that thing of his own creation with him that he took no more notice of him than if he had been a dog, or perhaps in the foul depths of his mind there was some spawning idea of heaping humiliation on humiliation both for the girl and his beaten slave. He edged towards her unsteadily, his glittering eyes leering with unutterable things, and she retreated from him as she would have done before a snake, until her back was to the wall and she could retreat no farther.

"Come to me, beautiful white rose!"

His arms reached out for her. She tried to slip sideways away from their clawing grasp, keeping her eyes out of sheer terror from looking full into that puffed lecherous face, but he caught her arm and held it with a strength greater than her own. She was drawn irresistibly into his hot embrace—she felt the horrible softness of his paunch against her firm young flesh, and shuddered until mists swam before her eyes. She could not possibly endure it much longer. Her senses reeled and she seemed to have lost all her strength . . .

And then, as his greedy lips found her face, her brain went out at last into merciful blackness, and she heard the shot that struck him down only as a dim part of her dream.

8

Simon Templar slammed the door of the glory hole forward, twisted the key, and snapped it off short in the lock. He heard a babel of shouts, and jabbering in heathen tongues break out behind it, and grinned gently. So far as he had been able to discover in a lightning reconnaissance, practically the whole of Osman's crew was congregated up there in the fo'c'sle; he had already battened down the hatch over their heads, and it would take them nothing less than an hour to break out. It was the moment for a speed of action that could be outdistanced by nothing less nimble than a Morality Squad discovering new vices to suppress—that speed of decision and performance in which the Saint had no equal. With the stillness of the ship still freshly bruised by the sharp thud of that single shot, it was a time when committee meetings and general philosophy had to take second place.

He raced down the alley-way towards the second door under which he had seen a strip of light; it was thrown open as he reached it, and an olive-skinned man in uniform, with his shirt unbuttoned, stared into his face from a range of twelve inches. In the cabin behind him, two others, apparently fellow officers, were frozen statuesquely around a table littered with cards. Just for the sharp etched half of a second there was an utter immobility and then Simon's fist crashed into the man's face and sent him staggering. In another second that door also was locked, and the key broken. Simon had located only one other danger point, and that was a few steps further down the passage. As he opened the door he saw that it was the galley, and the explanation of the light he had seen was provided by a coal-black Kano boy who was placidly peeling potatoes and humming one of his own weird melodies. The song died away in an abrupt minor as the Kano boy looked up at him with rolling eyes: Simon saluted him cheerfully, and turned the third key on the safe side of the door.

Then he went aft to the saloon, and as he went he saw another door hanging drunkenly open on its mutilated hinges.

Toby Halidom was pillowing Laura's head on one arm, babbling silly incoherent things to her. His other hand covered the doorway with the automatic that had killed Osman, and for one second Simon felt nearer death than he cared to stand at any time.

"Put that down, you ass," he said, and then Toby recognised him, and lowered the gun slowly.

"What are you doing here?"

"Getting you out of trouble," said the Saint briskly. "You needn't worry—the crew won't be interfering yet. I've just locked them up to keep them out of mischief."

His gaze swept comprehensively round the room—over the body of Abdul Osman, who lay stretched out on his back, half underneath a table that he had clutched at and brought down with him in his fall, with a slowly widening red stain on his white shirt-front; over the unconscious figure of Galbraith Stride; over the enslaved secretary, Clements, who sat without movement on one of the couches, his face hidden in his hands, with an empty hypodermic syringe lying where it had fallen on the dark tapestry beside him . . . He reached out and took the automatic from Halidom's unresisting fingers.

"I don't care if I hang for it!" said the young man hysterically. "He deserved everything he got."

Simon's eyebrows went up through one slow half-centimetre.

"If you hang for it?" he repeated.

"Yes. They can do what they like. I killed him—the swine. I shot him—"

The Saint's smile, that quirk of the lips which could be so gay, so reckless, so mocking, so debonair, so icily insolent, so maddeningly seraphic, as his mood willed it, touched his mouth and eyes with a rare gentleness that transformed him. A strange look, almost of tenderness, touched the chiselled lines of that mad buccaneering face.

"Hang you, Toby?" he said softly. "I don't think they'll do that."

The young man scarcely heard him. For at that moment Laura's eyes opened full of the horror of the last moment of consciousness, and saw the face of the young man bending over her with a queer little choking sob.

"Toby!"

She clung to him, raising herself against his shoulder, still wild-eyed with lingering nightmares, and then she shrank back as she saw Abdul Osman.

"Toby! Did you—"

"It's all right, darling," said Halidom huskily. "He won't trouble us again."

Then the Saint's hands touched each of their shoulders.

"I don't think you need to stay here," he said quietly.

He led them out on to the deck, out into the night air that was cool and fresh with the enduring sweetness of the sea. The motor-boat in which they had come was still moored at the bottom of the gangway, but now the *Puffin* was made fast behind it, with its spread sails stirring like the wings of a grey ghost against the dark water. Between them they helped the girl down to the motor-boat, and Simon sat on the half-deck and gazed aft to the seats where the other two had settled themselves. A match flared at the end of his cigarette.

"Will you try and listen to me?" he said in the same quiet tone. "I know what you've been through tonight, because I was listening most of the time. There were some things I had to know before I moved—and then, when the time came for me to interfere, there wasn't much for me to do. I did what I could, and no one will stop you going back to the *Claudette*."

The hand with a cigarette moved towards the *Luxor's* side in a faint gesture.

"A man was killed there tonight. I've never seen any good reason for buttering up a bad name just because it's a dead one. As Toby said, he deserved everything he got—maybe more. He was a man whose money had been wrung farthing by farthing out of the ruin and degradation of more human lives than either of you can imagine. He was a man who'll leave the world a little cleaner for being dead.

"But in the eyes of the law he was murdered. In the eyes of the law he was a citizen who had every right to live, who could have called for policemen paid for by every citizen to protect him if he'd ever been threatened, who could have been guiltless for ever in the eyes of the law until his crimes could have been proved according to the niggling rules of evidence to twelve bamboozled half-wits by a parade of blathering lawyers. And the man who killed him will be sentenced to death according to the law.

"That man was Galbraith Stride."

They were staring at him, intent and motionless.

"I know what you thought, Toby," said the Saint. "You burst into the saloon with murder in your heart, and saw Osman dead, and Laura with the gun close to her hand. You could only think for the moment that she had done it, and you made a rather foolish and rather splendid confession to me with some wild idea of shielding her. If I had any medals hung around me I'd give you one. But you certainly weren't in your right mind, because it never occurred to you to ask what Stride was doing there, or where Laura found the gun.

"Laura, I don't want to make it any harder for you, but there is one thing you must know. Every word that Osman told you was true. Galbraith Stride himself was just such a man as Osman. He has never been such a power for evil, perhaps, but that's only because he wasn't big enough. He was certainly no better. Their trades were the same, and they met here to divide their kingdoms. Osman won the division because he was just a shade more unscrupulous, and Stride sent you to him in accordance with their bargain.

"You might like to think that Stride repented at the last moment and came over to try and save you, but I'm afraid even that isn't true. He killed Osman for a much more sordid reason, which the police will hear about in due time."

Even in the darkness he could see their eyes fixed on him. It was Laura Berwick who spoke for them both.

"Who are you?" she asked, and Simon was silent only for a second.

"I am Simon Templar, known as the Saint—you may have heard of me. I am my own law, and I have sentenced many men who were lesser pestilences than Abdul Osman or Galbraith Stride . . . Oh, I know what you're thinking. The police will also think it for a little while. I did come here tonight to kill Abdul Osman, but I wasn't quick enough."

He stood up, and swung himself lightly back on to the gangway. His deft fingers cast off the painter and tossed it into the boat, and without another word he went up to the deck and down again to the saloon.

They sentenced Galbraith Stride for the murder of Abdul Osman on the first day of November, just over a month after these events had been recorded, after a trial that lasted four days.

One of the documents that played a considerable part in bringing the jury to their verdict was a sealed letter that was produced by a London solicitor at the inquest. It was addressed in Abdul Osman's own heavy sprawling calligraphy:

> *To the Coroner: to be handed to him in the event of my*
> *death in suspicious circumstances within the next three*
> *months.*

Inside was a comprehensive survey of Galbraith Stride's illicit activities that made the police open their eyes. It was typewritten, but the concluding paragraph was in Osman's own handwriting.

> *This is written in the expectation of a meeting between*
> *Stride and myself at which our respective spheres of influence*
> *are to be agreed on and mutually limited. If any "accident"*
> *should happen to me during this conference, therefore, the*
> *man responsible will certainly be Galbraith Stride, whom*
> *I should only expect to violate our truce as he has violated*
> *every other bargain he has ever made.*

> *Abdul Osman*

The defence made a valiant effort to save their case by making great play with the fact that the notorious Simon Templar was not only in the district, but was actually on board the *Luxor* when the murder was committed, but the judge promptly repressed all questions that were not directly concerned with the circumstances of the murder.

"The police," he said, "have charged Galbraith Stride with the murder, and I cannot have alternative murderers dragged in at this stage of the proceedings. We are here to decide whether the prisoner, Galbraith Stride, is guilty or not guilty, and if he should eventually be found not guilty it will be open to the police to bring charges against such other persons as they think fit."

There was also, somewhat inconsistently, an attempt on the part of the defence to represent their client as a repentant hero hastening to rescue his step-daughter from her fate. The case for the prosecution lasted two days, and this happened when the Crown's position was rapidly becoming unassailable. And then Clements was called, and that finished it.

He was a very different man from the whimpering wreck who had suffered all the indignities that Osman's warped brain could think of to heap upon him. From the moment of Osman's death he had become free of the supplies of cocaine that were stocked in that concealed cupboard in the saloon: he had used them liberally to maintain himself in the normal state that he would never be able to return to again without the help of drugs, keeping their existence secret until the case was transferred to the mainland and he could secure proper treatment. But there was no treatment that could give him back the flame of life, and so the police surgeon told him.

"Honestly, Clements, if I'd been told that a man could develop the resistance to the stuff that you've got, so that he would require the doses that you require to keep him normal, without killing himself, I shouldn't have believed it. You must have had the constitution of an ox before you started that . . . that—"

"Folly?" queried Clements with a flicker of expression passing over his wasted features. "Yes, I used to be pretty strong, once."

"There's no cure for what you've got," said the doctor bluntly; for he was still a young man, an old Rugger blue, and some of the things that he saw in his practice hurt him.

But Clements only smiled. He knew that the poisons they were pumping into him six times a day to keep him human would kill him within a matter of weeks, but he could not have lasted much longer anyway. And he had one thing to finish before he died.

He went into the witness-box steady-nerved, with his head erect and the sparkle of cocaine in his eyes. The needle that the young doctor had rammed into his arm half an hour before had done that, but that was not in evidence. They knew he was a cocaine addict of course— he told them the whole story of his association with Abdul Osman, without sparing himself. The defence remembered this when their turn came to cross-examine.

"In view of these sufferings which you endured at the hands of the dead man," counsel put it to him, "didn't you ever feel you would like to kill him?"

"Often," said Clements calmly. "But that would have cut off my supplies of the drug."

"Wouldn't it be quite conceivable, then," counsel continued, persuasively, "that if you had killed him you would be particularly anxious to keep yourself out of the hands of the police at any cost?"

Just for that moment the witness's eyes flashed.

"You'd better ask the doctor," he said. "He'll tell you that I shall probably be dead in a couple of months anyway. Why should I waste my last days of life coming here to tell you lies? It would make no difference to me if you sentenced me to death today."

Counsel consulted his notes.

"You had never met Galbraith Stride before?"

"Never."

Then came the attempt to represent the killing as an act in the defence of a girl's honour.

"I have told the court already," said Clements with that terribly patient calm of a man for whom time has no more meaning, which somehow set him apart from the reproof that would immediately have descended upon any ordinary witness who attempted to make a speech from the box, "that nothing of the sort was suggested. Miss Berwick had fainted, and during the time that she was being attacked I was only occupied with taking advantage of the confusion to get at Osman's supply of cocaine. I cannot make any excuses for that—no one who has been spared that craving can understand how it overrules all other considerations until it has been satisfied. Deprived of it, I was not a man—I was a hungry animal. I went to the cabinet and gave myself an injection and sat down to allow the drug time to take effect. When I looked up Galbraith Stride was there. He had a pistol in his hand, and he appeared to have been drinking. He said, 'Wait a minute, Osman. She's worth more than that. I'm damned if I'll let you have her and get rid of me as well. You can make another choice. If you take her, we'll divide things differently.' Osman flew into a rage and tried to hit him. Stride fired, and Osman fell. I thought Stride was going to fire again, and I caught hold of the nearest weapon I could find—a brass vase— and hit him with it. I hadn't much strength, but luckily it struck him on the chin and knocked him out."

"And it was you who went over to St Mary's and informed Sergeant Hancock what had happened?"

"Yes."

"On your own initiative?"

"Entirely."

"I suggest that Templar said 'Look here, Osman's dead, and there's no need for us to get into trouble. Let's go over to Sergeant Hancock and tell him that Stride did it.'"

"That is absurd."

"You remember the statement that Stride made to Sergeant Hancock when he was arrested?"

"Fairly well."

"You will recall, perhaps, that Stride described how he was attacked in his cabin on the *Claudette* by this man Templar, and that significant mention of a knife that was alleged to have been thrown into a door. Did you hear Sergeant Hancock give evidence that he examined the door in the saloon of the *Claudette*, and found the mark of a knife having been driven deeply into it?"

"Yes."

"How would you account for that?"

"If you ask me I should say that a man like Stride might well have foreseen the possibility of accidents, and he could easily have prepared that mark to substantiate his story in case of trouble."

It was on this point that the greatest weakness of the case for the prosecution seemed to rest. Simon Templar was recalled before the end, and his evidence re-examined.

"You have admitted that you went out to the *Luxor* on the night in question with the intention of assaulting Osman?"

"I've never denied it," said the Saint.

"Why, if you were so anxious to take the law into your own hands, did you confine your attentions to the deceased?"

"Because I'd heard of him, and I hadn't heard of Stride. Mr Smithson-Smith told me about Osman—that's already been given in evidence."

"And you," said counsel, with deliberate irony, "were immediately filled with such a passion for justice that you couldn't sleep until you had thrashed this monster that Osman was represented to you to be?"

"I thought it would be rather a rag," said the Saint, with a perfectly straight face.

"It has been suggested that you were the man who branded Osman five years ago—was that also intended to be rather a rag?"

"I never met the man before in my life."

"You have heard Galbraith Stride say that you told him that you had done that?"

"He must be dotty," said the Saint—a reply that earned him a three-minute lecture from the learned judge.

In his closing speech, the counsel for the Crown suggested that the difficulty might not be so great as it appeared.

"In this case," he said, "the only discrepancies which you need to take into consideration are those between the evidence given by Mr Clements and Mr Templar, and the story told by the prisoner. It is my submission to you that the defence has in no way succeeded in shaking the credibility of those two witnesses, and when you remember, in discarding the evidence of the prisoner, that it is not supported by any other witness at any point, and that the only alternative to discarding it as the fantastic story of a man lying desperately to save his neck is to regard all the stories of all the other witnesses as nothing short of deliberate conspiracy to send an innocent man to the gallows—then, ladies and gentlemen of the jury, in my humble submission, there is only one conclusion at which any reasonable person can arrive."

The jury was away for three hours, but to the reporters in the crowded press seats it was a foregone conclusion. The finger-prints of Galbraith Stride had been found on the gun, and that seemed to clinch it.

So they found him guilty as we know, and the warders had to hold him up when the judge put on the black cap.

9

Three weeks later an early post brought Toby Halidom a letter.

He was awake to receive it; for during that night the story as it concerned him had dragged through its last intolerable lap. It was the end of three weeks of dreadful waiting—three weeks in which the lines of strain that had marked themselves on the face he loved had been etched in indelible lines of acid on his own memory. It was not that either of them bore any more affection for the man who had made his infamous bargain with Abdul Osman, and who was now awaiting the final irrevocable summons of the Law; Galbraith Stride had placed himself beyond that, but they had known him personally, eaten at his table, seen him walking and talking as a human being of the same race as themselves instead of the impersonal deformed specimen in a glass case which the criminologists were already making of him, and they would not have been human themselves if that period of waiting for the relentless march of the Law had not preyed on their waking and sleeping hours like an intermittent nightmare. And that night had been the last and worst of all.

At midnight Toby had seen Laura sent to bed by a kindly doctor with a draught which would send her the sleep that could not have come naturally, and he had gone back to his bachelor apartment to get what rest he could. All her sufferings had been his by sympathy: he had seen her stared at in the court by goggle-eyed vampires with no better use for their time than to regale themselves with the free entertainment provided for them by her ordeal, had read with a new-found disgust the sensational journalism that was inevitably splurged on the case, and seen press photographers descending on her like a pack of hounds every time she left the court. He had knocked down one who was too importunate, and it had given him some relief. But the rest of it had remained, and it had been made no easier by the sudden inaccessibility of the one man who might have been able to help him. Simon Templar had been as elusive as a phantom; a couple of days after the case, Chief Inspector Teal, who came down with a watching brief, told him that the Saint had gone abroad.

Toby had slept fitfully until six o'clock, and had woken up unrested. He got up and brewed himself a cup of tea, and paced restlessly up and down his tiny sitting-room. The clatter of the postman's knock on his front door was a kind of relief: anything that would serve to distract his mind for a few minutes was welcome.

He went out and found that single letter. It bore a Spanish stamp, and was postmarked from Barcelona.

My dear Toby,

I know you've been thinking some hard things about me since I became so obstinately impossible to lay hands on during the trial of Galbraith Stride. Will you understand that I only did what I thought was best, and what I think in the future you also will see the best thing for you both?

You will remember that at our last meeting, after the police court proceedings, you told me what was on your mind, and I could only give you the vaguest possible comfort. I didn't want to try you too highly then, because not all of us are born to be self-appointed judges and executioners, and what you didn't know you couldn't possibly be tempted to reveal. We agreed that it would be better if you knew nothing until it was all over, and that Laura must never know.

Well, that time has nearly come, and it has been brought much nearer by a cable I had this morning, which removes the last reason I might have had for keeping silent. Clements is dead.

And he, Toby, was the man who killed Abdul Osman.

I know all the things you've been thinking. That confession you made in the saloon, when you told me that you had done it, wasn't quite such a foolish thing as I tried to make you believe, and perhaps you never did wholly believe it. Perhaps even now there are moments when you wonder . . . You couldn't ask her, of course. Well, that's one shadow I can take away from your young lives.

And then there were other times when you thought I'd done it myself. Toby, old lad, you may have gathered some idea of my views on the Englishman and Public School Man legend, but here's where I make an everlasting exception in your case. You rose to something much bigger then— something that makes me sorry you'll always have that Public School background behind you in your ordinary life, and go on to become a highly respected county magistrate, chairman of the golf club, and member of the Athenaeum. But even though it wasn't necessary I think a hell of a lot of the loyalty that kept you from breathing a word of it when they were grilling you in the box.

You figured to yourself that it was Galbraith Stride who sold Laura and I who saved her, and therefore even if I perjured myself to hell you had a debt to me that would never let you speak. And now, Toby, you've got to show yourself just as big a man to the memory of that poor devil who died the other day.

This is exactly what happened.

I arrived on the Claudette just as you and Laura were pushing off from the other side. I heard your boat buzzing away, and thought nothing of it at the time. I was after Galbraith Stride and Abdul Osman at the same time. You know all about me, and all the things I've done in the name of what I think is justice. I had decided that both Osman and Stride were far too foul to live any longer. I've killed men before, many of them—it didn't mean anything like the same thing to me as it would have to you. I meant to carry the pair of them off on the Puffin, rope them together with half a ton of lead for ballast, and drop them quietly into the sea away off beyond Round Island where there's forty fathoms of water and they could swing there on the tides till the lobsters had finished with them. There'd have been no bungling about it, no fuss, and I'd have had a peach of an alibi waiting back on St Mary's for me if there hadn't been other things doing that night which upset all my plans.

I hauled Stride up on to the Luxor, and whizzed over the ship to locate the crew so I'd know where to expect trouble coming from if there was any. Then I headed for the saloon, lifted the skylight half an inch to look in, and saw all the jamboree going on. Toby, I simply had to stay watching. Call it morbid fascination or what you like, there were things going on down there that I had to know more about. I heard most of it—and remember that I could have butted in at any time things started looking too rough. I might have spared you some of the things that happened, but my professional curiosity had to see the scene through as far as I dared let it go.

Osman was telling the truth about Stride's bargain—I could tell that at once. You remember that the torn note they found in the saloon, the one Laura was sent over with, was just a blank sheet of paper? Wasn't that proof enough? You saw it later, but I was looking down right over Osman's shoulder, and I saw it the minute he opened it.

You know what happened up to the time you were taken out of the saloon. Then Abdul started trying his sheik stuff on Laura, as you've been told. The only other person there was Clements—the man Abdul forgot—the man everyone always forgot. And Clements, crazed with the need for the drug that Abdul had broken him in to—he had been kept without it all day, as he told me afterwards, just for one of those spiteful whims of torture that Abdul's pleasant imagination was always producing—Clements's only idea was to take advantage of the confusion and help himself from the cupboard where the stuff was kept. I could see him stumbling towards it like a madman, and it seemed that that was the cue for me to butt in at last.

I'd started out unarmed—recent notoriety has made me rather cautious about running the risk of letting anyone catch me within miles of a gun—but Stride had an automatic when I captured him, and I'd shoved it away in a hip pocket that wasn't designed for a quick draw, after considering for some moments whether I should pitch it into the sea. I wanted it badly then, and I was trying to get hold of it with one hand while I held the skylight propped up with the other, when Clements pulled his big scene.

He'd got his hands into the cupboard, and there was an automatic there. He touched it, actually picked it up—heaven knows why. And then he looked round. Laura had just fainted, and Abdul was clawing at her.

I told you that I was my own judge and jury, but there are some things which even I will not presume to judge. You may say that Clements had every reason to hate Osman, that even he might know that Osman's death, whatever it cost him, would mean the end of a slavery that was worse than any hangman. You may say that Osman's demonstration on him that night before your eyes fanned his hate to a furnace that even the fear of being deprived of his drug could not quell. Or perhaps, Toby, you may like to think that even in that broken wreck of a man that Osman had made of him there was a lingering spark of the man that Clements had been before, a spark that had been awakened into a faint flame of new courage by that last brutal humiliation which you saw, a spark that even in his hopeless soul could feel the shame of that final outrage which he had been left to witness. You will think what you like, and so shall I. I shall only tell you what I saw.

Clements turned round, with the gun. His face was under the light, and it had a look—I can't say of hate or rage—a look of sudden peace that was almost glorious. He stepped up to Abdul Osman and shot him through the heart, and stood quite still and watched him fall, and then he dropped the gun—it just happened to fall near Laura, that's *all—and went back to the cupboard. And I should like to say that he didn't stagger back like a starving animal, as he had gone there at first: he went quite slowly, quite quietly, though I could see that every one of his nerves was a white-hot wire of agony with his hunger for that poison.*

Well, it seemed as if the inquest was the next thing, and I didn't want it to be held on any of us at the same time, with that heathen crew roused by the shot. I dashed round and locked them up pronto, after heaving the skylight wide open and dumping Galbraith bodily in to get him out of the way—he was still sleeping peacefully from the clout I'd given him on the jaw, and wasn't likely to make any trouble for some time.

I took you and Laura down to your motor-boat and left you—by the way, you must be a pretty hefty bird when you're roused, for the hinges of that door you'd bust open looked as if they'd been through an earthquake. I still had to go on thinking at a speed that nearly gave me brain fever, because when you've got to work out alibis that weren't prepared in advance in less than sixty seconds there isn't much time for writing poetry. I hashed up everything I told you in the boat straight out of my head, without coffee or ice compresses, and then I left you and went back to the saloon to try and stage it to look true.

Even on the spur of the moment you see, I'd made up my mind that Clements wasn't going to swing for what he'd done if I could possibly avoid it. Abdul had asked for it, and Abdul had got what was coming to him anyhow. Clements had simply paid off a debt of ten years of living death, and, Toby, after all, it had been Clements who actually saved your girl. I'd seen that look on his face when he shot Osman, that look which I can't hope ever to describe to you, and which I'd rather leave out of the story and leave for you to see in your own heart if you can. There seemed to be a much more suitable victim ready to hand; Galbraith Stride who had also had it coming to him that night. The only question was whether Clements could be pulled together sufficiently to catch on.

The dope had taken effect when I got back to him, and he was more or less normal. Also he was very calm. He used practically your own words.

"They can hang me if they like," he said. "It doesn't matter much."

I took him by the shoulders, and believe it or not, he could look me in the eye.

"They're not hanging you," I said. "They're going to hang Galbraith Stride."

"I don't mind what happens," said Clements. "I'm not sorry to have killed Osman. Do you see me? I'm only one man that he's ruined. There were thousands of others. I've seen them. You haven't been through it, and you don't know what it means."

"Perhaps I do," I said. "But Galbraith Stride is only another like him."

And I told him that I had meant to kill Stride as well that night, and who I was. Then he caught on.

"I haven't long to live anyway," he said. "But I should like to see this work finished."

He wanted to shoot Stride then and there where he lay and take the rap for the two of them, but I told him there was a better way. It didn't seem to mean much to him, but somehow I wanted to be able to think that that poor devil was going to see out the rest of his life decently in the freedom that he hadn't known for ten years. I talked to him for twenty minutes, working out the story we were to tell, and he took it in quickly enough. Then the crew bust down the door of the glory hole and came yelling down to the saloon, and it was lucky for me Clements could swing a good line of Arabic oratory and tell 'em the facts as we'd agreed on them.

And so we told our stories as you heard them, and Galbraith Stride will hang on the day you get this.

I've no excuses to make to you. Deliberately and with infinite malice aforethought I arranged to frame your stepfather-in-law-to-be to the gallows, and nothing that can ever happen can make me sorry for what I did. That was a just thing as I have always seen justice and as I shall see it all my life according to a law that is bigger than all your man-made laws. But you have been taught to respect those man-made laws, so this letter will help to set your conscience free. You guessed some of it, of course, and you're free now to say as much of it as you like. Clements is beyond your justice, but Chief Inspector Teal would like nothing better than a chance to send his sleuths trailing after me with extradition warrants overflowing from their pockets. They wouldn't catch me, of course, but they could have lots of harmless fun trying.

If you're interested in anything that Clements thought, after what I've told you, you might like to know the last thing I heard from him. It came to me in a letter, which he must have written when he knew that the sands had almost run out. There was just one line.

"Go on and prosper."

Not a very Public School sentiment, Toby, you may think. Rather more melodramatic than any English Gentleman should have been. But he had come back from depths that I hope you'll never see—from which, even if I hadn't been on board that night he would still have saved you. You will judge him and decide what to do according to what you think of that farewell. It is only right that you should make your own choice.

If that choice is what I think it will be, we may meet again.

Ever yours,
Simon Templar.

Toby Halidom lighted a cigarette and read the letter through again, word by word. In some way it lifted a terrible load from his mind, brought him a great breath of relief in the fullness of knowledge that it gave him. And, as he read, there was a queer little smile on his lips that any Headmaster of Harrow would have been surprised to see . . .

He put the letter in the empty grate, set a match to it, and watched the sheets flare and curl and blacken. "Go on and prosper." . . . And then, with a heart that felt suddenly light and clear, he went to the open window and leaned on the sill, looking out into the blue-grey lightening of that morning of the 22nd of November. Somewhere a clock was striking the hour of eight.

PUBLICATION

HISTORY

This book sees the start of a new trend, for the Saint and Leslie Charteris were now so well established that the pressure to make a magazine sale prior to publishing in book form was easing off; "The Gold Standard" first appeared in issue No. 193 of *The Thriller* on 15 October 1932, under the title of "The Gold Flood," and "The Man from St Louis" first appeared just five issues later on 19 November 1932, under the title of "The Saint—Hi-Jacker." But "The Death Penalty" was written exclusively for this book.

This book was first published by Hodder & Stoughton in January 1933 under the title of *Once More the Saint*. The Americans christened it *The Saint and Mr Teal* when Doubleday published their first edition in May that same year. Eventually, with their sixteenth edition in October 1950, Hodder & Stoughton adopted the American title and have used it ever since.

A French translation of sorts appeared in 1939, for the book *Ici le Saint!* includes translations of "The Gold Standard" and "The Death Penalty," however the French had to wait until the following year to read "The Man from St Louis" which appeared in *Les compagnons du Saint*. A Spanish translation, *Otra vez el Santo*, appeared in April 1935 whilst a Portuguese translation, *O Santo e o Sr Teal*, was first published in 1950.

A paperback edition published by Carroll & Graf of the USA in May 1995 caused some merriment, for on the spine it labeled the book as *The Saint and Mrs Teal*.

All three of the stories in this book were subsequently adapted for *The Saint* television series with Roger Moore: "The Death Penalty" was adapted by Ian Stuart Black and was shown during the third season of the show, initially airing on Sunday, 29 November 1964; "The Man From St Louis" was adapted by Paddy Manning O'Brine and retitled "The Set-Up," first broadcast on Thursday, 14 January 1965; and "The Gold Standard" was adapted by Brian Degas and first broadcast on Saturday, 3 July 1965 as part of the show's fourth season.

ABOUT THE AUTHOR

I'm mad enough to believe in romance. And I'm sick and tired of this age—tired of the miserable little mildewed things that people racked their brains about, and wrote books about, and called life. I wanted something more elementary and honest—battle, murder, sudden death, with plenty of good beer and damsels in distress, and a complete callousness about blipping the ungodly over the beezer. It mayn't be life as we know it, but it ought to be.

—Leslie Charteris in a 1935 BBC radio interview

Leslie Charteris was born Leslie Charles Bowyer-Yin in Singapore on 12 May 1907.

He was the son of a Chinese doctor and his English wife, who'd met in London a few years earlier. Young Leslie found friends hard to come by in colonial Singapore. The English children had been told not to play with Eurasians, and the Chinese children had been told not to play with Europeans. Leslie was caught in between and took refuge in reading.

"I read a great many good books and enjoyed them because nobody had told me that they were classics. I also read a great many bad books which nobody told me not to read . . . I read a great many popular scientific articles and acquired from them an astonishing amount of general knowledge before I discovered that this acquisition was supposed to be a chore."[1]

One of his favourite things to read was a magazine called *Chums*. "The Best and Brightest Paper for Boys" (if you believe the adverts) was a monthly paper full of swashbuckling adventure stories aimed at boys, encouraging them to be honourable and moral and perhaps even "upright citizens with furled umbrellas."[2] Undoubtedly these types of stories would influence his later work.

When his parents split up shortly after the end of World War I, Charteris accompanied his mother and brother back to England, where he was sent to Rossall School in Fleetwood, Lancashire. Rossall was then a very stereotypical English public school, and it struggled to cope with this multilingual mixed-race boy just into his teens who'd already seen more of the world than many of his peers would see in their lifetimes. He was an outsider.

He left Rossall in 1924. Keen to pursue a creative career, he decided to study art in Paris—after all, that was where the great artists went—but soon found that the life of a literally starving artist didn't appeal. He continued writing, firing off speculative stories to magazines, and it was the sale of a short story to *Windsor Magazine* that saved him from penury.

He returned to London in 1925, as his parents—particularly his father—wanted him to become a lawyer, and he was sent to study law at Cambridge University. In the mid-1920s, Cambridge was full of Bright Young Things—aristocrats and bohemians somewhat typified in the Evelyn Waugh novel *Vile Bodies*—and again the mixed-race Bowyer-Yin found that he didn't fit in. He was an outsider who preferred to make his own way in the world and wasn't one of the privileged upper class. It didn't help that he found his studies boring and decided it was more fun contemplating ways to circumvent the law. This inspired him to write a novel, and when publishers Ward Lock & Co. offered him a three-book deal on the strength of it, he abandoned his studies to pursue a writing career.

When his father learnt of this, he was not impressed, as he considered writers to be "rogues and vagabonds." Charteris would later recall that "I wanted to be a writer, he wanted me to become a lawyer. I was stubborn, he said I would end up in the gutter. So I left home. Later on, when I had a little success, we were reconciled by letter, but I never saw him again."[3]

X Esquire, his first novel, appeared in April 1927. The lead character, X Esquire, is a mysterious hero, hunting down and killing the businessmen trying to wipe out Britain by distributing quantities of free poisoned cigarettes. His second novel, *The White Rider*, was published the following spring, and in one memorable scene shows the hero chasing after his damsel in distress, only for him to overtake the villains, leap into their car . . . and promptly faint.

These two plot highlights may go some way to explaining Charteris's comment on *Meet—the Tiger!*, published in September 1928, that "it was only the third book I'd written, and the best, I would say, for it was that the first two were even worse."[4]

Twenty-one-year-old authors are naturally self-critical. Despite reasonably good reviews, the Saint didn't set the world on fire, and Charteris moved on to a new hero for his next book. This was *The Bandit*, an adventure story featuring Ramon Francisco De Castilla y Espronceda Manrique, published in the summer of 1929 after its serialisation in the *Empire News*, a now long-forgotten Sunday newspaper. But sales of *The Bandit* were less than impressive, and Charteris began to question his choice of career. It was all very well writing—but if nobody wants to read what you write, what's the point?

"I had to succeed, because before me loomed the only alternative, the dreadful penalty of failure . . . the routine office hours, the five-day week . . . the lethal assimilation into the ranks of honest, hard-working, conformist, God-fearing pillars of the community."[5]

However his fortunes—and the Saint's—were about to change. In late 1928, Leslie had met Monty Haydon, a London-based editor who was looking for writers to pen stories for his new paper, *The Thriller*— "The Paper with a Thousand Thrills." Charteris later recalled that "he said he was starting a new magazine, had read one of my books and would like some stories from me. I couldn't have been more grateful, both from the point of view of vanity and finance!"[6]

The paper launched in early 1929, and Leslie's first work, "The Story of a Dead Man," featuring Jimmy Traill, appeared in issue 4 (published on 2 March 1929). That was followed just over a month later with "The Secret of Beacon Inn," starring Rameses "Pip" Smith. At the same time, Leslie finished writing another non-Saint novel, *Daredevil*, which would be published in late 1929. Storm Arden was the hero; more notably, the book saw the first introduction of a Scotland Yard inspector by the name of Claud Eustace Teal.

The Saint returned in the thirteenth issue of *The Thriller*. The byline proclaimed that the tale was "A Thrilling Complete Story of the Underworld"; the title was "The Five Kings," and it actually featured Four Kings and a Joker. Simon Templar, of course, was the Joker.

Charteris spent the rest of 1929 telling the adventures of the Five Kings in five subsequent *The Thriller* stories. "It was very hard work, for the pay was lousy, but Monty Haydon was a brilliant and stimulating editor, full of ideas. While he didn't actually help shape the Saint as a character, he did suggest story lines. He would take me out to lunch and say, 'What are you going to write about next?' I'd often say I was damned if I knew. And Monty would say, 'Well, I was reading something the other day . . .' He had a fund of ideas and we would talk them over, and then I would go away and write a story. He was a great creative editor."[7]

Charteris would have one more attempt at writing about a hero other than Simon Templar, in three novelettes published in *The Thriller* in early 1930, but he swiftly returned to the Saint. This was partly due to his self-confessed laziness—he wanted to write more stories for *The Thriller* and other magazines, and creating a new hero for every story was hard work—but mainly due to feedback from Monty Haydon. It seemed people wanted to read more adventures of the Saint . . .

Charteris would contribute over forty stories to *The Thriller* throughout the 1930s. Shortly after their debut, he persuaded publisher Hodder & Stoughton that if he collected some of these stories and rewrote them a little, they could publish them as a Saint book. *Enter the Saint* was first published in August 1930, and the reaction was good enough for the publishers to bring out another collection. And another . . .

Of the twenty Saint books published in the 1930s, almost all have their origins in those magazine stories.

Why was the Saint so popular throughout the decade? Aside from the charm and ability of Charteris's storytelling, the stories, particularly those published in the first half of the '30s, are full of energy and joie de vivre. With economic depression rampant throughout the period, the public at large seemed to want some escapism.

And Simon Templar's appeal was wide-ranging: he wasn't an upper-class hero like so many of the period. With no obvious background and no attachment to the Old School Tie, no friends in high places who could provide a get-out-of-jail-free card, the Saint was uniquely classless. Not unlike his creator.

Throughout Leslie's formative years, his heritage had been an issue. In his early days in Singapore, during his time at school, at Cambridge University or even just in everyday life, he couldn't avoid the fact that for many people his mixed parentage was a problem. He would later tell a story of how he was chased up the road by a stick-waving typical

English gent who took offence to his daughter being escorted around town by a foreigner.

Like the Saint, he was an outsider. And although he had spent a significant portion of his formative years in England, he couldn't settle.

As a young boy he had read of an America "peopled largely by Indians, and characters in fringed buckskin jackets who fought nobly against them. I spent a great deal of time day-dreaming about a visit to this prodigious and exciting country."[8]

It was time to realise this wish. Charteris and his first wife, Pauline, whom he'd met in London when they were both teenagers and married in 1931, set sail for the States in late 1932; the Saint had already made his debut in America courtesy of the publisher Doubleday. Charteris and his wife found a New York still experiencing the tail end of Prohibition, and times were tough at first. Despite sales to *The American Magazine* and others, it wasn't until a chance meeting with writer turned Hollywood executive Bartlett McCormack in their favourite speakeasy that Charteris's career stepped up a gear.

Soon Charteris was in Hollywood, working on what would become the 1933 movie *Midnight Club*. However, Hollywood's treatment of writers wasn't to Charteris's taste, and he began to yearn for home. Within a few months, he returned to the UK and began writing more Saint stories for Monty Haydon and Bill McElroy.

He also rewrote a story he'd sketched out whilst in the States, a version of which had been published in *The American Magazine* in September 1934. This new novel, *The Saint in New York*, published in 1935, was a significant advance for the Saint and Leslie Charteris. Gone were the high jinks and the badinage. The youthful exuberance evident in the Saint's early adventures had evolved into something a little darker, a little more hard-boiled. It was the next stage in development for the author and his creation, and readers loved it. It became a bestseller on both sides of the Atlantic.

Having spent his formative years in places as far apart as Singapore and England, with substantial travel in between, it should be no surprise that Leslie had a serious case of wanderlust. With a bestseller under his belt, he now had the means to see more of the world.

Nineteen thirty-six found him in Tenerife, researching another Saint adventure alongside translating the biography of Juan Belmonte, a well-known Spanish matador. Estranged for several months, Leslie and Pauline divorced in 1937. The following year, Leslie married an American, Barbara Meyer, who'd accompanied him to Tenerife. In early 1938, Charteris and his new bride set off in a trailer of his own design and spent eighteen months travelling round America and Canada.

The Saint in New York had reminded Hollywood of Charteris's talents, and film rights to the novel were sold prior to publication in 1935. Although the proposed 1935 film production was rejected by the Hays Office for its violent content, RKO's eventual 1938 production persuaded Charteris to try his luck once more in Hollywood.

New opportunities had opened up, and throughout the 1940s the Saint appeared not only in books and movies but in a newspaper strip, a comic-book series, and on radio.

Anyone wishing to adapt the character in any medium found a stern taskmaster in Charteris. He was never completely satisfied, nor was he shy of showing his displeasure. He did, however, ensure that copyright in any Saint adventure belonged to him, even if scripted by another writer—a contractual obligation that he was to insist on throughout his career.

Charteris was soon spread thin, overseeing movies, comics, newspapers, and radio versions of his creation, and this, along with his self-proclaimed laziness, meant that Saint books were becoming fewer and further between. However, he still enjoyed his creation: in 1941 he indulged himself in a spot of fun by playing the Saint—complete with monocle and moustache—in a photo story in *Life* magazine.

In July 1944, he started collaborating under a pseudonym on Sherlock Holmes radio scripts, subsequently writing more adventures for Holmes than Conan Doyle. Not all his ventures were successful—a screenplay he was hired to write for Deanna Durbin, "Lady on a Train," took him a year and ultimately bore little resemblance to the finished film. In the mid-1940s, Charteris successfully sued RKO Pictures for unfair competition after they launched a new series of films starring George Sanders as a debonair crime fighter known as the Falcon. But he kept faith with his original character, and the Saint novels continued to adapt to the times. The transatlantic Saint evolved into something of a private operator, working for the mysterious Hamilton and becoming, not unlike his creator, a world traveller, finding that adventure would seek him out.

"I have never been able to see why a fictional character should not grow up, mature, and develop, the same as anyone else. The same, if you like, as his biographer. The only adequate reason is that—so far as I know—no other fictional character in modern times has survived a sufficient number of years for these changes to be clearly observable. I must confess that a lot of my own selfish pleasure in the Saint has been in watching him grow up."[9]

Charteris maintained his love of travel and was soon to be found sailing round the West Indies with his good friend Gregory Peck. His forays abroad gave him even more material, and he began to write true-crime articles, as well as an occasional column in *Gourmet* magazine.

By the early '50s, Charteris himself was feeling strained. He'd divorced his second wife in 1943 and got together with a New York radio and nightclub singer called Betty Bryant Borst, whom he married in late 1943. That relationship had fallen apart acrimoniously towards the end of the decade, and he roamed the globe restlessly, rarely in one place for longer than a couple of months. He continued to maintain a firm grip on the exploitation of the Saint in various media but was writing little himself. The Saint had become an industry, and Charteris couldn't keep up. He began thinking seriously about an early retirement.

Then in 1951 he met a young actress called Audrey Long when they became next-door neighbours in Hollywood. Within a year they had married, a union that was to last the rest of Leslie's life.

He attacked life with a new vitality. They travelled—Nassau was a favoured escape spot—and he wrote. He struck an agreement with *The New York Herald Tribune* for a Saint comic strip, which would appear daily and be written by Charteris himself. The strip ran for thirteen years, with Charteris sending in his handwritten story lines from wherever he happened to be, relying on mail services around the world to continue the Saint's adventures. New Saint books began to appear, and Charteris reached a height of productivity not seen since his days as a struggling author trying to establish himself. As Leslie and Audrey travelled, so did the Saint, visiting locations just after his creator had been there.

By 1953 the Saint had already enjoyed twenty-five years of success, and *The Saint Detective Magazine* was launched. Charteris had become adept at exploiting his creation to the full, mixing new stories with repackaged older stories, sometimes rewritten, sometimes mixed up in "new" anthologies, sometimes adapted from radio scripts previously written by other writers.

Charteris had been approached several times over the years for television rights in the Saint and had expended much time and effort during the 1950s trying to get the Saint on TV, even going so far as to write sample scripts himself, but it wasn't to be. He finally agreed a deal in autumn 1961 with English film producers Robert S. Baker and Monty Berman. The first episode of *The Saint* television series, starring Roger Moore, went into production in June 1962. The series was an immediate success, though Charteris himself had his reservations. It reached second place in the ratings, but he commented that "in that distinction it was topped by wrestling, which only suggested to me that the competition may not have been so hot; but producers are generally cast in a less modest mould." He resented the implication that the TV series had finally made a success of the Saint after twenty-five years of literary obscurity.

As long as the series lasted, Charteris was not shy about voicing his criticisms both in public and in a constant stream of memos to the producers. "Regular followers of the Saint saga . . . must have noticed that I am almost incapable of simply writing a story and shutting up."[10] Nor was he shy about exploiting this new market by agreeing to a series of tie-in novelisations ghosted by other writers, which he would then rewrite before publication.

Charteris mellowed as the series developed and found elements to praise too. He developed a close friendship with producer Robert S. Baker, which would last until Charteris's death.

In the early '60s, on one of their frequent trips to England, Leslie and Audrey bought a house in Surrey, which became their permanent base. He explored the possibility of a Saint musical and began writing some of it himself.

Charteris no longer needed to work. Now in his sixties, he supervised the Saint from a distance whilst continuing to travel and indulge himself. He and Audrey made seasonal excursions to Ireland and the south of France, where they had residences. He began to write poetry and devised a new universal sign language, Paleneo, based on notes and symbols he used in his diaries. Once Paleneo was released, he decided enough was enough and announced, again, his retirement. This time he meant it.

The Saint continued regardless—there was a long-running Swedish comic strip, and new novels with other writers doing the bulk of the work were complemented in the 1970s with Bob Baker's revival of the TV series, *Return of the Saint*.

Ill-health began to take its toll. By the early 1980s, although he continued a healthy correspondence with the outside world, Charteris felt unable to keep up with the collaborative Saint books and pulled the plug on them.

To entertain himself, Leslie took to "trying to beat the bookies in predicting the relative speed of horses," a hobby which resulted in several of his local betting shops refusing to take "predictions" from him, as he was too successful for their liking.

He still received requests to publish his work abroad but had become completely cynical about further attempts to revive the Saint. A new Saint magazine only lasted three issues, and two TV productions—*The Saint in Manhattan*, with Tom Selleck look-alike Andrew Clarke, and *The Saint*, with Simon Dutton—left him bitterly disappointed. "I fully expect this series to lay eggs everywhere . . . the only satisfaction I have is in looking at my bank balance."[11]

In the early 1990s, Hollywood producers Robert Evans and William J. Macdonald approached him and made a deal for the Saint to return to cinema screens. Charteris still took great care of the Saint's reputation and wrote an outline entitled *The Return of the Saint* in which an older Saint would meet the son he didn't know he had.

Much of his time in his last few years was taken up with the movie. Several scripts were submitted to him—each moving further and further away from his original concept—but the screenwriter from 1940s Hollywood was thoroughly disheartened by the Hollywood of the '90s: "There is still no plot, no real story, no characterisations, no personal interaction, nothing but endless frantic violence . . ." Besides, with producer Bill Macdonald hitting the headlines for the most un-Saintly reasons, he was to add, "How can Bill Macdonald concentrate on my Saint movie when he has Sharon Stone in his bed?"

The Crime Writers' Association of Great Britain presented Leslie with a Lifetime Achievement award in 1992 in a special ceremony at the

House of Lords. Never one for associations and awards, and although visibly unwell, Leslie accepted the award with grace and humour ("I am now only waiting to be carbon-dated," he joked). He suffered a slight stroke in his final weeks, which did not prevent him from dining out locally with family and friends, before he finally passed away at the age of 85 on 15 April 1993.

His death severed one of the final links with the classic thriller genre of the 1930s and 1940s, but he left behind a legacy of nearly one hundred books, countless short stories, and TV, film, radio, and comic-strip adaptations of his work which will endure for generations to come.

I was always sure that there was a solid place in escape literature for a rambunctious adventurer such as I dreamed up in my youth, who really believed in the old-fashioned romantic ideals and was prepared to lay everything on the line to bring them to life. A joyous exuberance that could not find its fulfilment in pinball machines and pot. I had what may now seem a mad desire to spread the belief that there were worse, and wickeder, nut cases than Don Quixote.

Even now, half a century later, when I should be old enough to know better, I still cling to that belief. That there will always be a public for the old-style hero, who had a clear idea of justice, and a more than technical approach to love, and the ability to have some fun with his crusades.[12]

---

1 *A Letter from the Saint*, 30 August 1946
2 "The Last Word," *The First Saint Omnibus*, Doubleday Crime Club, 1939
3 *The Straits Times*, 29 June 1958, page 9

4 Introduction by Charteris to the September 1980 paperback reprint of *Meet—the Tiger!* (Charter), the last ever print edition.

5 *The Saint: A Complete History*, by Burl Barer (McFarland, 1993)

6 PR material from the 1970s series *Return of the Saint*

7 From "Return of the Saint: Comprehensive Information" issued to help publicise the 1970s TV show

8 *A Letter from the Saint*, 26 July 1946

9 Introduction to "The Million Pound Day," in *The First Saint Omnibus*

10 *A Letter from the Saint*, 12 April 1946

11 Letter from LC to sometime Saint collaborator Peter Bloxsom, 2 August 1989

12 Introduction by Charteris to the September 1980 paperback reprint of *Meet—the Tiger!* (Charter).

WATCH FOR THE SIGN

OF THE SAINT!

THE SAINT CLUB

*And so, my friends, dear bookworms, most noble fellow
drinkers, frustrated burglars, affronted policemen, upright
citizens with furled umbrellas and secret buccaneering
dreams that seems to be very nearly all for now. It has been
nice having you with us, and we hope you will come again,
not once, but many times.*

*Only because of our great love for you, we would like
to take this parting opportunity of mentioning one small
matter which we have very much at heart . . .*

—*Leslie Charteris,* The First Saint Omnibus *(1939)*

Leslie Charteris founded The Saint Club in 1936 with the aim of
providing a constructive fanbase for Saint devotees. Before the War, it
donated profits to a London hospital where, for several years, a Saint
ward was maintained. With the nationalisation of hospitals, profits
were, for many years, donated to the Arbour Youth Centre in Stepney,
London.

In the twenty-first century, we've carried on this tradition but have
also donated to the Red Cross and a number of different children's
charities.

The club acts as a focal point for anyone interested in the adventures of Leslie Charteris and the work of Simon Templar, and offers merchandise that includes DVDs of the old TV series and various Saint-related publications, through to its own exclusive range of notepaper, pin badges, and polo shirts. All profits are donated to charity. The club also maintains two popular websites and supports many more Saint-related sites.

After Leslie Charteris's death, the club recruited three new vice-presidents—Roger Moore, Ian Ogilvy, and Simon Dutton have all pledged their support, whilst Audrey and Patricia Charteris have been retained as Saints-in-Chief. But some things do not change, for the back of the membership card still mischievously proclaims that . . .

The bearer of this card is probably a person of hideous antecedents and low moral character, and upon apprehension for any cause should be immediately released in order to save other prisoners from contamination.

To join . . .

Membership costs £3.50 (or US$7) per year, or £30 (US$60) for life. Find us online at www.lesliecharteris.com for full details.